D0016106

What Readers Are Saying About
Karen Kingsbury's Books

"I have read many of Karen's books, and I cry with every one. I feel like I actually know the people in the story, and my heart goes out to all of them when something happens!"

—Kathy N.

"Novels are mini-vacations, and Karen's are my favorite destination."

—Rachel S.

"The best author in the country."

—Mary H.

"Karen's books remind me that God is real. I need that reminder."

—Carrie F.

"The stories are fiction; their impact is real."

—Debbie L. R.

"Every time I read one of Karen's books I think, 'It's the best one yet.' Then the next one comes out and I think, 'No, *this* is the best one.'"

—April B. M.

"Whenever I pick up a new KK book, two things are consistent: tissues and finishing the whole book in one day."

—Nel L.

"Karen Kingsbury is changing the world—one reader at a time."

—Lauren W.

More Life-Changing Fiction™ by Karen Kingsbury

Stand-Alone Titles
Fifteen Minutes
The Chance
The Bridge
Oceans Apart
Between Sundays
When Joy Came to Stay
On Every Side
Divine
Like Dandelion Dust
Where Yesterday Lives
Shades of Blue
Unlocked
Coming Home—The Baxter
 Family

Angels Walking Series
Angels Walking
Chasing Sunsets
Brush of Wings

The Baxters—Redemption
 Series
Redemption
Remember
Return
Rejoice
Reunion

The Baxters—Firstborn Series
Fame
Forgiven
Found
Family
Forever

The Baxters—Sunrise Series
Sunrise
Summer
Someday
Sunset

The Baxters—Above the Line
 Series
Above the Line: Take One
Above the Line: Take Two
Above the Line: Take Three
Above the Line: Take Four

The Baxters—Bailey Flanigan
 Series
Leaving
Learning
Longing
Loving

9/11 Series
One Tuesday Morning
Beyond Tuesday Morning
Remember Tuesday Morning

Lost Love Series
Even Now
Ever After

Red Glove Series
Gideon's Gift
Maggie's Miracle
Sarah's Song
Hannah's Hope

www.KarenKingsbury.com

Brush of Wings

Book 3 in the Angels Walking Series

KAREN KINGSBURY

HOWARD BOOKS

An Imprint of Simon & Schuster, Inc.

New York   Nashville   London   Toronto   Sydney   New Delhi

Howard Books
An Imprint of Simon & Schuster, Inc.
1230 Avenue of the Americas
New York, NY 10020

This book is a work of fiction. Any references to historical events, real people, or real places are used fictitiously. Other names, characters, places, and events are products of the author's imagination, and any resemblance to actual events or places or persons, living or dead, is entirely coincidental.

Copyright © 2016 by Karen Kingsbury

Scripture quotations are from the Holy Bible, English Standard Version, copyright © 2001, 2007 by Crossway Bibles, a division of Good News Publishers. Used by permission. All rights reserved.

Published in association with the literary agency of Alive Literary Agency, 7680 Goddard Street, Suite 200, Colorado Springs, Colorado, 80920, http://aliveliterary.com.

All rights reserved, including the right to reproduce this book or portions thereof in any form whatsoever. For information address Howard Books Subsidiary Rights Department, 1230 Avenue of the Americas, New York, NY 10020.

First Howard Books hardcover edition March 2016

HOWARD and colophon are trademarks of Simon & Schuster, Inc.

For information about special discounts for bulk purchases, please contact Simon & Schuster Special Sales at 1-866-506-1949 or business@simonandschuster.com.

The Simon & Schuster Speakers Bureau can bring authors to your live event. For more information or to book an event, contact the Simon & Schuster Speakers Bureau at 1-866-248-3049 or visit our website at www.simonspeakers.com.

Interior design by Davina Mock-Maniscalco

Manufactured in the United States of America

10   9   8   7   6   5   4   3   2   1

Library of Congress Cataloging-in-Publication Data

Names: Kingsbury, Karen, author.
Title: Brush of wings : a novel / Karen Kingsbury.
Description: Nashville, TN : Howard Books, 2016. | Series: Angels walking ; 3
Identifiers: LCCN 2015042249
Subjects: | BISAC: FICTION / Christian / Romance. | FICTION / Christian / General. | FICTION / Religious. | GSAFD: Christian fiction. | Love stories.
Classification: LCC PS3561.I4873 B78 2016 | DDC 813/.54--dc23
LC record available at http://lccn.loc.gov/2015042249

ISBN 978-1-4516-8753-8
ISBN 978-1-4516-8754-5 (ebook)

To Donald:

Maybe the best thing we ever did as a couple was this past year's "Fifty-Two Date Nights" adventure! I'll never forget the waiter at that coffee shop taking our picture and looking at us like we were on a first date. We told him we'd been married twenty-seven years and about our fifty-two dates and he was amazed. He made us promise to come back at the end of the year to show him all fifty-two pictures. And now we're already on our second year of weekly date nights! Our family is so grown-up now. Sometimes I walk by a young mom sitting with her kids at Starbucks and tears automatically sting my eyes. Not that I'm sad—I'm not. I'm just so grateful to God for every wonderful season we've loved each other through. Kelsey and Kyle well into their fourth year of marriage and raising little Hudson, Tyler a graduate changing the world for Jesus, Sean finishing his year with YWAM, and Josh and EJ halfway finished at Liberty University. In a few weeks Austin will graduate and celebrate one last summer here before heading off to Liberty also. People ask, where did the time go? But I don't have to ask. I already know. The time went to a million beautiful moments with you and our kids, times I will cherish forever. And even still we are making memories—as grandparents and parents! I pray God lets us dance together until the final page. Thank you for being steady and strong and good and kind. Hold my hand and walk with me through the coming seasons—the graduations and grandchildren, the growing up and getting older. All of it's possible with you by my side. Let's play and laugh and sing and dance. And together we'll watch our children take wing. The ride is breathtakingly wondrous. I pray it lasts far into our twilight years. Until then, I'll enjoy not always knowing where I end and you begin. Can't wait for our next date night! I love you always and forever.

To Kyle:

Kyle, you are the answer to so many of our prayers, our son-in-love who is forever part of our family, and such a wonderful new daddy!! Because of you, our five boys have someone besides their dad to follow behind. You have set the bar as high as it could be in your daily example of loving Jesus, His word, and our precious daughter and grandson. Somehow you find a way to balance it all. We're so proud of how your music is changing lives, more so every season. Keep writing and singing for God—He's got such good plans for you as an artist! We're also proud of the book you and Kelsey wrote—*The Chase*—and how it is impacting a generation of young girls everywhere. On top of all that you're so much fun, Kyle. We love hanging out with you and Kelsey, double dating, and watching you with little Hudson. God is growing your family into world changers for Him. Love you always!

To Kelsey:

My precious daughter, what an amazing year it's been! You are a mommy now to Hudson—and the most beautiful, wonderful mom ever! You and Kyle are such great parents! So patient and gentle and attentive. So loving. And your book—*The Chase*—debuted at number 1 on the bestseller list!! I'm so happy for how God is using you and Kyle. Your heart for the youth of this generation is now clear for all to see! On top of that your dreams of acting and designing for Jesus are firmly taking shape. But even still it is your beautiful heart that best defines you. Time and again I point to you and Kyle as proof of God's faithfulness. Whatever the next seasons in life bring, your dad and I will be here for you and Kyle. We love our tennis dates and together times and dreaming about all that's ahead. And we love being grandparents to Hudson! But most of all we love being right here, right now in this beautiful moment in time. You're in my heart always. I love you, Kels.

To Tyler:

You're already grown up, out on your own, and finding the path God has for you. It's been one of my life's greatest gifts, watching you grow up, Ty. Watching you graduate from college last year was a surreal moment, because life really does happen in a blink. It's so easy to see you as a baby and a little boy—directing those cousin plays—and flash forward to you on a stage as Tony in *West Side Story*. And every amazing moment in between. You can write and direct, you can act and sing. One day I have no doubt you'll find a way to do it all, using the power of the visual story to bring hope to a hurting world. I'm so proud of how you continue to show the light of Christ to your peers. Keep letting God's word be a lamp unto your feet, Ty. He knows the good plans He has for you. And wherever the journey takes you, we'll be cheering from the front row. I love you always.

To Sean:

You knew you needed something to take you from being a boy to standing tall as a man, and together we prayed and God showed us the answer: YWAM. You still have another few months before you're ready to go back to Liberty University again, but this much is obvious—God is doing amazing work in your life. We believed this year would be life changing, and so it has. You have moved from being a comfortable spectator in your faith, to knowing deep in your heart that serving and loving God are all that matter. This is part of your story, son. A part we are very excited about and proud of you for choosing. The beautiful thing about this season in life for you is that you are finding the answers. God is meeting you right where you are. Whatever the seasons ahead hold, you'll be successful for Jesus and with Him. I know that with all my heart. I'm so proud of you, Sean. Keep loving and serving God! Love you so!

To Josh:

What a wonderful journey it's been watching you discover yourself at Liberty University! You're a junior now, and making strides in every area of life. Most of all I love watching your very deep heart come to the surface. The poem you wrote for Dad and me last Christmas, the beautiful texts, the realization that sometimes we're closer to God when we have a week of struggle. Amazing revelations, and proof that God is working a very good plan in your life. Keep being yourself, Josh! You're one in a million, and the world needs your very bright light for God. So proud of you! Love you always!

To EJ:

Can I just say how very proud of you I am? There were days when you weren't sure about even attending college, and now you've nearly finished your sophomore year at Liberty University. It's been one of my greatest joys watching you blossom and grow in your faith and confidence at that incredible school. How wonderful that you're considering a career in film—and not just any moviemaking, but films that glorify God. I can't measure the blessings, EJ. And now I know for sure whatever is ahead, you will choose a path that shines God's light and love on a hurting world. God will see you through it all. He has great plans for you and a wonderful future ahead. So glad you're such a part of our family! I love you so!

To Austin:

Austin, how can you already be finishing your senior year in high school? Just yesterday we were handing you off to a surgeon at three weeks old, praying as you underwent emergency heart surgery, and thanking God as you survived that day. We wondered whether you'd be small and sickly like the doctors predicted. Now that you are six-five, we can confidently say that only God can decide your future. He's in the midst of your life and He always has been, Austin. This year we have loved seeing you grasp new dreams, dreams of acting and filmmaking! You're a very bright light on the media arts team, a young man people turn to for encouragement. We are so proud of you for that. I remember earlier in the school year when one of the administrators pulled Dad aside and said, "Austin is an amazing young man." She went on to explain that you stand up for the smaller, bullied kids, and you help pick up trash when you think no one is looking. Small things, you tell us. But they shine the love of God amid a hurting world. And very soon you will share that light away from home at Liberty University. Only a handful of weeks now and you'll be out the door. I'm so proud of your determination to live healthy and to protect your heart, so proud of your academic success and your leadership among your peers. You have a special heart, for sure. In every possible way. Keep shining for Jesus! Trust Him with your future. Love you forever!

And to God Almighty, the Author of Life, who has—for now— blessed me with these.

Prologue

Angel Town Meeting—Heaven

ORLON'S MIND WAS MADE UP. There would not be a new team of angels, not for this final stage of the mission. Earth had suffered much heartache in the past year. The angels on his team specialized in desperate matters of the heart. They were needed now more than ever.

In places around the globe.

Orlon took his place at the front of the room and felt an assurance come over him. He was leader of this group of angels, and he'd made the right decision. He was sure of it. Ember and Beck. Jag and Aspyn. In the coming season, the four would face intense struggles and challenges, greater than any they'd encountered before. But they were the right angels for the terrible times ahead.

Orlon was sure of that.

He breathed deeply. *Stay strong,* he told himself. *These*

four must believe the mission is possible. Even now. A heavenly peace filled him. The room was empty, the angels still a few minutes from gathering. Orlon turned toward the window, toward the bright light that streamed through the opaque glass and filled the room.

He closed his eyes. *Help us, Father. You know my concerns.* Using the same teams of angels would present difficulties. A greater chance of being discovered. For humans to recognize an angel meant interrupting events that needed to play out. Events that must play out. Orlon sighed. *But You know all this, God. Give us wisdom. Go before us. In Jesus' name, amen.*

The first angels entered the room. They arrived in twos and threes. A few spoke in whispered voices, but many were quiet. Somber. They didn't fully know the challenges ahead, but they knew this much:

The stakes had never been higher.

Ember and Beck, Jag and Aspyn sat near the front. They were among the first to arrive, and of course, their hearts were already deeply invested in the mission. When the rest of the angels were seated, Orlon waited a few silent moments. *Thank You, God, for this team.* What would Earth be without them?

Orlon straightened himself. "You know why you're here. I've been alerted by Michael that the Father is ready for the final stage of this great mission—the one involving Tyler Ames and Sami Dawson, Mary Catherine Clark and Marcus Dillinger."

A few of the angels nodded. The four already involved leaned closer, completely focused.

"You remember that ultimately a baby's life is at stake, a

baby who will grow up to be a very great teacher. His name will be Dallas Garner, and he will turn the hearts of the people in the United States back to God, the Father." Orlon paused. He needed to be clear. "This baby will be an evangelist, a great teacher. A modern-day C. S. Lewis or Billy Graham. He will stand firm on the Word of God." Orlon hesitated. "His teachings will capture the attention of the world—but particularly Americans."

Orlon paced a few steps toward the window, toward heaven's crystal blue sky. He turned and faced the angels again. "There was a time when Christ's followers in the United States were an example of love and truth for all the world." He felt the heaviness of the mission ahead. "Today people have strayed from the truth. Dallas Garner will help return a generation back to God's word." He paused. "If . . . he is born at all."

The weight of Orlon's words seemed to settle on the shoulders of every angel in the room.

Orlon explained that all four humans must stay alive, and together. In friendship and relationship. Despite the enemy's attempts to tear them apart. Otherwise the mission would fail. And this stage of the mission involved life and death—but not like the last time.

He returned to the podium and checked his notes. "Previously, Jag and Aspyn faced gang violence and murderous attempts on the humans. This time the threats will be random and deadly. Accidents aimed at these four. And the greatest danger will come from within Mary Catherine. Her heart."

The very great problem, Orlon explained, was that Mary Catherine still planned to leave for Africa. "There, she will face every kind of danger."

A restless anticipation came over the room. The angels wanted to take action. It was how they were wired. Orlon stepped out from behind the podium, his voice determined. "I have already decided which Angels Walking team will be sent."

A few of the angels blinked, looking about the room, surprised. Usually the angels volunteered for a given mission. This would be different.

Orlon turned to the angels at the front of the room. "Ember and Beck, Jag and Aspyn. You know the humans well, you've studied them and prayed for them, followed alongside them and intervened for them. You've wept over them."

The expressions on each of their faces shifted from shock to holy determination. They sat a little taller in their seats, their attention fixed on Orlon.

"All four of you will work this final part of the mission. You will meet together often and decide which angel is best for each situation."

Jag looked at his three peers and each of them nodded in agreement. "We are willing. And we are ready."

Orlon glanced around the room at the others. "We will no longer stay here in heaven, planning and praying about what happens next." He took a few steps closer to the group. "The people of Earth suffer more each day. Every team in this room will be on an Angels Walking mission by the end of the week."

Several angels exchanged looks. This was definitely different.

Orlon took a quick breath. It was time to get to work. "Let's pray."

Around the room the angels closed their eyes and bowed

their heads. Some raised their hands toward the Father, and others lifted their faces to the light. After the prayer, Orlon walked with Beck and Ember, Jag and Aspyn to the back door. "This will be your most difficult assignment yet." He looked each of them in the eyes. "Pray constantly. Believe."

The four angels looked set, determined. As they left the room, Orlon silently begged God that although the mission seemed doomed to fail, the four angels might succeed. He prayed also for Dallas Garner, the baby whose life hung in the balance.

And for a generation who might never find redemption otherwise.

FOUR EMPTY CHAIRS faced each other at the center of the adjacent room.

Jag took the lead as they entered the space and shut the door behind them. Windows lined the walls, flooding the place with light and peace.

When they were seated, Jag studied his peers. "Are you surprised?"

Beck leaned back. Rays of sunshine streamed through the windows and flashed in his green eyes. He breathed deep, clearly bewildered. "Shocked."

"It's true, we know the humans better." Ember ran her hand over her long, golden-red hair. Concern knit itself into her expression. "But if they suspect us, it could alter their choices. We must be so very discreet."

Jag nodded. "Discretion will be key." He planted his elbows on his knees, leaning closer to the others. "We'll need a strategy."

"For every minute." Aspyn crossed her arms. She had the most street sense of anyone in the room. "I want this mission. But it's risky." She looked at Ember and then at Jag and Beck. "I'm concerned."

Aspyn sighed. "It won't be easy."

"Remember what Orlon said." Beck narrowed his eyes. "The baby has only a two percent chance of being born. The odds of failing are high."

Silence like dense fog hung over the room for more than a minute. Then Jag rose to his full towering height. "If the odds are against us, then we will better prepare ourselves this time, more than for any of the missions before." He felt his determination build. "We will commit to pray and we will always have each other's backs."

Jag sat down again, intensity filling his soul. "Here's what we'll do." He could see the mission coming into view. "Let's start with Mary Catherine . . ."

An hour later they had a plan. There were great risks, of course. Jag had never taken an Angels Walking mission without them. But this one would be even more dangerous. They would leave heaven later that afternoon and begin the assignment first thing in the morning. Jag was grateful about the immediacy of their actions.

Every hour could mean the difference—not only for the mission.

But for all mankind.

1

BECK CROSSED OCEAN AVENUE, the sea behind him.

Determination welled up in his heart. The team had chosen him to make the first move, and Beck was ready. Anxious. He walked east along Santa Monica Boulevard toward a brilliant Southern California sunrise. It was several blocks to Mary Catherine's apartment.

Beck stayed in the shadows.

He wore board shorts and a tank top, flip-flops and sunglasses. Over one shoulder he carried a faded black backpack. *Take it slow,* he told himself. *You're just any other surfer headed off the beach for breakfast.*

Beck caught a glimpse of his reflection in the front window of a seafood restaurant. His brown arms looked fit, athletic. Like he spent his days conquering waves. No one would suspect he was an angel.

After a few minutes he reached her apartment. Immediately he spotted her car—an old Hyundai. Beck glanced down the street. Several drifter types sat huddled on park benches or tucked up against the buildings. None of them seemed to notice Beck.

He stopped, lowered the backpack, and pulled a tire gauge from it. This first part of the plan was brilliant. Frustrating for Mary Catherine, maybe. But necessary. The gauge slipped easily into the tire stem of the Hyundai's right rear tire. A hissing sound signaled the release of air. When the back tire was obviously flat, Beck moved to the front of the car.

As he did, a couple of police officers turned the corner and headed his way. Beck felt his heartbeat quicken. *Come on, Jag. You gotta help me.* He stood, not sure whether the officers had seen him. At the same time another officer, tall and blond, built like a gladiator, stepped out from a doorway and approached the first two.

Jag.

Beck felt himself relax. He could hear Jag's voice—friendly and confident—as he talked to the officers. The words of their conversation weren't clear, but that didn't matter. Jag would hold them off until Beck finished the job.

He worked quickly and in less than a minute both right tires were completely flat. That should do it. She wouldn't have two spares. Beck tucked the tire gauge away, slid the backpack onto his shoulder, and turned toward the beach. At the bike path that bordered the sand, he slipped around a busy bicycle shop and disappeared.

MARY CATHERINE WOKE UP early for one reason—she wanted to feel the ocean against her skin, and she was nearly out of time.

In two weeks she would leave for Africa—no matter what anyone thought. Once she reached Uganda, there would be no beautiful spring mornings for riding waves. No chance to walk along the beach.

Today was perfect. It was early March and not a stitch of fog hung over Santa Monica. Nothing but sunny skies and the cool ocean breeze. Last night her roommate Sami had wanted to stay up and talk, but Mary Catherine had turned in early. All so she could drive to the ocean this morning. Lately, she didn't have the energy to walk, not since her heart had gotten worse.

Sami couldn't join her. She'd already left for an early breakfast meeting at the Chairos Youth Center. Which was okay with Mary Catherine. The more time she had alone out on the beach, the better. She had much to say to God, much to think about.

She could hardly wait to feel the sand beneath her feet.

Mary Catherine slipped on her wetsuit, grabbed her beach bag and towel, and hurried through the apartment. She pulled her boogie board from the front closet and headed out the door for her car.

The moment she was outside, she stopped. The tires on her Hyundai were completely flat.

"No!" A groan slipped from her lips as she walked closer. "Come on!" She scanned the roadway. No broken glass, no pieces of metal. Why in the world would this happen?

Without her car she'd have to pass on the beach. Which

was frustrating because she had the morning off. Once a week everyone at her office came into work late. And this was that day. She would have only one more like it—and only if she didn't need the time to finish her final projects.

She took her things back into her apartment and dropped them on the floor. Disappointment darkened her mood. If only she didn't tire so easily, she could walk there. But she couldn't take the risk on a work day. Maybe she could get to the beach later this week. In the afternoon. Once her tires were fixed.

Mary Catherine called a tow truck company, found her journal from beside her bed, and made a cup of decaf tea. She situated herself at the small kitchen table and stared at the weak-tasting hot drink. Coffee was another of her losses. Caffeine would speed the demise of her heart.

Mary Catherine closed her eyes.

She hesitated and then looked at the journal. The book was one of her closest friends. She opened it and found what she'd written yesterday. As far back as Mary Catherine could remember she had kept a journal. Not an accounting of her days, but a record of her dreams and goals. The very specific things she was learning in the Bible, wisdom she'd gleaned from quiet moments with God.

But lately her journal entries had taken a turn. She tended to write more about things she'd never see, the wedding she'd never have. Children she'd never hold. She wrote about her feelings, too. Her fear and excitement over what lay ahead in Uganda and the way she missed Marcus Dillinger.

These things consumed her.

In all likelihood she would never see Marcus again. He

still emailed her and texted her from spring training in Phoe-
nix. Sometimes she replied. Usually on days when she could
still feel his kiss, still remember the touch of his embrace.

Mary Catherine took a sip of her tea. The days ahead
would be easier if she could forget him. But forgetting Marcus
Dillinger was like forgetting how to breathe. Impossible, no
matter how hard she tried.

Even if all she gained by remembering him was the assurance that—for the briefest moment—she had known what it
felt like to be in love.

Something she would never know again.

Mary Catherine started at the top of the next page and
wrote, *Things I Need to Do Before Africa.* Beneath that she
scribbled a brief list.

> *Get shots and extra heart medicine. Call Mom and*
> *Dad. Buy school supplies for the kids at the orphanage.*

She paused.

This wasn't how she wanted to spend her morning. She
didn't need a list to know what she had to do before leaving
for Africa. She turned the page and poised her pen at the first
line. Her heart overflowed with dreams and hopes, doubts and
fears. She didn't have time for lists.

And like that every thought of her heart began pouring
onto the page.

> *Sometimes I close my eyes and I'm there again, I can*
> *feel the creaking boards beneath my feet, dancing on*
> *that back deck with Marcus. He holds me in his arms,*

*and his quiet laughter fills my soul. The stars hang in
the night sky and I can feel his breath against my skin,
his lips against mine. And I do everything I can to hold
on to the moment, to etch it into my heart in a place
where I can relive it whenever I want. The truth is, I'm
lonely and afraid. Marcus is gone, and I'll never see him
again. And the scant days ahead are slipping through
my fingers.*

Mary Catherine closed her eyes. Maybe God would allow
her to keep the memory alive—even till her dying day. And
since that could be sometime this year, she was even more determined to find a way to hold on to the brightest and most
beautiful moments of her life.

Like the one she should've had this morning out on the
beach.

Never mind that her doctor didn't want her in the ocean.
Too much exertion. Too much adrenaline. She had been taking medication to prepare her for a heart transplant, but it
could be years before a donor heart became available. She had
to take care of herself, give herself the greatest chance at living long enough to get a heart. If Mary Catherine ran her
heart into the ground before a donor could be identified,
then . . . well, then she would go home to heaven and she'd
spend every morning at the beach.

Forever.

But she would never have another chance to see Marcus.

Mary Catherine read what she'd written. Why was she
running off to Africa, anyway? Maybe she should go to Phoe-
nix. Walk up to Marcus at a break in his practice and tell him

she was wrong to send him away without a bit of hope, wrong to believe they could never have anything between them.

As soon as the crazy idea landed on her, she dismissed it. The reason then was the reason now. She was dying. It'd be different if she and Marcus had been dating when the news came. If that were the case, she couldn't deny him the chance to ride out this season with her if that's what he wanted.

But they weren't dating. Marcus was just finding a relationship with God, just realizing what was important in life. He needed a love who could walk that journey of faith at his side. Someone who would be there for him through the years.

Not someone who needed a new heart.

She began to write again.

> *Love isn't God's plan for my life. It never was. I wasn't that girl with the long line of guys trying to get my attention. Real guys . . . guys who loved Jesus . . . they weren't at my school and they weren't around at college.*

She thought for a moment. Sure she had dated a little bit, but no guy had ever turned her head.

Until Marcus Dillinger.

Star pitcher for the Los Angeles Dodgers. Of all people. She put his face out of her mind and moved her pen across the page once more. *Your love is enough. It is. Thank You, Lord, for that.*

A smile lifted the corners of Mary Catherine's mouth. She breathed in and felt the presence of God in the most real way possible. *Look at all the things I've done, Lord . . . all because*

You let me live. Really live. She closed her eyes again and she could see herself, skydiving over a field near Castaic Lake, and riding her bike down Ocean Avenue and across hundreds of miles of paths that ran along the beach from Will Rogers to Redondo. She had known what it was to have the sea breeze against her face, the sunshine in her long hair.

She had swum with the dolphins and looked long at the horizon. She had taught second-graders at church and sat bedside with elderly people at the Santa Monica Summer Hospice Home. She had walked foreign soil in a number of countries to tell people about the hope of Jesus.

Yes, God had already allowed her so much life. Mary Catherine could never complain about the fact that she was running out of time. No matter how sad the next six months might be, she couldn't dwell on what she would never have. The love she would never know. She would anchor herself instead on what God had given her, the ways she had lived. Some people never had a minute of the wonderful life she'd already experienced.

She moved her pen to the bottom of the page.

As for the dreams that will never be . . . maybe, God, You'll let me live them out at night when I sleep. The unimaginable joy of standing face-to-face with a man like Marcus and promising him forever. The precious warmth of my very own newborn in my arms and the journey of growing old next to the love of my life.

Together loving You and loving people for a hundred years.

If You'll let me live those things out when I sleep,

Lord, that will be enough. I promise. No tears, no
complaining, no doubting. I am Yours, always. No
matter how many days You give me.

There was one more adventure just ahead, one more
dream that actually would come true. Her dream of going
back to Africa. The orphanage in Uganda had just opened. Already forty-three kids called the place home. Mary Catherine
would organize it and make a plan for food and schooling. She
would teach, and hire other teachers, and bring in caretakers
for the children.

Yes, Mary Catherine would make sure the orphanage
thrived. She knew exactly what needed to be done. God had
given her this mission—she had no doubt.

She opened her eyes. Long ago when no guys seemed interested, when no one invited her to the prom and all of her
friends were finding someone special, Mary Catherine had
made a pact with God.

She could live without love, as long as she could love
where she lived.

And that place—she had known from the minute she
went on her first African mission trip—would be Uganda. At
times she had hoped she might have years there, pouring herself into the people, helping them know the salvation of Jesus
and giving them a purpose. Teaching trades and digging wells
for clean water and providing education to better their
chances at a future.

She moved to Los Angeles intent on making a difference
and saving money before moving to Africa. But she hadn't
known how little time she actually had.

A text from Sami flashed on her phone.

How was the beach?

Mary Catherine felt a ripple of guilt. That was something else. She had told Sami about her valve condition, but her friend had no idea that without a heart donor, Mary Catherine might have less than a year to live.

No one knew but the doctor. Mary Catherine hadn't even told her parents—although she needed to find a way to do that. Probably before Africa. The problem was, she didn't want her family or her best friend feeling sorry for her or worrying about her. She wanted them to believe in this trip, and to pray for a miracle. And if she didn't get one, then she wanted them to rejoice that she had lived a full life.

Regardless of how the news was perceived, Mary Catherine had promised her doctor that sometime soon she would tell Sami. Her, at least. She would make Sami promise not to tell Tyler or Marcus. Nothing good could come from them knowing how sick she was. They needed to focus on the coming baseball season.

But in case something happened in Africa, she really should have at least one friend who knew the truth, who could get word to her cardiologist in an emergency. Sami would be that friend. No matter how much Mary Catherine didn't want to tell her.

Mary Catherine closed the journal. She could still see the concern on Dr. Cohen's face when she told him she was serious about spending six months in Africa. He had tried to talk her out of it, but ultimately he had agreed. Six months, no longer. And only if she had easy access to transportation back home.

In case she became sicker.

And so with what might be the final months of her life, she would live out the one dream she could still make a reality. The dream of helping orphans. And at night, when the strange sounds of the African plains kept her awake, she would allow herself to go back. Back to Marcus Dillinger, and a love that would only ever be possible when she fell asleep.

In the quiet of her dreams.

2

SAMI ONLY HEARD FROM TYLER every few days—whenever he had a spare moment and no one needed him to run a meeting or stage a coaching conversation or help out in the dugout. Spring training in Arizona kept him constantly busy.

Sami missed him with every breath.

So when Tyler's call came that morning midway through a long meeting at the Youth Center, Sami immediately stepped into the hallway.

"Hello?" Her heart skipped a beat. "Tyler?"

"Baby." He was breathless, as if hearing her voice had given him permission to inhale. "I'm so glad you picked up."

She closed her eyes. "I miss you."

"I knew it would be a long month, but it feels like a year." He sounded so close, like he was holding her in his arms. "I need you, Sami."

She leaned against a cool wall and pictured him, Dodgers

baseball cap, shorts, and a polo shirt. "I can't wait to see you."

"Me, too." Wherever he was, the spot was quieter than usual. More intimate. "Skype tomorrow?"

"You have time?"

"I do. Finally." He sighed. "Where are you?"

"At the Youth Center. Back-to-back meetings this morning." She peered into the room. A volunteer was speaking to the group. "Things are great here, Tyler. Every program is full. And the teen mentoring class starts tonight." She smiled. "Lexy will be here. I just wish we could have Mary Catherine."

"She leaves in two weeks, right?"

"Yes." Sami glanced back at the meeting. "My friends from college are helping tonight in her place. Five of them."

Tyler laughed. "It'll take five of them to replace Mary Catherine."

"True." Sami exhaled. She would miss Mary Catherine so much.

The subject bounced back to Tyler and Marcus and spring training.

Tyler sounded subdued as the conversation ended. "Sometimes . . . I think about the past. My years in the minors. I was such a fool, Sami." He fell quiet for several seconds. "I'd give anything to have that time back. To never have left you." His sincerity rang through the phone line. "I love you."

"I love you, too." She was touched to the depths of her heart. "The past is behind us. All that matters is now."

When the call was over, for a long moment Sami could only stand there and relive the conversation. God was so good to give her this new, faithful Tyler Ames. The conversation was proof of something that filled Sami with joy.

Nobody would ever love her the way Tyler Ames did.

THE LAST TIME IN program had always been a short-term answer to a long-term problem. Scare teens with the reality of prison and follow up with a series of counseling meetings.

But then what?

Sami and Mary Catherine had worked together when the program ended last year to come up with a next step. A place where troubled girls could find hope and faith and a future.

In the end the answer was obvious—a mentoring program for teenage girls. Another way the Chairos Youth Center could make a difference in Los Angeles.

Tonight's meeting was the first, but Sami believed it would be the start of a long-running forum where girls were given an alternative to gangs and crime. She had prayed that many girls from the Last Time In program would come tonight, and sure enough, several were among the twenty-four teens from the community who showed up for the meeting.

But Lexy Jones was not one of them.

When Sami asked about Lexy, the response from the teens was guarded. Maybe Lexy was hanging out with her new boyfriend, one girl said. The thought broke Sami's heart. She made a mental note to contact Lexy tomorrow, maybe take her for lunch.

For now, the conversation was already going deep, something else Sami had wanted. A slender, slightly graying coun-selor, Lauren Sandall, sat quietly in one corner of the room. The woman had trained Sami and her friends from UCLA earlier today. Mainly advising them to listen well and hold off on giving advice until the girls were ready for it.

Before the teens arrived Lauren explained that she wouldn't lead the discussion, just monitor it. In case one of the girls showed signs of abuse or criminal activity. Something that would need private follow-up.

Sami's friends were split up around the circle, so the teens could sit between them. For this first meeting, everyone stayed in the large group. In later weeks they would break off into separate areas in the Youth Center so the girls could have more talk time.

In an effort to meet the girls where they were likely strug-gling the most, this first conversation was about sex. What it should be . . . what it shouldn't be. God's plan for intimacy in married relationships. Sami led the discussion.

"God designed sex to be a beautiful part of a married rela-tionship between a man and a woman." Sami was ready for push-back. "Let me be clear—this isn't *my* plan. It isn't some-thing I made up. It's God's plan. He defined marriage that way in the Bible. So for the purpose of our group, the Bible will be our standard."

A few girls covered up quiet giggles. Some of them ex-changed sarcastic looks. Sami didn't care. If she was going to help them, she had to offer them the greatest source of love available. God's word, His truth. She drew a slow breath. "Why do you think God created sex and then confined it only to marriage?"

One girl snapped her fingers, her brow raised. "Because He doesn't want us to have any fun."

Her remark elicited laughter from a few of the girls.

Sami's friends looked nervous. But Sami was ready. "Okay." She lifted her Bible off the floor and put it on her lap. She opened it to Song of Solomon, chapter 3, verse 4. "One of my favorite Scriptures is in Song of Solomon. That's a book in the Bible. Sort of a love letter. It says, 'I have found the one my heart loves.'"

The girls were quiet. Skeptical, but listening.

Sami set the Bible down. "In my life, I've found that man. Or he found me. How do I know?" She didn't wait for them to answer. "Because he loves God more than he loves me. He's kind. He treats me with respect. He prays for me and reads the Bible with me. He cherishes me like I'm a princess. But we're not married yet . . ."

"You're saying you two don't have sex?" The question came from one of the youngest teens in the room. Probably not a day over thirteen.

"That's right." Sami needed to be honest and transparent. "We want to, of course. Sex is going to be wonderful. God designed it that way. But . . . He created it for marriage."

The girl seemed shocked. "And your boo don't get mad at you?"

"No. He doesn't get mad. He sets boundaries for us. He reminds us when it's time to go home, when we've hung out long enough. God made men to be leaders." She looked straight into the girl's eyes, all the way to her heart. "If the guys you're around aren't like that, then they're the wrong guys."

The thirteen-year-old tilted her head back, showing a glimpse of the tough girl she wanted to be. "Where we supposed to find guys like that?"

Sami kept her tone even. "You have to wait for them."

"Till I'm eighty." It was the first girl again, the one who liked getting a laugh. She nodded her head at Sami. "You seen the guys we got around here?"

A chorus of voices added their agreement. Another girl was more respectful. "You didn't find your man in the projects."

Sami let that settle for a moment. *Give me the words, God . . . this isn't easy.*

Her friend Megan Winters took the lead. "The truth?" She made eye contact with several of the girls. "God is enough." Megan was from Kenya and lived in the projects before getting a scholarship to UCLA. "My first boyfriend was in a gang." She hesitated, noting the looks of surprise. "It's true. I used to think I needed a guy to feel good about myself." She leaned in, her voice filled with intensity. "But then I realized something. God loves me so much, I don't need a guy. Having the Lord in my heart, by my side. That's enough." She leaned back in her chair.

Again the girls were listening.

"There's another reason I'm okay with being single." Megan looked around the circle again. "I sure don't want to be with the wrong guy when the right one comes along."

Sami remembered her relationship with Arnie. How it had almost been the reason she and Tyler never found their way back together. Megan's advice was dead-on.

The first girl's expression softened. "What if we don't want to be single forever?"

"Don't worry about being single. Always looking for the right guy." Megan was on a roll. "Worry about yourself. Spend time becoming that special girl, the one the right guy would want." She looked at Sami. "Right?"

"Yes." She leaned over her knees. "The right guy will love God first. He will be honest and hardworking and kind. He will treat you with respect and lead your relationship so that both of you stay pure." She paused. "Pure means not having sex before you're married. Or making a decision right here . . . tonight . . . to stop having sex until then."

A few of the girls nodded, curious.

One of them let out a single defeated laugh. "Girl, I lost my purity when I was twelve. And every weekend after that." She laughed again. "Ain't nothing I can do about that. And ain't no Prince Charming gonna want me now."

"I'll be honest." Sami took a breath. Tyler had told her to share his story if it would help. "Tyler—my boyfriend—had sex before. With different girls." She waited, measuring their surprise. "He walked away from God and his life became miserable. But now . . . now he's committed to being pure. We won't have sex until and unless we get married." She looked straight at the girl who had just spoken. "With God, you can start again. He'll help you."

"Not everything can be forgiven." The girl's eyes filled with tears. "Some things are too bad."

"That's not true." Sami slid to the edge of her chair, her tone more passionate than before. "Jesus died on the cross to forgive us from *all* our sins." She motioned at the circle of girls. "All of us. Everything we've ever done." Her eyes met the girl who asked the question. "No matter how many times you've done it."

Sami went on to explain that next week they would talk about Jesus. Who He was and who He is, why He came to Earth and what it meant that He died on the cross. "You can have a certainty—because of Jesus—that you'll go to heaven when you die. But more than that, you can be sure you're for-given." She hesitated. "Purity can be part of your life again . . . because Jesus is the God of second chances."

A few of the girls nodded. Others still looked skeptical.

When the hour was up, Sami closed by reading one of her favorite verses. "In the Bible, in Jeremiah, chapter twenty-nine, verse eleven, it says, 'For I know the plans I have for you, says the Lord. Plans to give you a hope and a future and not to harm you.'" The verse was personal for Sami. "A hope and a future." She allowed a long pause for the words to sink in. "Let's think about that until we meet next week."

A few of the girls thanked Sami and her friends before they left. Three neighborhood moms had shown up, and they lingered when the meeting was over. Each of them made their way to Sami and thanked her for the meeting. "This could change my baby's life," one of them said. Tears glistened in her eyes. "Thank you."

As her friends drove away, Sami peered at the starless sky and smiled. *Thanks, God . . . tonight was perfect.* Her heart felt suddenly heavy again. *But Lord, wherever Lexy is, please get her attention. She needs this.*

There was no quiet whisper, no audible response. Only a certainty that Sami needed to call Lexy tomorrow. Sami stepped back inside the center and found her things. Good changes were happening . . . she could feel them. Tonight didn't hold all the answers.

But it was a beginning.

WHEN SAMI GOT HOME, Mary Catherine was sitting at the kitchen table. She seemed quiet. Distracted. Sami looked at the baked chicken and broccoli on the counter. "Smells amazing."

"Have some. I already ate." It looked like she'd been crying. "Tell me about the meeting."

Sami served her plate and sat down. She studied Mary Catherine. "Something's wrong."

"I'm fine. I've been going through my closet." A smile lifted Mary Catherine's lips. "Just a lot on my mind." She leaned her forearms on the table. "Come on. I want to know everything."

Sami was still hesitant about whatever seemed to be troubling Mary Catherine, but since her friend wanted to know the details, Sami told her. "Okay . . . so it went better than I ever thought . . ."

When she was finished she paused. "Except one thing . . . Lexy wasn't there."

Mary Catherine's shoulders sank. "I'm worried about her."

"I know." Sami set her fork down. "She hasn't been by the center at all."

For a moment Mary Catherine stared at her hands. "Sometimes I think I should skip Africa and help kids here.

Kids like Lexy." She lifted her eyes to Sami. "It'd be a lot easier."

"Then do that." Sami felt a glimmer of hope. She hated seeing Mary Catherine leave for so long. Especially with her heart condition. Sami was concerned about something else, too: that once Mary Catherine got settled in Africa and started working with orphans, she might never come back.

Mary Catherine made herself a cup of green tea. She swirled the hot liquid and stared at it. "I have to go. I promised myself."

"Hmmm." Sami took a bite of her chicken and set her fork down. She looked at her friend. "What about your heart? The valve replacement?"

Mary Catherine shrugged. Her answer came a little too quickly. "My doctor said I could go."

"All right." Sami didn't want to push. If Mary Catherine's doctor was okay with her going, then the trip must be okay. "And God? What does He say about you going?"

A surprised look lifted Mary Catherine's eyes. "He wants me to go. Of course. I mean, who do *those* kids have?" She looked distant, distracted. "Besides, I've always dreamed about going back."

Sami cleared her dishes and washed the chicken pan, letting a little space settle between them. Something was definitely bothering Mary Catherine. When she was finished she dried her hands and turned to her friend again. "Have you talked to Marcus?"

"He calls." Mary Catherine kept her eyes on her cup of tea. "We don't talk long. There's no point."

The two of them had been over this. "I still disagree."

Sami crossed her arms and kept her tone kind. "You and Marcus had something special. I was there, remember?"

Mary Catherine lifted her eyes to Sami. "It's over. You know that." She stood and joined Sami in the kitchen. "How are you and Tyler?"

The message was clear—conversation closed. Sami understood. She breathed in, thinking back to her phone call earlier with Tyler, how much he missed her. "We're great. We're Skyping tomorrow night."

"Good." Mary Catherine smiled. "You two are perfect."

Sami would miss this, her time with Mary Catherine. "Thanks." She hugged her. "You're a great friend."

"You, too." Mary Catherine pulled back. Her smile remained, but Sami could see the hint of tears in her eyes.

As Sami fell asleep that night she figured she understood why Mary Catherine was more emotional tonight. In just a few weeks she would be leaving everything behind. Not only that, but her friend had worked too hard making it clear she wasn't interested in Marcus. If Sami had to guess, she'd say her friend was missing him. Maybe more than even Mary Catherine herself expected.

If she wasn't so stubborn, she and Marcus could have a beautiful love. One as great as Sami and Tyler's. A love that—as Mary Catherine said—wasn't only beautiful.

It was perfect.

THE SITUATION WITH Mary Catherine was getting critical.

Aspyn and Ember had been there tonight—invisible—in

the apartment when Sami came home from the Youth Center. They had hoped Mary Catherine would tell Sami the truth. About her need for a heart transplant. If Sami knew, then she would encourage Mary Catherine to immediately fly home from Africa when her symptoms grew worse. Or better, convince her to stay in Los Angeles.

If Mary Catherine didn't make it back from Africa in time, she would die. In which case, the mission would fail.

Earlier in the day, Ember had arranged for an extra project to land on Mary Catherine's desk. Because of that she left work late and didn't make a trip to the ocean. A victory for Aspyn and Ember. They had to keep Mary Catherine away from the beach. Even a few hours of exertion on her already damaged heart could take days off her life.

Days she didn't have.

The angels had done everything right. But still Mary Catherine had avoided the conversation about her heart. Now Aspyn and Ember were headed once more to Camelback Ranch for another idea, one that involved Marcus Dillinger.

If only Mary Catherine would cooperate.

3

MARY CATHERINE HAD BEEN dreading this appointment for weeks.

A few days ago she'd gone into Dr. Cohen's office for another round of tests. Today he would give her the results. The nurse called her name minutes after she arrived.

The floor shifted as she stood, and spots clouded her vision. *Calm down,* she told herself. *Don't be afraid. Breathe.* Whatever was happening inside her chest, God already knew. He had a plan for her life—a good plan. Mary Catherine believed that completely. But somehow her heart felt tight as she followed the nurse down the hallway to an exam room.

Mary Catherine slipped into a paper gown and crossed her legs. Outside temperatures were in the mid-eighties. Warm for Los Angeles in early March. But here on the exam table, Mary Catherine's teeth chattered. Her fingers were freezing.

Not more bad news. Please, God . . . not now.

Again the wait was brief. Dr. Cohen knocked first, and then joined her. He shut the door behind him and immediately she knew. The look on his face told Mary Catherine two things: The news wasn't good. And she was about to get more restrictions.

Dr. Cohen held her chart in his hands and for a few seconds he looked at her, his expression pained.

"Bad news?" Mary Catherine's voice trembled, her words soaked in fear. *I need more time, God . . . please.*

She held her breath and waited.

"Your functions are worse." He sighed and opened the folder. "The insufficiency is more pronounced. Your heart's enlarged and thicker—which is a precursor to heart failure, as you know."

Mary Catherine nodded. She pulled her paper gown more tightly around herself. "Did you expect it to happen more slowly?"

The doctor brought his lips together and stared at the contents of the folder. "I had hoped."

Her trip to Uganda was set, so Mary Catherine didn't mention it. "What happens next?"

"I'd like to officially place you on the heart transplant list. But even then I'm not sure we'll have enough time. You're deteriorating very quickly." He breathed in sharp through his nose and looked at her. "How's your activity level? We talked about adrenaline last time you were in, trying not to overexert yourself."

Mary Catherine stared at the floor for a few heartbeats. She hated this, hated having to ration her brightest moments, the times that took such a toll on her life. She looked at Dr. Cohen. "I haven't been skydiving."

He smiled, patient with her. "You know what I mean. What about the ocean?"

She thought about her flat tires and the late assignment the other day. "I haven't been. Not lately."

"Mary Catherine . . ." The tension in the room doubled, and a heaviness weighted the doctor's tone. "This is very serious. You absolutely cannot spend time in the ocean. I'd like you to walk five to ten minutes a day, no more. And only at an easy pace." His expression was intense. "No bike riding, no running, nothing that will put extra strain on your heart." He hesitated. "You understand, right?"

"Adrenaline is bad for my heart." It wasn't a question. Mary Catherine already knew.

"Not just that." He straightened and set her file on the counter. "Any unnecessary activity means heart strain. The harder your heart works, the fewer days you'll have before you need a transplant." He let that sink in. "Do you remember the statistics about getting a heart transplant?"

Mary Catherine had memorized them.

God worked outside the numbers, but even so, the reality was grim. Between five and ten thousand people were on the wait list for a heart at any time. But only two thousand transplants were performed in the United States each year.

Which meant most patients died waiting.

Dr. Cohen didn't ask her to recite what she knew. Instead he pulled a piece of paper from her folder and handed it to her. "I'd like you to look over this information sheet. It's about the transplant. I'd like to put you on as a Status Two patient. The less urgent ranking."

Panic took punches at Mary Catherine's calm demeanor. She looked over the fact sheet and her mouth felt dry. "You remember . . . I'm headed to Uganda?"

A frown darkened Dr. Cohen's face. "You were still planning on going?"

"I was." She paused. "I am." Never mind her hesitancy the other night. With this news, nothing could change her mind. "It might be my last chance."

Dr. Cohen shook his head. "We'll talk about Uganda in a minute." He narrowed his eyes. "The transplant list has two levels—Status One is for patients already in the hospital. That's the urgent list. People in grave condition with very little time. Days, in some cases."

Mary Catherine caught a full breath. Finally, something to be thankful for. At least she wasn't Status One.

He continued. "The other is Status Two. Patients who need a new heart to survive, but the situation isn't as urgent." Dr. Cohen nodded at the fact sheet. "You'll notice Status Two patients can wait six months to several years in some cases." He crossed his arms. "Which is why your name will be added today. As long as you want to be considered for a new heart."

Want to be considered? Dizziness washed over Mary Catherine again. She gripped the sides of the exam table so she wouldn't fall off. "I'm sorry?" Was she really sitting here? Listening to a doctor tell her it was time to be added to a transplant wait list? She blinked slowly, keeping her eyes shut extra long. *Focus,* she told herself. *Dear God, what's happening?* "I'm . . . I'm not sure what to say."

"Mary Catherine . . . do you want a new heart?"

Of course she did. She wanted to live. Absolutely. If she could blink and walk out of here with a new heart she would do so without any hesitation. If only it were that easy. "Yes." She uttered the word and nodded her head. "Yes, I do."

"So then"—he paused—"you need to be on the wait list. When a heart becomes available it is evaluated against the profiles of those waiting. We look for a blood match first, from the urgent list, and then at the health of the recipient, how long he or she has been on the wait list, location, that sort of thing. If we don't find a match on the Status One list, we move to Status Two." He paused. "Are you okay with that?"

What choice did she have? Some of the fog in her mind cleared. "I can still go to Uganda?"

A quiet sigh slipped between Dr. Cohen's lips. He took hold of her file again and opened it. For a long time he sorted through the pages. Finally he lifted his eyes to hers. "If your name is called while you're in Uganda, you will lose your chance at a heart. That will go on your file, and you may be passed over the next time a matching heart comes up. We typically give transplant patients a beeper so you'll know immediately when a heart is available. Of course, a beeper does you no good in Uganda, Mary Catherine."

Tears welled in her eyes. "You said it could take a while to get a heart." She wiped at a couple of tears. "Can I be on the list and pick up the beeper when I get back?"

"It's risky." Dr. Cohen looked nervous. "I'd rather you stay here, catch up on your reading, and keep your beeper as close as your cell phone."

Another tear slid down her cheek. She forced herself to stay composed. "The thing is"—she searched his eyes—"I could do that and die waiting." She sniffed. "Right?"

It was a rhetorical question. They both knew the answer. Most people died waiting. "I'm trying to help you live."

"Me, too." She sat a little taller, unwavering this time.

They were at an impasse. Mary Catherine found a new strength, something deep inside her soul. "For me, there'll never be a better time to go to Uganda. After the transplant— if I get a transplant—I'll have medicines and follow-ups and every day will be a gift. I won't be able to leave for at least six months."

Dr. Cohen didn't speak. Clearly he could say nothing to refute her.

"Here's the thing . . . I'll never get married or have children. I won't skydive or ride the waves at Santa Monica Beach. I promise." It took everything to keep her composure. "But Uganda . . . that's something I can do. It's *very* important to me. Besides, there's a hospital there. I can let them know about my situation."

He nodded, his eyes softer than before. After a long while he exhaled again, resignation in his tone. "I understand." He stood and put his hand on her shoulder. "I'll hold the beeper for you."

Fresh tears blurred her eyes and Mary Catherine could do nothing to stop them. She covered her face with her hands. When she spoke her voice was barely a whisper. "Thank you."

"One thing . . . you need to tell your family and friends about the transplant. You'll need a support team."

Mary Catherine said nothing. She hated this part of the conversation. Her parents would be devastated about the news. She wanted to wait as long as possible before telling them. Marcus was busy with spring training and Sami was in the happiest season ever. Why tell any of them now about the transplant? They'd find out soon enough.

"Every heart patient needs a support team." The doctor took a pen from his pocket and reached for her file again. "Why don't you give me three names and their contact information?"

She let her eyes drift to the window. As long as she was the only one who knew, the idea of a transplant seemed like something from a nightmare. Not altogether real.

"Mary Catherine?" Dr. Cohen still had the pen poised over her file. "The names?"

Her heart pounded harder. She looked at the doctor. "Can I get that to you? Later? I can call the office in the next few days."

Dr. Cohen looked doubtful. "That part isn't optional."

"I understand."

"Okay." He came closer. "Lie back. I'd like to listen to your murmur." The doctor listened to several locations across her chest. Then he put the stethoscope away and took a seat opposite her. "You'll need to get the proper shots before you go. Each of them holds a greater risk because of your condition." He paused. "But I don't think that's going to change your mind."

"It isn't." She sat up, holding the gown closed again.

He thought for a few seconds. "In an ideal world you'll come back from Africa right about the time we find you a heart."

"I think that's what's going to happen." She nodded, convincing herself. "The timing could be perfect."

"Yes." Dr. Cohen stood and looked at her, right through her. "You believe in prayer, right? You've told me several times."

"I do." She was reminded of God's role in her life and it brought a surge of hope. "Absolutely."

"Well." The doctor shook her hand. "This would be a great time to start praying."

"Yes, sir." She didn't need to go into the fact that she prayed constantly about her heart. He seemed ready to get to his next patient.

The doctor turned for the door and then looked back at her. "And Mary Catherine?"

"Yes, sir?"

"Be careful in Uganda." His slight smile was colored with concern. "I'll see you in six months."

Mary Catherine got dressed, checked out at the front desk, and headed for her car. The news was terrible and getting worse. She turned on the radio, rolled down her car windows, and took Pacific Coast Highway home to her apartment. Along the way she let the ocean breeze fill her lungs. She would not cry again, no matter how discouraged she felt. No matter what tomorrow held, today she would choose joy.

She remembered the mission trip to Africa and the orphans she'd helped when she was in high school. The team of women had handed out gifts of food and built a kitchen for the village. The children clamored around the volunteers, starving for attention. The looks on their little faces was something that had stayed with Mary Catherine. It was as if they'd never been loved like that before. From that moment on, Mary Catherine knew that one day she would be back, loving kids like those again. What was the purpose of life if she couldn't take a season to make a difference?

Now that time had finally come. A sense of joy and happiness replaced any sadness from earlier. She wouldn't have her own children, but she would have the orphans in Uganda. Nothing could've made her happier.

This wasn't a day to grieve her heart condition. It was a day to celebrate.

After all, she was one day closer to packing her bags.

ASPYN AND EMBER kept up with Mary Catherine's car. Their Angels Walking mission had included much heartache. Little Jalen, who'd been nearly killed by gang gunfire. The broken relationship between Mary Catherine and Marcus. But this—seeing Mary Catherine relegated to the sidelines of life, knowing her days were short, her desperate need for a heart—this was the most difficult time yet.

"She needs to tell Sami." Ember looked worried. "Her, at least."

"Maybe tonight." Aspyn watched Mary Catherine pull up in front of her apartment and go inside. "She thinks telling people will make it more real."

"It's real either way." Ember kept her attention on the beautiful girl below them. "This is crucial."

It was true. Aspyn and Ember had brainstormed every possible way to get Mary Catherine's attention, to persuade her to talk about her impending heart transplant. They'd been successful earlier today at the Arizona ballpark. Now the two of them took a spot on the bench across the street from Mary Catherine's apartment—a couple of tourists in floppy sun hats thinking up plans for the evening. Sitting there, with Mary Catherine in for the night a few dozen feet in front of them, Aspyn and Ember did the most powerful thing they could do.

They prayed.

MARY CATHERINE WAS STILL REVELING in her renewed joy over the upcoming trip to Africa. She didn't feel sick—not at all. The last thing she planned to do tonight was put together her support team, the one Dr. Cohen wanted. There was no point. If she grew sicker in Africa, then she would email Sami and tell her everything. But odds were—if she stuck to teaching and loving the kids, and if she didn't overexert herself—her heart wouldn't get too much worse. She might even get better. God could do that. It was something she would pray about.

Then she would tell Sami and her parents when she came back home. So they wouldn't worry about her.

The lights were off inside the apartment. A chill passed over her. *How cold is it in here?* She walked to the thermostat. Seventy-four. *So why am I freezing?* Mary Catherine kicked it up a few degrees, found a blanket from the end of her bed, and grabbed her laptop from the table in the kitchen.

She sat on the sofa and spread the blanket over her lap. The sun was setting outside, but she left the lights off.

How could anything be wrong with her heart? She let her head fall against the back of the couch. She almost felt fine. Just a bit more tired. A walk to the beach would wake her up. If she could grab her boogie board and hurry to the shore, ride waves till it was pitch dark.

But she wouldn't. That was one promise she'd make good on. She had no choice if she wanted to stay well in Uganda. A yawn came over her and she opened her computer. She went to the Front Line Studios website. Sure enough. Her marketing materials had been uploaded for their fall film.

Mary Catherine sat up straighter. Her work looked great. She hadn't found a love for design until the end of her college days. But maybe she had a real gift. She grinned at the designs on the various pages. The look and brand of faith films needed to be exceptional. At least if it was ever going to compete in the marketplace.

She opened her email—in case her boss had feedback about her design work. But she saw a different letter instead. The name on it made her catch her breath. Marcus Dillinger. The second letter he'd sent since he left for spring training.

The ache inside returned without warning and the memories played out all over again. His voice and his laugh, his hand around hers. She opened the email.

Like it was water to her parched soul, she drank in every word.

Hey . . .

I've tried to give you space, like you asked. But today I
came in from the field and my computer was open and
there it was—your last email. You sent it weeks ago, but for
some reason it was there. Staring at me like some kind of
sign. Like someone had gotten into my computer and left it
out—all so I'd write to you.

So here goes.

The chills on Mary Catherine's arms had nothing to do
with the cold in the apartment. She kept reading.

I have to be honest. I have the strangest thought that
something's wrong with you. Maybe I just don't want you
to leave for Africa. Or maybe it's something else. Only you
know, I guess. But Mary Catherine, do me a favor, please. If
something is wrong, will you tell me? If you're struggling or
worried about something . . . if you're sick . . . please talk to
me. Or at the very least talk to Sami.

Mary Catherine shivered. The goose bumps ran the lengths
of her legs now, too. The timing of his message was uncanny. As
if he'd known somehow that she'd been at the doctor's earlier
today. She ignored the way the ground felt suddenly unsteady,
and instead she found her place in the email again.

See, you have this way of keeping everything locked in. And
that's not good for you. I'm here, Mary Catherine. I want you
to talk to me.

Okay, well . . . I have to run. If I wrote to you every time
I thought about you, you'd have an email every hour.
Normally I resist.

Today I couldn't.

Oh, and by the way . . . sometimes I'm warming up for a game and I'm supposed to be thinking about the ball and the glove and the speed and control it'll take to stay at the top of this crazy game.

But all I can see is you in my arms that night on my back deck. All I can hear is your laughter. Just thought you should know.

I'll let you go. It never feels right being so far away. Just remember I'm always thinking of you. Praying for you.

Missing you.

Love, Marcus

Not until she finished the letter did she notice the tears on her cheeks. She read the email one more time and wished with everything in her that Marcus could've been here, sitting beside her, telling her these things in person.

But the fact that his words had come through a cold, impersonal computer did not lessen their impact. She set the laptop down and pulled the blanket up to her shoulders. God was clearly trying to tell her something. First the doctor, then Marcus.

It was more than she could ignore.

If the Lord wanted her to talk about her heart transplant with someone, then she would. The next time she had a chance she would tell Sami. Because apparently that's what she was supposed to do.

But what she wouldn't do—what she would never allow her heart to consider—was to tell Marcus. Or even write back to him. Whatever her brief future held, Marcus Dillinger didn't deserve to take on her medical issues. He would forever be only a part of her past.

Which meant it was okay to cry. Because this was harder on Mary Catherine than anything: the pain of missing Marcus. The man with the beautiful, real soul, and his way of making her feel loved.

For the first and only time in her life.

4

J AG COULD FEEL THE building intensity of the mission, feel it gaining on them.

An hour had passed since their work at the ballpark, and now Jag walked along a sidewalk in the Signature Collection Estates, an elite neighborhood in prestigious Westlake Village. He wore a suit and tie and carried a professional leather bag. The only way he wouldn't look out of place here. A blond woman in a black Cadillac Escalade drove by and waved absently at him.

He returned the wave.

His sunglasses hid the brightness of his blue eyes. No way the woman thought he was an angel. Even so, Jag didn't have long. If residents thought he was soliciting, they'd call the police.

It was that type of neighborhood.

Jag pulled the postcard from the outside pocket of his leather bag. He heard a hissing sound and then felt something whiz past him. Demons. Scattering in the presence of light, off to wreak havoc on someone else's family.

There were more demons in neighborhoods like this than there were in the projects. More ways to be tempted by the darkness.

Jag focused on the matter at hand. The street was free of traffic for now. Jag looked at the postcard, checking the details. Matthew West in concert. Monday night. 7:00 p.m. Central Community Church, Thousand Oaks, California, and the address. It looked good.

He opened the mailbox, placed the postcard inside with the bills and miscellaneous letters, and closed it again.

Then Jag walked down the street to a parked delivery truck.

He slipped around behind it and disappeared.

EXHAUSTION WAS SOMETHING new to Mary Catherine, and she hated it. She longed for time alone so she could ask God to renew her spirit of adventure, her energy. In a few weeks she'd be living in Uganda, after all. This was no time to be tired.

She and Sami were just home from church, and already Sami was heading back out to meet the new volunteers at the Youth Center. A couple of times during the service, Mary Catherine caught her friend wiping tears. The message was very relatable: People might fail you. They might leave. God never would.

Sami opened the fridge and grabbed a string cheese.

"Come with me." She looked over her shoulder at Mary Catherine. "We can talk on the drive."

She could tell her friend was already missing her, and normally Mary Catherine would've jumped at the chance. But today she didn't have the energy. "I'm too tired. Thanks, though." Mary Catherine did her best not to look as run-down as she felt. "I have too much to do before I leave. I think I'll walk to the beach and sort through my thoughts."

Sami managed a smile. "I understand. I feel like you've already left for Uganda and things have changed between us." She peeled back the plastic wrapper on her string cheese. "I'm going to miss you so much."

"I'm sorry." Mary Catherine hugged her friend. "I've been so distracted lately. I'm going to miss you, too. More than you know. "

This was when Mary Catherine should've told Sami about her impending heart transplant. But she couldn't bring herself to talk about that now. Not when Sami was already sad, and Mary Catherine didn't have the energy.

She waited until Sami was gone before heading to the bathroom and slathering sunscreen on her arms and face. All she wanted was to feel the sun on her skin. If she couldn't ride the waves, she could at least walk the beach.

The weather outside was perfect. The sky a forever blue, temperatures in the low eighties. Mary Catherine slipped a few bottles of water, her keys, her phone, and a towel into her beach bag, locked the door behind her, and set out.

Despite being so tired she decided to walk. Even if she was a little slower than usual. The fresh air was bound to do her good—as long as she didn't push herself. But the walk was harder than she expected. Fifteen minutes later when she stepped onto the sand she had to stop and stretch her arms over her head. Her breathing wasn't normal. Faster than usual.

Come on, MC, don't be afraid. Peace . . . Jesus is with you. But her next breath wasn't easier. A wheezing came from deep inside her lungs. Everything felt tight and her chest hurt. She tried again, but no matter how hard she worked she couldn't catch her breath.

Her heart began to race and black spots danced in front of her eyes. Panic grabbed at her, surrounding her, suffocating her. *I can't breathe, God! Help me!* Dizziness swept over her and she grabbed at a nearby signpost. What was happening?

Mary Catherine bent at the waist and put her forearms on her thighs. *Lord, let me breathe.*

Exhale. Breathe out, my daughter. I am with you.

She closed her eyes. *Thank You, Father. You're with me. I can feel You with me. Calm me down and help me breathe.*

With deliberate patience, she exhaled. That was the difficult part, getting the old air out of her lungs. She breathed out again. A few more times and gradually the panic subsided. She straightened and drew a slow breath. The air seemed to fill only the top half of her lungs and her heart rhythm seemed off. But at least she didn't feel like she was being strangled. If a simple walk to the beach was causing this kind of struggle, the doctor was right. Her heart didn't have long—no matter how much she didn't want to believe that. No matter how much she prayed about her health.

For a few minutes she stood there, not moving. She was sweaty, the insides of her palms and her forehead. Her eyes found the distant shore. Was this how it was going to be? She'd gradually suffocate to death? In her darker moments she'd read articles about how a person died of heart failure. Most people who suffered through it described it as a slow drowning.

An inability to breathe.

The sweat on her forehead evaporated after a minute and her heart settled into a normal rhythm. She was going to be okay. This time. Mary Catherine took a swig of water from the bottle in her bag, and then pushed her way toward the water. Santa Monica Beach had a forever stretch of sand before the shore. Normally she loved walking through it, feeling the burn in her legs and knowing the effort was good for her. Today every step felt like a battle. She wasn't sure how much more she could ask of her heart.

When she reached the water she was exhausted. She spread her towel out on the sand, sat down, and stared at the horizon, at the place where the ocean met the sky. *God, I know You love me. I feel Your Spirit at work inside me. Even now. But is this really it? Would You please heal me, Lord?* She thought about her breathing, the terrifying feeling of not being able to draw a breath. *Is my heart that bad?*

This time there was no quick response, no easy answer. The breeze off the water played with her hair and soothed her soul. *I don't need to hear Your voice, God. I only need You.* She lifted her eyes to the cloudless sky. This time her whispered words mingled with the wind. "Please help me walk the road ahead. That's all. If You don't heal me . . . just help me."

She didn't want to move, didn't want to walk too fast and feel the frightening breathlessness again. All her life Mary

Catherine had taken life a hundred miles an hour, her hair flying behind her. She had raced the wind and won. Time and time again. Nothing she couldn't do. No fear. God had come to give her life to the full and she was going to take hold of every minute of it.

Until this week.

Now the only way to get the most out of life was to go slow. Just like the doctor said. To measure her steps and monitor her activity. And focus on breathing. She couldn't imagine a time when breathing was the most difficult thing she'd do in a given day. But that was coming. Mary Catherine could feel it.

Life would be slower, simpler in Africa. She would take it easy and maybe she'd even rebound a little. She pulled her phone from her bag and called Janie Omer, the coordinator for her trip to Uganda. Janie explained that she'd emailed the list of necessary shots. "You have to get on that." The woman sounded worried. "The malaria medicine has to be in you for at least a week before you arrive in Africa."

"I'll take care of it." Mary Catherine tilted her face to the sun. "First of the week for sure."

They talked another minute about what to pack. Mary Catherine planned on bringing an extra suitcase with school supplies.

"We have a few cargo containers being shipped to the new orphanage." Janie paused for a moment. "We could use small boxes of crayons. We weren't able to get those. And maybe some children's books."

Mary Catherine took a slow breath. "I'm on it." The thought of shopping made her feel even more tired.

"We're meeting a week from Wednesday. New York's LaGuardia Airport." Janie rushed through the details. "Our flight will leave around three that afternoon. I need everyone there by noon. We'll go over the details before we fly out."

"I'll be there."

The call ended and Mary Catherine tried to imagine all she had to do over the next ten days. Get her shots, shop for school supplies, pack, and figure out a way to say goodbye. She had booked her trip to New York with a three-day layover in Nashville. Time with her parents. Originally she had planned for a week with them. But her work schedule hadn't allowed it. Besides, they didn't know she was coming, didn't know about Africa.

They didn't even know about her need for a heart transplant.

A ribbon of guilt wove itself through her conscience. They would be distraught if they knew about her health. That's why Mary Catherine didn't see the point in telling them. That would happen soon enough. The last thing she wanted was her parents panicking over her trip to Africa. A person could die in a car accident or in their sleep.

Going to Africa wasn't going to increase her chance of dying.

Right?

She stared at the whitecaps on the far-off waves. The problem was the timing. She might *not* have six months. After the way she felt walking here today, she might not have half that. Which was why she needed to make the goodbyes count.

The only person she wouldn't be able to tell goodbye, or even see—maybe ever again—was Marcus.

She exhaled, and the weight of his memory settled around her shoulders like a blanket. *I miss you, Marcus. You'll never know how much.* She leaned back on her hands and for a moment she could feel him beside her again, here on this beach, the two of them sharing bits and pieces from their past.

Gradually letting down their walls.

Mary Catherine hadn't written back to him after his last email. She hadn't seen the point. But that wasn't right. Marcus had done nothing to deserve her silence. And since she probably wouldn't see him again, she could at least write. She'd do that before the day was over.

She decided to call her parents. The most amazing thing had happened with them. They were back together. They had gotten remarried before a judge and were even talking about having another wedding—something small for family and close friends.

After their divorce, Mary Catherine had prayed every day for her parents to reconcile. Now they had. Which meant God could do anything. He could even heal her heart while she was in Africa.

She checked the time on her phone. Her parents would be finished with dinner by now, doing dishes, talking about the church service. Her mother answered on the third ring. "Mary Catherine! What a wonderful surprise!"

She didn't realize how much she'd missed them until the sound of her mother's voice. Tears blurred her sight, and she blinked them back. "Hi, Mom. How are you?"

They spent five minutes catching up. Her parents' health was better than ever, their diet radically changed. "You were right about ketosis. Your father and I have so much more energy eating a high-fat, low-carbohydrate diet. In fact, we're hardly eating any carbs, and all our blood levels are better." Her mother sounded a decade younger. "No more insulin for your father's diabetes. It's like a miracle. Really, we feel amazing."

"That's great." Mary Catherine smiled. "You'll both live to be a hundred. Together. Which is the best part of all."

Her mother's laugh filled the phone lines. "I wouldn't mind it." She caught her breath. "You're still eating that way, right? Low carb, higher fat. Protein."

"For the most part." Mary Catherine remembered the nachos she'd had with her work team yesterday. The carbs absolutely hurt her ability to breathe. She needed as little inflammation as possible. "I could be more intentional."

"Well, you're young." Her mom's happy tone fell off a little. "How's your heart, Mary Catherine? You haven't told us in a while."

"It's still beating." The panic rose within her again. She wasn't about to have this conversation with her mother. "Hey, I have a surprise for you."

"I still want to know about your heart." Her mother wouldn't be easily fooled. She'd been tracking Mary Catherine's health since they found her heart defect at three weeks old. The smile returned to her mom's voice. "What's the surprise?"

"I'm coming to see you! I'll be there in a week." Suddenly she could hardly wait. "I'll be there for three days."

"Why not a week?" Her mother sounded confused. "I mean, we'll take it! I'd love to see you for any amount of time."

Telling her mom about her heart could wait. Africa could

not. She stood and walked slowly toward the water. "I need to be in New York on Wednesday morning. I'm meeting with a mission team there and flying to Uganda." She forced a giddy tone. "Isn't that incredible?"

Her mother didn't answer.

"Mom?" Mary Catherine allowed a lighthearted laugh. "Aren't you excited? I've seriously always wanted to go back to Africa. You know that."

Her mother drew a long breath. "It's just . . . how come you're only telling us now?"

"Everything just came together." Not quite the truth. Mary Catherine winced. She put her toes in the water. "I'll be there for six months. I'm helping open an orphanage and a school." She hesitated. "We'll get it up and running and then someone else can step in and take over." Another pause. "Isn't that great?"

"Six months?" Her mother sounded shocked. "What about your job?"

"They've given me a leave." Mary Catherine stopped trying to sound happy. "Mom, this has been on my list forever. You know that." In the silence that followed, her mother began sniffling. "Please . . . you're not crying, are you?"

"Honey, Africa?" She was definitely crying. "For six months?" She seemed to struggle to find her voice. "What about your health?"

"I'll be fine." Mary Catherine hated this. "My doctor gave me permission. I wouldn't go if he didn't."

It was a slight exaggeration, but she wasn't lying.

Her mom hesitated. "You're sure?"

"Yes." Mary Catherine hurt for her mom. It couldn't have

been easy all these years having a daughter with heart trouble and diabetes. "I'll come home earlier if I'm not feeling well."

"All right." Her mom clearly didn't agree with the plan. "So you'll be here Sunday?"

"I will." Relief came with the next breeze off the ocean. Her mom sounded a little happier when they hung up. She would be okay. And the less time she had to worry about the heart transplant, the better.

Mary Catherine turned off her phone and slipped it into her pocket.

She thought about her parents again. Having them worry the entire time she was gone would do none of them any good. She'd tell them about her heart once she got back from Africa. And if she never returned . . . then her time was up. Her parents would understand. Spending her final months knowing her parents were worried and upset was not what Mary Catherine wanted. She breathed in little bits of ocean air until her lungs were filled. Shoulders back, hair blowing in the breeze, she closed her eyes and faced the sun.

The time waiting for a transplant would go faster in Africa. The orphans and some workers had already moved in and she couldn't wait to join them. Mary Catherine pictured their little faces. Children who had nothing, no one. Afraid and alone. Mary Catherine could hardly wait to love them. *There's no other way I'd want to spend my time, Lord.* She sighed.

And if God were willing, she would come home and have her surgery.

Mary Catherine moved back toward her spot and dug her toes in the sand. Maybe her breathlessness had nothing to do with her heart. She might just be tired. A good nap and she'd feel like herself. She gathered her things, picked up her towel, and headed back to her apartment. This time she forced herself to walk more slowly. Because of that—and because she knew God was answering her prayers—she didn't have any breathing troubles all the way home.

She barely made it to her bed and flopped on her side before falling asleep. Three hours later she woke to the setting sun. She sat up in bed and blinked a few times. Why was she sleeping in the middle of the day? She looked around her room. What day was it? Gradually the answers came to her. Today was Sunday. She'd gone to church with Sami and then for a walk to the beach. She must've really needed the nap.

Mary Catherine slipped out of bed and felt the room tilt a little. She stayed in one spot till she had her bearings. At least her breathing seemed back to normal. She moved to the sofa beneath her bedroom window, sat down, and grabbed her laptop. Food would take care of the dizzy feeling and restore her energy. But she had something to do before she could eat.

She opened her email and found Marcus's letter. The one where he had asked her if she was okay and told her he missed her every hour. She was wrong to let this much time pass without responding to him. Especially since he was worried about her.

Mary Catherine read his words again, let them soak their way into her heart.

I have to be honest. I have the strangest thought that something's wrong with you. Maybe I just don't want you to leave for Africa. Or maybe it's something else.

A shiver ran down her arms. How could he have known something was wrong? He had no idea about her heart defect. Mary Catherine finished reading his letter. When she reached the end she read his last words through teary eyes.

> I'll let you go. It never feels right being so far away. Just remember I'm always thinking of you. Praying for you.
>
> Missing you.
>
> Love, Marcus

Why hadn't he just faded into this next season of life the way Mary Catherine had expected? She had set him free for his own good. He deserved more than her damaged heart and uncertain future. There was no point to the two of them. Yet she loved him more now than ever before. Like he'd woven himself into the fabric of her soul.

She hit the reply button and started to type.

> Dear Marcus,
>
> I'm sorry I didn't write back sooner. I should have. Things have been busy at work and at home, trying to get ready for the big trip. I'm nowhere near organized. You'd laugh at this, but I haven't even gotten my shots. Queen of procrastination, I know.

She stopped and looked out the window. The evening was perfect. She wished she was still at the beach.

Instead she was trying to find the right words to tell Marcus Dillinger goodbye—again. One last time. She blinked back fresh tears and sighed. "I'm just glad you're not here in person," she whispered. Because after today she might actually cancel her flight to Uganda and stay here with Marcus. Glad for every minute they might have together. Even if she only had a handful of months.

Focus, she told herself. *Your plans are set.* She looked at the computer screen again and her fingers began to move across the keys.

> Anyway, I wanted to thank you for writing, for telling me how you felt, and for your concerns.
>
> I think God's given you a special discernment when it comes to me. Yes, I'm definitely distracted about this trip. Honestly, sometimes I wonder if I should really be going for six months. But then I remember how I've always wanted to go back. I don't want to miss my chance.
>
> That's probably why you've been worried about me. I'm fine. Really. Just a little anxious about leaving. So if you could pray about that, I'd appreciate it.

She stared at her letter. Awfully superficial. Borderline dishonest. And she hadn't dealt with the rest of what he'd written. The hardest part.

She started typing again.

> About the missing, it's not much fun, is it?

She hesitated.

> I think about you, too. Sometimes I actually hurt from wishing I could see you again. But the important thing is we've each got our dreams to follow. I'll be gone six months . . . and you've got the season. Everything you've ever wanted, Marcus. You're the best pitcher in baseball,

you've got the Youth Center, and a faith that's growing all
the time.

You'll forget about me eventually.

She read that line again and winced. *Too harsh.* She de-
leted it.

You might not forget about me—I certainly hope not,
anyway. I'd like to think I'm fairly unforgettable. But
eventually you'll come to understand this is for the best.
God will bring someone into your life where the timing
is better for both of you, where you both want the same
things.

Two tears slid down her cheeks. She wiped them with the
back of her hand and tried to see the computer screen.

I guess I just wanted to thank you for your letter, and for
praying for me, and to tell you I'm okay.

Tears blurred her eyes again.

Oh . . . and I think it's all right if we both hold on to that one
memory, the two of us dancing on your balcony.
Some people live their whole lives and don't have a night
like that.
Play for God. I'll pray for you, too.
Love, Mary Catherine

By the time she finished the letter, Mary Catherine had
lost her appetite. For food, anyway. She read it again and hit
send. Then she closed her computer and dried her eyes. *That's*

it. She sniffed and hurried to her feet. *No more.* She wasn't going to sit here crying about Marcus.

Their time had passed.

Get organized, she ordered herself. *You're going to run out of days.*

She went to her closet, pulled out her suitcase, and set it on the bed. Her second suitcase went on the floor, where it would stay—a reminder that she needed to buy crayons and kids' books.

For the next hour—until Sami came home—Mary Catherine went through her clothes, sorting out what to take and what to leave behind. The chore helped. She felt more organized, more focused on her flight out of LA next week.

But it didn't stop her from thinking about a private balcony, an LA night sky clearer than most, and a song falling gently around her.

And the dancing she'd done in the arms of a man she would miss as long as she lived.

Even if she never saw him again.

5

EMBER PLACED THE CALL to Front Line Studios just after two o'clock.

Mary Catherine answered on the first ring. "Hello?"

"Hi, I'm looking for Mary Catherine?"

"This is she." Her voice sounded weary.

She's sick, Ember thought. *We don't have long.* She felt the heaviness of anxiety. Something angels felt only on Earth. She closed her eyes and continued. "Yes, hello. I'm with Janie Omer's team, helping with details." It was true. Angels always helped with details of mission trips. Whether humans knew it or not. Ember steadied her voice. "I'm checking to see if you've gotten your shots?"

Mary Catherine uttered a soft groan. "Not yet. I keep meaning to."

"Okay, well, here's what you need to do." Ember explained that the clinic around the corner from Mary Catherine's office could handle all the shots she needed. "They close at five."

"Hmmm." Mary Catherine hesitated. "I don't get off work till six or so."

"Ask your boss for the time." Ember tried to sound convincing. "You need the shots today for the medicine to work in time."

Another pause and then a quiet laugh from Mary Catherine. "I guess I don't have any choice."

"Right." Ember could hear her own smile in her voice. "Thanks. Janie will be glad you took care of this."

MARY CATHERINE HATED asking to leave early, but it was only Monday. If she still had work to do, she could stay late another day this week. And the volunteer from Janie's team was right. If she didn't get the shots today, she wouldn't be protected by the time she reached Uganda. And in her case vaccination was crucial. Her heart couldn't take a serious illness right now.

At four fifteen and with her boss's blessing, Mary Catherine walked out the door of the studio offices, but before she could take a single step she stopped. Her breath caught in her throat. "Marcus . . ."

He was standing there, leaning against a light pole, his eyes locked on hers. He wore dark jeans and a lightweight white cotton button-down, sleeves rolled up. His eyes shimmered in the afternoon sunlight. He took a few steps toward her. "Figured if I wanted to have a real conversation with you, I had to come here."

"Is that right?" A rainbow of emotions colored Mary Catherine's soul. Suddenly her energy soared and she felt a smile fill her face. He was here! Marcus had come all the way to Los Angeles for her! To talk to her. Her knees felt weak and her resolution weaker.

He held out his hands. No man ever had kinder, deeper eyes than Marcus had right now. "Mary Catherine . . . come here. Please."

She had missed him more than she knew, even more than she'd been willing to admit. And here, with him standing a few feet from her, Mary Catherine felt like they were the only two people in the world. What else could she do but go to him?

As soon as his arms were around her Mary Catherine forgot every reason why she had tried to put him out of her mind. In this moment, her heart was well and she wasn't leaving for Uganda and everything was absolutely right with the universe.

All because she was in Marcus Dillinger's embrace.

Her words came in a whisper. "I missed you." She held on to his waist, protected, safe. Whole.

"There." He kissed the side of her head, stroking her hair. "That's what I wanted to hear."

After a while, Marcus drew back and studied her. "How can you be more beautiful than I remembered? Your face, your eyes. Your heart. You're perfect."

Mary Catherine ignored the irony. At least she looked nice. She wore new jeans and a white T-shirt with a navy button-down cardigan. She'd lost weight since being sick. New clothes were a necessity.

She caught her breath and looked down the street. "Wanna walk with me?"

"Always." He smiled, but there was no denying the depth in his expression. "Where to?"

She wrinkled her nose. "I need shots. For Uganda." She pointed. "A few blocks away there's a clinic."

He took her hand. "It's a date."

The feel of his fingers between hers made her want to stop time. Live in this single day, this walk with Marcus. She grinned at him. "I told you, I'm the queen of procrastination. I was supposed to get these weeks ago."

"Me, too." They walked slowly, their arms brushing against each other with every step.

She raised an eyebrow at him. "You're getting shots?"

"Yes!" He tried to keep a straight face. "Didn't you hear?"

"You're quitting baseball and going to Africa?" She laughed and the sensation was freeing. How long had it been since she'd laughed out loud? Since she'd even had the energy to laugh?

He stopped and faced her. "You already know?" He nodded, still playing serious. "Hanging up the ball and glove, moving to Uganda. I'll run the orphanage next to yours."

"Mmmm." She started walking again. "Because every village needs two orphanages."

"Exactly."

Mary Catherine laughed, and again the feeling was wonderful. "Perfect. We'll do recess together."

"Right." He chuckled. "I'll teach them to play baseball."

"And I'll teach them to dance."

"And to skydive." He winked at her. "If they ever get the chance."

Mary Catherine laughed once more, but this time it fell a

little flat. She would never skydive again or share recess with Marcus in Uganda. They had today. She would have to hang on to that. They grew quiet, and she was intensely aware of his presence. "When do you go back?"

"Tonight. Ten o'clock." He sighed and lifted his face to the blue sky, then turned back to her. "Too soon."

Mary Catherine stopped, stunned. "You flew in today?"

"Landed at three thirty. Took Uber to your office." Marcus raised his brow. "Matthew West is the reason I'm here."

"The singer?"

Marcus laughed. "Coach's wife loves the guy's music. He took her to a show and gave us today off."

"I always did love Matthew West." She smiled and started walking. "You're here by yourself?"

"Tyler wanted to come. He had training." He gave a slight shake of his head. "Poor guy can't wait to get back."

She hesitated just outside the door of the clinic. His eyes were so beautiful, the man behind them more so. Mary Catherine had to catch her breath again. This time the dizziness had nothing to do with her heart. Not physically, anyway.

The shots didn't take long. Even though Marcus didn't get any, he stayed at her side. The nurse looked concerned as she checked the list for Uganda. "You're leaving Wednesday for Africa?"

"Yes, ma'am." Mary Catherine squeezed her eyes nearly shut for the last shot.

"You should be okay." She checked a chart. "Our clinic is more conservative. We prefer giving shots ten days before travel. Just to be sure. Malaria is on the increase in Uganda."

"Wait . . ." Marcus spoke before Mary Catherine could respond. "She'll be protected still, right?"

"I think so." The nurse smiled. She finished filling out the shot record and handed it to Mary Catherine, along with a bottle of pills to prevent malaria and instructions.

Mary Catherine tucked the paperwork and pills into her purse and thanked the woman. She only wanted to think about Marcus and how they would spend the rest of the day. As much as she was looking forward to being in Africa, the reality of leaving Marcus again darkened her enthusiasm.

When they were back on the city street outside the clinic, Marcus faced her. "Something's wrong."

She shook her head and found a smile. "No . . . I'm fine. Just wishing we had longer."

"Says the girl who wouldn't answer my emails." His eyes sparkled. "Come on." He took her hand. "Let's go to the beach."

"Yes!" Mary Catherine grinned. "Perfect!" And like that the sadness and futility lifted. Never mind that it was a ten-block walk and she already felt breathless around Marcus. Tomorrow didn't matter.

Not as long as she and Marcus could have one more time at the beach.

MARY CATHERINE WALKED until she couldn't breathe. Then she would stop to share anecdotes from her work week or look at the crystal blue sky or laugh at something he said. He held her hand and stayed at her side, never seeming to notice the slow pace.

Each slight break gave her time to catch her breath.

By the time they reached their spot on the beach it was just after six o'clock. The temperature had dropped into the low sixties—normal for mid-March, but still chilly. The cool air felt wonderful to Mary Catherine. She slid her shoes off, rolled up her jeans, and dropped cross-legged to the dry sand. "I want to swim."

Marcus took off his shoes and rolled up his jeans, as well. He sat beside her and rubbed his bare arms. "You might need your wetsuit."

"True." She laughed. "We should've stopped by my apartment first." But even as she said the words she knew a swim now wasn't possible. The cold water combined with her health would make it impossible to breathe. Besides, her doctor had forbidden it.

A quiet fell over them, intimate and sacred, their eyes on the pretty blue horizon. This time Marcus left a little room between them. The space gave Mary Catherine the chance to think more clearly, to convince herself this wasn't a dream. After so long apart Marcus Dillinger really was sitting beside her, on her favorite beach.

But what about after this? He'd fly back to Arizona tonight.

She felt a ribbon of fear work its way through her. Marcus would get on a plane and a few days later, she would do the same. And that would be that. These would be their last few hours together for a very long time. Maybe forever.

She narrowed her eyes and blinked back the beginning of tears.

"What are you thinking?" Marcus turned to her, his expression warm and kind.

"Lots." She smiled, taking her time. The pull she felt toward him was magnetic. Stronger than the ocean tide. "I wish I could stop time."

"Mmm. Me, too." He slid closer, and their bare arms touched again. Once more he faced the water. "Maybe I really will quit baseball and move to Africa."

"Sure." A giggle escaped before she could stop it. "The Dodgers will love that."

"Mary Catherine . . ." He turned his body so he could see her better. He hesitated for a long moment. "If you want to stop time, why do you push me away?"

The sting of her tears grew stronger. "I'm sorry."

"I know." His tone was gentle, his voice mixed with the breeze off the Pacific. "But why?" He sighed and hung his head for a beat. When he looked up, she could see the muscles in his jaw. "Can't you feel it? The way we are . . . the way it is between us?"

"Yes." She stared at the ocean. "I feel it." *God, what am I supposed to say?* She couldn't tell Marcus the truth. She refused to burden him with her struggles. Finally she turned to him again. "I'm not like other girls. I need crazy adventure. Something different." She hated this, hated not telling him the truth. "What if I don't come back from Africa?"

He drew back, as if he'd been slapped. "Ever?"

"Right." She felt her head spinning. *Because I might not live that long.* The sad reality swept over her. She squeezed her eyes shut. This time she could do nothing to stop her tears.

He leveled his gaze at her. "What happened to the girl who wanted someone present, in the moment? Someone she could be real with?" He paused. "Someone who would listen?"

Mary Catherine could see herself that long-ago night, walking beside Marcus in his neighborhood, the two of them getting to know each other. He was right. She'd said those exact words. Now she searched his eyes. "Things changed." At least that part was true. "I'm going away."

"For six months, Mary Catherine. So what?" Marcus shook his head. "Don't you get it?" He chuckled but the sound was mostly sad. "I'm not leaving. One day you'll be back and I'll be here. Waiting for you." He hesitated. "If you'll let me."

Two tears slid down her cheeks. *I want to,* she thought. *Dear God, You know I want to.* She stood and walked to the water's edge. Her feet ankle-deep in the cold surf, the tears came harder. She wanted to run to him and beg him to never leave, never let her go.

Which was why she needed to end things with Marcus.

She hated losing him but she had no choice. Africa was now or never—and this trip had been a dream of hers for too long to give it up now. Sure, if she were healthy she could agree to let Marcus wait for her. But there was no point. Her situation was what it was.

Mary Catherine felt his arms around her before he reached her. The bond between them was that strong. He put his hands on her shoulders and drew her close. She didn't turn around, didn't want him to see her crying. Instead she leaned her head back on his chest and closed her eyes.

"Hey." His words came with a gentleness that belied his great strength. He eased her around so she was facing him. He caught her next few tears with his fingertips. "Is it me?"

He looked pained even asking. "I'm just . . . not the one? Is that it?"

She searched his eyes. Somehow she could breathe better when he was this close. "It's never you." She put her hand on his cheek. "I told you before. If I was going to love someone . . . it would be you."

At first he looked like he might argue, press for an answer that made more sense. Instead he slowly pulled her into his arms and held her. Mary Catherine memorized the feeling as they swayed ever so slightly to the sound of the nearby waves. She had never felt more safe and secure.

More loved.

Finally he eased back and moved his hands to her shoulders. "Then I'll wait." His breath was sweet against her skin, his words like balm to her heart. "When you come back in six months I'll be here."

"I might not come back and then—"

"I'll move to Africa." He searched her eyes. "Or to the moon. Wherever you are."

Mary Catherine fell quiet. "No." Her heartache had nothing to do with her health. "I asked you to be my friend."

It was true. Last time they were together she had asked him to be content with that. And he had promised he would. That he would be the best friend she'd ever had.

A smokiness filled his eyes. He ran his hands lightly down her arms and looked to the deepest parts of her soul. "Does this . . . feel like friendship?"

She hesitated, trying to remember which way was up. Gradually she shook her head and whispered just one word. "No."

"Then I'll wait." His words filled up every lonely, hurting place inside her.

Then, just when she thought he might kiss her, he took her hand. "Let's walk."

The beach was empty except for an occasional surfer. They headed north toward the pier, and again Mary Catherine felt winded. A constant reminder that she had to keep resisting him. Every twenty yards or so she stopped and stared at the sunset. The pace allowed them time to talk about other things. Marcus was involved in a weekly chapel Sunday mornings at the Camelback Ranch spring training facility.

"I had no idea so many major leaguers were Christians." Marcus smiled. "A few of us meet for Bible study every morning. I'm learning a ton."

"Like what?" She loved being with him, loved the way his fingers felt between hers.

"About living different from society. Living out God's ways not only in love, but in truth." He squinted at the sunset. "I want my life built on God's word." He picked up a handful of sand and let it sift through the fingers of his free hand. "Nothing else lasts."

Mary Catherine felt her attraction to him double. They walked a little more and then turned to face the water. The golden light was just hitting the place where the sky and sea came together. She shaded her eyes with her free hand. "It's so pretty."

The air was even cooler now. Marcus put his arm around Mary Catherine's shoulders. "I wish I could ask God to stop the sun . . . right there."

"Mmmm. Yes." She smiled. It was seven o'clock. They had

an hour at best. "Just freeze it. With a million shades of blues and pinks spread across the sky."

He took her hands and faced her again. The cold sand beneath her feet sent chills up her legs. Mary Catherine let herself get lost in his eyes. "I still can't believe you're here."

"Figured if I could see you even for an hour it was worth it." He brushed her long hair back with his fingers.

"You're crazy." She smiled, drawn to him, flattered by him.

"You can't get rid of me." His eyes sparkled, back to his familiar teasing. "I'm building that orphanage next to yours."

She laughed and the sound hung in the air between them. The sun was already gone, dropped below the horizon. She ran her thumbs along the tops of his hands. "We have to go."

"Can you pretend?" He moved closer, his breath soft on her cheek. "Please, Mary Catherine. Just for today?"

Her mouth was dry. "Pretend?" She could smell the faint scent of his cologne. All she wanted was to kiss him.

"Yes," he whispered. "That I'm more than your friend."

Tears blurred her eyes again. She closed the gap, brushing the side of her face against his. "I don't have to pretend." She met his eyes. "Nothing ever felt more real."

This time he framed her face with his hands and in a way Mary Catherine never thought she'd experience again, he kissed her. Passion swirled around them, making her forget the chilly breeze off the ocean. She would've been breathless with a perfectly healthy heart.

His breathing was faster, too. "How can I ever be just your friend?"

Mary Catherine had no answers. She looped her arms around his neck and this time the kiss came from her. Yes, she could pretend. She could pretend that she was healthy and whole and Africa was only a distant dream, something she wanted to do one of these years when she got around to it. She could pretend that Marcus was the man she'd been waiting for. The one. Real and good and true.

The kiss was wonderful, and when they parted and caught their breath, the sky was already growing dark. A sad smile played on the corners of his lips. "We need to get back."

She nodded, and he took her hand. They didn't talk as they made their way across the stretch of sand and crossed Ocean Avenue. She wasn't as breathless this time. Maybe she was too distracted by the sadness of it all. The fact that this could be the last time she'd ever see him.

When they were a block from her apartment, Marcus called for a ride. They had only a few minutes in front of her building. He kissed her again. "I'm not giving up."

She closed her eyes and let her forehead fall against his chest. "If I don't see you again—"

"Mary Catherine, you have to believe—"

"Please. I need to say this." She looked up. "If I don't see you again . . ." Tears welled in her eyes. "Just know I'll always remember this. You surprising me. These hours."

He looked like he still had more to say. But just then a black sedan pulled up. Marcus signaled to the driver to give him a minute. They kissed one final time.

"Remember something." He breathed the words against the side of her face.

She waited, fighting tears.

"Friends talk." He framed her face with his hands and searched her eyes. "Write to me, okay? Please."

She nodded. "I will."

They held on to each other until he kissed her cheek and whispered the word she never wanted to hear. "Goodbye."

She blinked back tears, her voice strained. "Bye. Thanks for coming."

He looked back once as he walked to the waiting sedan. But neither of them said another word. There was nothing to say. His plane was leaving in a few hours.

The setting sun had gotten the final word, after all.

6

JAG AND BECK'S NEXT TASK would be the toughest yet for one reason.

Marcus Dillinger was discouraged.

He'd been back from Los Angeles for nearly a week and though he'd texted Mary Catherine every day and emailed her twice, she hadn't responded. Last night Marcus told Tyler he couldn't understand what he'd done wrong. He was willing to cut ties with her for now. If that's what she wanted. But the possibility made him feel defeated.

Jag and Beck had a plan to inspire the man.

Dressed like janitors, they moved stealthily to the back of the clubhouse. Beck had a key, so the two of them made their way into the building and then down a hallway to Coach Ollie Wayne's office. Beck stood outside the door, keeping watch. Jag went inside and on the man's desk were his notes for the morning. The title read, "Using Your Gifts for God."

Good, Jag thought. *Not good enough.*

He opened a desk drawer and slid the notes in the back of a file marked "Messages." Then he thumbed through the front of the file until he found the one he wanted.

Yes. Jag smiled. *This'll work.* Jag set the document on Coach Wayne's desk. Sunday morning chapel was about to have a change of plans.

Jag hurried out of the office, where he and Beck turned a corner and disappeared.

They would spend the night praying.

TYLER AND MARCUS took their time walking to chapel that Sunday morning. It was just before eight and the Arizona sun was already hot overhead. Marcus had almost skipped this one. He kept thinking about Mary Catherine leaving Los Angeles later today. She'd spend a few days in Nashville with her parents and then be off to Uganda.

"You're quiet." Tyler glanced at him. "Mary Catherine?"

Marcus drew a deep breath. "Yeah. I can't figure her out."

"She's a tough one. Sami can't explain it, either." Tyler looked as baffled as Marcus felt. "She could at least write back. Especially after your visit. It sounded perfect."

A darkness washed over Marcus again. "It was." He shrugged. "At least I've been pitching better. Gotta credit her for that."

Tyler gave him a sad smile. "I'm sorry."

"It's okay. If it's supposed to happen, it'll happen." He breathed deep. "Maybe I just need to let it go. For now anyway."

They walked into the clubhouse and followed a few others to the chapel room. "I guess just pray. God will make it clear."

"Either that or He'll help me forget her." Marcus hated even saying the words. He and Tyler took seats next to each other in the second row. The room was like any other office in the building. But for spring training it was a place guys could get away and think if they needed to. Somewhere they could pray.

Marcus opened his Bible app. Then he anchored his elbows on the desk and rested his forehead against his fists. Why did she do this? Just cut him off like they hadn't had the most amazing day together? Was it all an act? He had asked her to pretend, after all. He remembered holding her in his arms, feeling her beside him. The crazy chemistry when they kissed.

It wasn't an act. She had answered that question there on the beach. Nothing had ever been more real. That's what she had said. No, what they shared wasn't pretend. It was real. So then why? He clenched his jaw. There was something she wasn't telling him, but what?

He looked up as Coach Wayne took his spot at the front of the room. A few times they'd had guest speakers for Sunday mornings. But usually Coach took the job. It was one more reason Marcus felt close to the man.

"Good morning." Coach looked around the room and then let his eyes land on Marcus. "Glad you're here."

"Thanks, Coach." Marcus managed a smile. A chorus of responses came from the twenty guys gathered.

"Today should be interesting—at least for some of you." He chuckled. "I had one message planned for today, but when

I got to my office I found a different set of notes on my desk."

Strange, Marcus thought. He shifted in his seat.

"I'm going with the new message. *Godly Men Take Risks.*" He shrugged. "Someone here must need this." He paused and his demeanor grew more serious. "This is something we don't talk about enough in the church. The fact that godly men have to take risks. They have to go after the things God is calling them to do." He paused. "Even if it costs them everything."

Marcus felt chills on his arms and legs. He glanced around at the other guys. Did that opening line hit anyone else the way it just hit him? Or was he the guy Coach Wayne was talking about?

The message was brief and powerful, and Marcus hung on every word. God brings opportunities and people into the lives of believers. But it's up to each one to pursue what God presents.

"You hear guys banter around a popular phrase. 'If it's supposed to happen, it'll happen.'"

Tyler kicked him under the desk. Marcus barely felt it. He looked down at his hands, at his phone still opened to the Bible app. He had said those exact words to Tyler on the way here. How could Coach have known?

God, if this is from You, I'm listening.

"Find Deuteronomy 31:8." He hesitated as he opened his Bible. "God's people were in battle through much of the Old Testament." Coach Wayne looked at them. "Whatever battle you're in—whatever you're facing—the words here will give you direction. I believe that."

Marcus found the section in Deuteronomy.

"Starting with verse eight." Coach waited a few seconds. "It says, 'The Lord, Himself, goes before you and will be with you; He will never leave you nor forsake you. Do not be afraid; do not be discouraged.'"

God would go before him? What did that mean when it came to Mary Catherine? Was he supposed to go to her again, tell her even more definitively how much he cared? Marcus listened intently.

Coach Wayne referred to other verses. "Turn to 1 Chronicles 28:20. Let's read it together." He waited. "David is talking to Solomon and he says, 'Be strong and courageous and do the work. Do not be afraid or discouraged, for the Lord God, my God, is with you. He will not fail you nor forsake you . . .'"

Marcus felt the words hit straight at the center of his soul. Something about the way Coach emphasized the words. Then they turned to 1 Chronicles 20. Marcus read along with Coach Wayne as he spoke the Scripture out loud. "'You will not have to fight this battle. Take up your positions; stand firm and see the deliverance the Lord will give you . . . Do not be afraid, do not be discouraged. Go out to face them tomorrow, and the Lord will be with you.'"

The Lord will be with me. Marcus felt his head spin. Maybe this was his answer, the message straight from God to his heart.

Coach was winding up the message, encouraging them to be brave and courageous. What was God calling them to do? Walk away from some addiction or sin struggle? Have a conversation they'd been putting off? "Or maybe just make your intentions known in a certain situation. Letting your faith direct you to speak your mind. Finally."

Marcus felt a deep courage stir within him. What was God calling him to do? That was the question. Maybe if he went to Mary Catherine one more time and told her how he really felt—how serious he was—then he would finally know. Her answer might set them both free to love . . . or it might break his heart. But in that case, the Bible was right. God would be with him.

Whatever the situation, he wouldn't have to walk the road ahead alone.

When chapel was over, Marcus thanked Coach Wayne. Then he walked with Tyler back to their rooms. "Powerful." Tyler raised his brow at Marcus. "Right?"

"Man, I thought he was talking straight to me."

"Me, too." He laughed. "I need to get that ring. Sami's waited long enough."

"Good for you." Marcus patted his friend on the back.

They made a plan to meet in an hour for their next workout. Once Marcus was alone in his room, he walked to the window, slid the sheer curtain aside, and stared at the barren Arizona mountains. Marcus smiled. Tyler was going to buy a ring. His friend was right—it was time.

The message this morning left no room for doubts.

His smile faded and he found the single cloud in the sky. If only it were that easy for him and Mary Catherine. Marcus was slated to pitch later this afternoon. He wouldn't have time today or tomorrow. He checked his schedule and chills ran down his arms again. Other than a few meetings and a single workout, he had Wednesday off.

The day Mary Catherine was flying to Africa.

Yes, he'd just seen her, and true, she'd told him not to wait for her. But something had to be wrong. Something more than her trip to Africa. Her feelings were as real as his—so she had to be keeping things to herself. Some problem he wasn't aware of.

Well, maybe if he told her how committed he was, that he didn't just want to wait for her and date her. Maybe then she would explain what was really holding her back.

He opened his computer and his fingers began flying across the keyboard. It wasn't enough to tell her he wanted to wait for her, or that he hoped she might pretend for a single day.

He wanted to marry her.

It was time he said so.

7

MARY CATHERINE NEEDED EVERY MINUTE of
the four-hour flight. Not just to rest, but to wrap her mind
around all that had happened last week. The events about to
happen. She settled into her seat and looked out the window.

The jet took off over the Pacific Ocean, over the water
and waves she loved. Over every wonderful memory from the
last few years. Her stomach felt nervous, a mix of excitement
about her time in Africa and sorrow over the life she was leaving behind. She put her hand on the plastic window. *Will I
ever be back, God? Is this my last goodbye?*

Like most flights departing Los Angeles International Airport, the plane made a U-turn a few miles over the ocean.
Mary Catherine could see it all clearly. One last look at the
beach, and then the city, the places where she'd worked, the
streets where she rode her bike. And then Castaic Lake and
the desert where she'd landed after skydiving.

All of it blurred together like the most beautiful kaleidoscope of laughter and living color and life. She lifted her eyes to the deep blue sky. The adventure ahead would provide a host of new memories, fulfilling times that she had looked forward to for years. Africa would be amazing. Instantly she would have a few dozen children—kids who would love her like the mother they didn't have. She could hardly wait.

But that didn't ease her anxiety.

She closed her eyes. Sleep. She needed sleep. Then she'd be better able to handle the clash of heartache and happiness whirling together in her heart and mind.

She leaned her head back against the seat.

A host of recent memories lined up on the screen of her heart. Starting with last night.

The beach had been calling to her all day, but she wasn't finished packing. So instead of a final walk to the shore, Sami helped her organize her bags.

"Four suitcases?" Sami had laughed. Both of them had tried to keep things light. "You're coming back after six months, right?"

Mary Catherine never actually answered. She laughed about not really needing so much, and how two of the bags were school supplies. By then Mary Catherine had made her decision. She wouldn't tell Sami about the transplant, not until she returned from Africa. Besides, she would only be an email away.

When they finished zipping up Mary Catherine's bags, they talked about the teen mentor program. "I'm still worried about Lexy." Sami's eyes clouded over. "Did she ever get ahold of you?"

"No." Mary Catherine hated that she and Lexy never talked. "I called her a few times and left messages." She shook her head. "Nothing."

Otherwise the Youth Center was doing better than ever. More neighbors on board, more people finding life outside the gangs. Their conversation continued through dinner until they watched *Saving Mr. Banks*. Both of them were wiping tears when it ended.

Sami had turned off the TV and looked at Mary Catherine. "I don't want to say goodbye."

"I know. I hate this." Mary Catherine had forced a smile. "Six months will go quickly." She had used her savings to pay six months' rent up front. So she would have a home to come back to. If she lived that long.

Like when she was with Marcus last week, Mary Catherine hated not telling Sami the whole story. She might love Africa so much that she would choose to stay until her heart gave out. Yes, she'd paid her rent in case she returned to LA. But truthfully she had no idea if she'd ever come back.

Before turning in for the night, the girls had hugged. Sami promised to pray for her every day. "I try to think about the kids you'll be helping." She put her hand on Mary Catherine's shoulder. "So I don't feel sorry for myself."

Her mention of the African children made Mary Catherine smile. This was her purpose now, her passion. "I can't wait. I've dreamed about going back for so long."

They prayed together, that God would bless Mary Catherine's time in Nashville with her parents, and that He'd guard and protect her on the way to Uganda and every day she was there.

"Until we're back here together again." Sami finished the prayer. "In Jesus' name, amen."

"Amen." Mary Catherine had felt exhausted. So many goodbyes, so much finality.

Sami had still been asleep this morning when Mary Catherine took a cab to the airport. Sami had offered to drive her, but Mary Catherine gently declined. Better to take a cab and not drag out their goodbyes. As for her car, rather than sell it, she left it behind. Sami planned to drive it a couple of times a week—just to keep the engine working. Mary Catherine would ask Sami to sell it if she stayed longer than six months or if . . .

The thought dangled in the shadows of her mind. *What if . . .*

A voice came over the plane's PA system. The captain introduced himself and gave a rundown of the hours ahead. They expected clear skies, a smooth flight. "Right now we're flying over Arizona." He paused. "Let our flight attendants know if you need anything at all. For now, sit back, relax, and enjoy the flight."

Arizona.

Mary Catherine opened her eyes and looked out the window again. The desert stretched out below, and somewhere in the landscape was the Camelback Ranch facility. She had checked the Dodgers' schedule. Marcus would be getting ready to pitch later today. He'd tried to reach her a number of times, and always—though it hurt her terribly—she hadn't responded.

What was the point? He needed to get on with his life. The greatest gift she could give him was her silence. *I'm sorry, Marcus . . . God, let him know I'm sorry. Please.*

After a while Mary Catherine fell asleep. She woke up as they were landing in Nashville. This time the window gave her a glimpse of everything familiar. The deep green rolling hills and picturesque trees. From the air, Nashville looked like Mary Catherine expected heaven to look.

One day soon she would know if she was right.

THE TIME WITH HER PARENTS was special for all of them. Mary Catherine and her mother made dinner each night, taking turns with favorite new recipes—all of them ketogenic and low carb.

"You look beautiful." Her mother commented on the fact often. "A little thin, though. And your blood sugars are good?"

Sometimes Mary Catherine's mother would look at her a little longer, as if maybe she suspected something was wrong. Once while they were making Mary Catherine's no-carb pizza, her mom stopped and stared at her. "You're sure you're okay? You seem quieter. Like something's on your mind."

Mary Catherine only smiled. "Just thinking about Africa." It was the truth. Her dream trip filled her mind more than thoughts of her failing health. "I can't wait to meet the kids."

Her mom nodded, but her expression made it clear she wasn't quite convinced. "You're taking care of yourself? Your heart . . . your diabetes?"

"I am." Mary Catherine cracked several eggs over the bowl of grated mozzarella. "I'm staying in ketosis. Eating less than twenty carbs a day." She stirred the eggs and cheese. "I can breathe easier."

That part was true, too. She'd been very careful with her diet these past few days and she was less out of breath. Clearly her heart responded to healthier eating.

She and her parents seemed happier than ever, their marriage better than it had been in their early years. The three of them felt like a family again. Together they took walks each night around the neighborhood Mary Catherine grew up in. Maybe it was the clearer air in Nashville or the way she was eating—but she wasn't as winded as before. They talked about her childhood days, the time she tried to ride a two-wheel bike the day before kindergarten and knocked out one of her teeth, and the summer she was eight years old, when she won the blue ribbon at the fair in a race against all the boys.

Her mother laughed. "Every one of those boys thought they had you beat."

"But no!" Her dad grinned. "My girl took the prize."

At night they played spades and Password and watched old home movies. Mary Catherine loved her time with her parents more than she could've imagined. They had accepted the fact that Mary Catherine would be in Africa for six months, but she avoided the conversation about her pending heart transplant. No need to ruin the mood for everyone.

In a blur of happy times, the visit was over and her parents were taking her to the airport. They stepped out of the car at the curbside departure area. Her father helped her with her bags and then hugged her. "You'll be so far away." He paused. "Be careful, sweetie. Please."

"I will, Dad." Mary Catherine kissed his cheek. "I'll check in every few days. Promise."

He looked satisfied. "We'd like that."

Mary Catherine turned to her mom. She loved her parents so much. And seeing them together again was nothing short of miraculous. Mary Catherine looked deep into her mother's eyes. "It means a lot that you understand this." The two of them hugged and Mary Catherine fought the tears.

"We're proud of you, honey." Her mom's smile emanated kindness and support.

A memory rushed at Mary Catherine. She was twelve and so excited for her first day of middle school. Her mom had smiled as she said goodbye, but every sort of concern showed in her eyes.

It was that way between them now. Mary Catherine searched her mom's face. "It'll be okay." They hugged again. "Really."

Her mom put her hand gently on Mary Catherine's cheeks. "You being here . . . made me realize how much I've missed you." She stood a little straighter, clearly trying to be strong. Her mom wiped a single tear from her cheek. "Go. I love you."

Mary Catherine stepped into the curbside baggage line, and for a long moment she held on to the image of her parents standing there. They exuded the kind of love a girl could only get from her mom and dad. She waved one more time as they climbed back into the car and drove away.

Was this it? The last time she would ever see them? Mary Catherine closed her eyes and forced herself to be brave. Was she wrong not telling them about her heart? The conflict tore at her. If her parents knew, they would never agree to her trip to Africa. And she wanted this so badly. She could already see the children's faces. *Lord, please . . . let me live long enough to be back here one day.*

She blinked and focused on the passengers ahead of her. The line wasn't long. A couple more people and then she'd check her bags and get her boarding passes.

Now that the goodbyes were behind her, she could hardly wait for Uganda.

BECK RAN THROUGH THE AIRPORT, dodging tourists and slow-moving families, just another passenger late for a flight.

He was a businessman today, black suit and tie, racing through the ticketing area and darting outside just as Mary Catherine was about to step up to the skycap counter and check her bags.

"Excuse me!" He was still running, and he glanced at Mary Catherine. "Sorry. I checked the wrong bag."

Mary Catherine stepped back and waited.

Beck shook hands with the man behind the counter. "Sorry for cutting the line, but I'll miss my flight if I don't get this figured out."

The skycap looked confused. "Did I help you today?"

"Yes." Beck waved his thumb toward the cars dropping off passengers. "My buddy dropped me off here. I checked two bags." He shook his head. "One of them was supposed to be carry-on." He checked his watch.

"Do you have your baggage claim tickets?"

Beck drew a blank. He needed to make this moment last as long as possible. Timing was everything. He patted his pants pockets, checked them, and then did the same to his suit coat pockets. Behind him he could feel the people getting antsy.

He turned around and looked at Mary Catherine. "So sorry." He gave her a weak smile. "Gotta find my claim tickets." He looked on the ground around the baggage center and then checked his pockets again.

"What's your name?" The skycap looked frustrated. "Maybe we can find your tags that way."

Beck gave the man a last name with six syllables. It took three minutes just to enter the spelling correctly in the computer. Every minute or so, Beck looked over his shoulder and apologized to Mary Catherine. Each time she nodded, pleasant.

Another minute and then the skycap shook his head. "No passengers by that name. Not on any flight."

"You're kidding." Beck crossed his arms and did his best to look baffled. "Maybe you entered the name wrong."

Another three minutes getting his name into the computer again and this time when it didn't turn up, the man behind the counter shook his head. "I need the claim tickets. Maybe your wallet?"

"Yes!" Beck pulled out his wallet. In the process he fumbled and it fell to the ground, credit cards and receipts scattering on the cement. He crouched down and made an effort at gathering each piece and dusting it off. *Come on,* he thought. *Hurry . . . I can't do this forever.*

There were a dozen people behind Mary Catherine now. Out of the corner of his eye, Beck watched her check the time on her phone and glance through the window at the counter inside. The line there was even longer. Beck was certain Mary Catherine wouldn't leave when she was next up.

Three people behind Mary Catherine, a large man shouted, "Hey, buddy. Maybe step to the side and look." His face was red and sweaty. "We got planes to catch!"

The skycap walked out from behind the counter and tapped Beck on the shoulder. "Sir, I've got a long line. Wait over there." He pointed toward the wall near the doors. "Until you find the claim tickets."

"Okay. Hold on." Beck could feel his heart racing. He should be here by now. Where was he? Beck had killed nearly ten minutes but he was out of reasons to hold up the line any longer.

Then from his place crouched on the ground, still collecting the contents of his wallet, Beck saw something that allowed him to relax again. He returned the cards and receipts to his wallet, stood and nodded at Mary Catherine, and then at the others. "Sorry." He pointed to the doors. "I'll look inside."

A smile lifted the corners of his lips. Success. Beck slid his wallet back in his pants, walked inside the airport, headed for the men's restroom, and disappeared.

8

⧽⧼⧽⧼⧽

MARY CATHERINE FELT SORRY for the people behind her. She'd never seen such a holdup—especially checking bags curbside. The poor businessman couldn't have been more flustered. But none of it bothered Mary Catherine. God had allowed this trip to Africa. Nothing could touch her peace and excitement about all that lay ahead.

The skycap was helping her with her third bag when she heard someone run up behind her and touch her elbow. *The businessman again,* she thought. But when she turned around she gasped. "Marcus . . ."

He hugged her, breathless. His words were soft, for her alone. "I can't believe I found you."

Was she dreaming? Could he really be here? And why had he come when . . . "How did you . . . ?"

"We had the day off." He seemed suddenly aware of the line behind them. "Finish with your bags." He put his hand on her shoulder. "We need to talk."

Butterflies filled her stomach, and she could feel her heart beating hard against her chest. He had come all the way from Arizona to Nashville for this? To be with her for an hour? She could barely collect her boarding passes and tip the sky-cap. Her knees trembled as Marcus took her hand and led her inside the airport.

The terminal was loud and chaotic, but they found a couple of seats in a quiet alcove adjacent to the ticketing area. Mary Catherine couldn't believe this was happening, that he was really here. "Is everything okay?" She turned her knees toward him and searched his face.

"Yes." He smiled, but the look in his eyes was deeper than before, more intense. He took hold of her hands. "How long before you have to get through security?"

She checked her time. "Forty-five minutes."

"Perfect." His expression relaxed. "Sami told me what time your flight was leaving for New York." He laughed. "My flight was delayed out of Arizona and by the time I got here, I figured I'd missed you."

Mary Catherine grinned. "When do you go back?"

"Three hours."

"What?" Her face felt flushed but she didn't mind. He'd come to see her and he was here. For now, nothing else mattered. She laughed. "You're crazy."

"I probably looked it." Something about his smile made the moment feel personal. "Ran up and down the line and then it hit me. Maybe you were checking your bags outside."

He talked about his week, spring training, and he asked about hers. "Of course"—he laughed again—"all I wanted to do was get on a plane and get those shots. I can't move to Africa without them."

He laughed and the conversation continued. Mary Catherine checked her phone. Ten minutes had passed, then twenty. Time was slipping through their hands and still she wasn't completely sure why he had come. Especially after she'd been so clear last time that they needed to move on.

"It's so good to see you, Mary Catherine." The sincerity in his eyes was a window to his soul. "I prayed I'd find a way."

Mary Catherine thought about the businessman. If he hadn't cut in front of her and made such a scene trying to find his claim ticket, Marcus would've missed her. "I guess . . . God answered."

"He did." He ran his thumbs over her hands. "When you wouldn't answer my emails, I was worried. I couldn't let you go all the way to Uganda without making sure you were okay. And without being very clear . . . about how I feel."

A dizziness swept over her. Every word he spoke was balm to her soul. Listening to his calming voice and savoring the way he made her feel loved. Looking into his handsome face. She wanted to cancel her flight and stay with him forever.

Wherever he went, however long she had.

Mary Catherine blinked and tried to keep her senses in order. "You said you wanted to talk." The noisy crowds from the nearby terminal seemed to fade. Right here, right now it was just him and her.

"I do." His expression was serious. "I had to know what was wrong . . . and I had to tell you something."

A thread of anxiety wove itself through the moment. He

hadn't come all this way for an hour just because he was worried about her. Whatever else was on his mind, she was about to find out. "Tell me what?" She studied him. "Why did you come here? Really?"

The easy sparkle in his eyes was gone now. "Can I hug you first?"

Hugging him was all she'd wanted to do since she first saw his face. "Please."

He helped her to her feet and like a scene from a movie they came together, no longer aware of anyone or anything around them. In his arms she felt small and safe, whole and well. As if they really might have forever to fall in love and live a life together. She breathed in the smell of his shampoo, the freshness of his skin.

With the greatest tenderness he placed his hands on either side of her face and first he kissed her cheek. "You captivate me, Mary Catherine."

A whirling sense of wonder and joy swirled around her, enveloping the moment and making Mary Catherine more aware of him. "I'm sorry." She breathed the words against his face.

"Don't be." This time he kissed her lips.

Mary Catherine knew better. She was wrong to captivate him, wrong to kiss him. But she couldn't help herself. *Just for this hour,* she told herself. *Just this one last time.*

He was looking at her, and she felt lost in his eyes. *That's all,* she told herself. She couldn't do this. She forced herself to press back just an inch or so. Enough so she could catch her breath and find her common sense. "The reason . . . you're here?"

Again he looked serious. They lowered themselves to the seats again, and once more he took her hands in his. He pursed his lips and exhaled as if he needed a minute to collect his thoughts.

"Well . . ." He leaned his forearms on his knees, his face closer than before. "I'm in a tough spot. I needed to know you were okay. And I couldn't figure things out until I saw you again." He hesitated. "Until I looked in your eyes and really talked to you."

A tough spot? *Please, God, give me the words to end things with him. I need to release him.* She blinked and shook her head. She checked her phone again. They had seven minutes before she needed to leave. "I . . . I'm not sure what you mean?"

For a long time he didn't say anything. Finally he narrowed his eyes. "See, I understand what you've said." He still had hold of her hands. "You want to be friends, you're not interested in dating." A sigh slid through his lips. "I've heard you each time, Mary Catherine."

She nodded. Her mouth was dry. Words wouldn't come even if she could think of something to say.

"But every day I've thought about this, how I feel for you, what I believe you feel for me." He paused. Then very gently he lifted one of her hands to his lips and kissed it. When his eyes met hers again it looked like his heart was breaking. "The thing is . . . I don't want to date you."

Mary Catherine could feel her heart beating hard, racing just beneath her skin. "You don't?"

"No." He lowered her hand again, his eyes never leaving hers. "I want to marry you."

The walls began moving toward her, closing in, suffocating her. A part of her wanted to twirl around in joy and tell him yes! Yes, she wanted to marry him, too! But the whole thing was impossible. She was the girl who had never been asked to the prom, the one who had found a way to love life despite being alone. And now she was about to realize her greatest dream by moving to Africa.

And Marcus wanted to marry her?

Nothing about her situation would allow it. Marriage was absolutely impossible, and now . . . now her words would hurt both of them.

She squeezed her eyes shut. Had the air left the building, or was it her lungs? She couldn't take a full breath.

"Mary Catherine, talk to me." Marcus hesitated, as if he was searching for the right words. "I'm not saying marry me now. But in a year, maybe. When you come back." His voice was quieter, so soft that Mary Catherine could barely hear it. "Please. You don't have to be afraid."

Her heart was racing now, faster than before. Nothing about this was good for her, minutes before boarding. She hung her head and searched for something to say, whatever might be the least painful. But it was too late for that. "Marcus, I'm so sorry." She lifted her head and looked at him. "I've told you."

"I know." A hint of frustration colored his tone. He seemed to will himself to stay calm. "But I thought maybe . . . if you knew how serious I was . . ."

"That doesn't change the situation." She glanced around the airport, desperate to make him believe her. "I'm not the marrying type, okay?" She steadied her gaze at him. "I don't

want a house in the suburbs or the picket fence. I want this."
She blinked a few times. "Adventure, travel, mission work.
Uganda. Where I can make a difference." That part was true.
But she hated doing it again, leaving out the most important
part, the truth about her health.

Marcus waited a minute, watching her, as if he was trying
to grasp the finality of her declaration. Slowly he released her
hands and leaned back in the seat. He looked like he wanted
to argue with her, or debate the truth in what she said. Instead
he stayed quiet.

The ache in Mary Catherine's heart was worse than anything she'd ever felt. She wanted only to be in his arms once
more. But she couldn't let that happen. Never again. She
leaned forward, searching his eyes. "Does that make sense?"

"Yes." He stood and helped her to her feet. "You have to go."

They were always saying goodbye. A sudden strange awk-
wardness clouded the air around them. "I told you, Marcus."
Tears choked her voice before they reached her eyes. "If there
was anyone, if I wanted that life, there would only be you."

After having her hands in his for so long, she felt distant
now. Like there was already a continent between them. He
looked like he might just turn and walk away. But then the
depth in his eyes returned and he embraced her a final time.
But already things were different. His hug was different.
More like a brother bidding his sister goodbye as she went off
to college.

In his arms for the last time, Mary Catherine spoke in little more than a whisper. "Please understand, Marcus. I'm
sorry." Two tears slid down her cheeks. "I'm telling you the
truth. I'm just not the marrying type." She was right. But not

for the reasons she'd given him. She was dying. It'd be cruel to both of them to allow love now.

He looked at her then and spoke the first words he'd said since she turned him down. "You know something, Mary Catherine?"

She waited.

"I don't believe you." He leaned in and slowly kissed her cheek.

"Marcus, I—"

"I don't." He caught her tear with his thumb. "Your eyes say something else." Tears gathered in his eyes, too. He smiled and stepped back, slipping his hands into the pockets of his jeans. "Be safe." A few steps farther and he mouthed one last word. "Goodbye."

She raised her hand. "Bye."

And then, like she'd done too many times already, she watched Marcus turn around and walk past the ticketing counter through the double doors and outside. She had no idea where he was going. He still had a few hours before his flight back to Arizona.

Her tears came harder then, and sobs overcame her. *Marcus . . . I didn't mean it. You were right.* Mary Catherine wanted to run after him more than she wanted her next breath. She waited to see if he'd turn around and come back, if he'd beg her to be honest and tell him why she wouldn't love him.

But this time he didn't come for her. The beautiful unthinkable moment was over.

Mary Catherine dried her cheeks with the sleeve of her sweater, took hold of her carry-on bag, and headed for security. Every step put distance between them. This time Marcus was truly a part of her past. Running after him would do neither of them any good. She had a plan, and she needed to work it. Africa would be her swan song, her final adventure, her last prayer.

But her final act of love was a sacrifice only she would understand.

Letting go of Marcus Dillinger.

THE EVIL PRESENCE around the airport was palpable. Beck could feel it. The whirring of leathery wings and dark shadowy figures. He waited at the airport, watching Marcus cross the street and step into a cab. The man was clearly devastated.

His sunglasses did nothing to hide the fact.

Beck felt the weight of the loss. Today had been a disaster. The entire mission was in jeopardy. Dressed as the businessman again, Beck stayed close to Mary Catherine, seated at the same gate, praying for her health, her heart, her trip. Prayer was his strongest weapon now. It always would be.

Especially when the task ahead appeared impossible. Getting Mary Catherine back to Los Angeles.

He watched Mary Catherine as she boarded the plane, one of the last ones on. She kept to herself, talking only when necessary. Clearly she missed Marcus the way he missed her. Beck felt the pain of human heartache. So much pain.

When the plane was boarded and the gate shut, Beck remained. Praying. Begging God for a next move. Some way to keep the mission on track.

Suddenly, he felt a brush of wings.

"The plane." It was Jag, beside him. "It's in danger."

Beck felt the urgency. "Let's go."

A minute later they were dressed as mechanics, complete with heavy headphones. They headed for Mary Catherine's plane. Beck began to jog. "Hurry."

The jet's engines were running, and the pilot was about to back up. Jag and Beck began running toward the guy, waving their arms. The noise was louder than anything Beck had heard on Earth.

Jag pointed to the plane and held up credentials showing he was a lead engineer. Beck did the same. The man signaled to the pilots and like that one of them killed the engines.

Jag moved quickly, long strides, stern face. The tarmac was still loud, so Jag yelled his orders. "Get the other mechanics over here."

"Yes, sir," the man shouted in response. He looked confused. "What is it?"

"Something's wrong with the engine." Jag pointed to the plane's right side. "We just reviewed the inspection report." He yelled again. "Damaged fuel line."

Beck felt sick to his stomach. The 747 would've gotten partway over the Atlantic and run out of fuel.

The groundsman listened to his radio. "They're on the way. Any minute." His face was a grayish white. "Thank you. This . . . this wouldn't have been good."

Beck felt chills run down his arms and legs. The work of the enemy. No wonder he'd felt a sense of evil around the airport. The dark one planned to take down Mary Catherine's plane. And if that had happened, the mission would be over.

Failed for this generation and generations to come.

Again he felt a brush of wings.

Beck looked up and his soul flooded with relief. Not one angel, but an army of angels. Strong and capable. The airport was being surrounded. Beck exchanged a look with Jag. Mary Catherine's flight would be safe. Darkness would not have the final word.

Not today.

Not ever.

9

MARY CATHERINE HAD BEEN gone forty-four days. Marcus had counted every lonely one of them, but today he made a decision. He had to let her go. After she didn't respond to his first email, he kept hoping. But now . . . well, now he had to be honest with himself. If she didn't want him, then he wouldn't email her.

What was the point?

Marcus pulled into the parking lot of Hotel Bel-Air and left his car with the valet attendant. He was back in Los Angeles, the season under way. Today was the middle of a three-day break, so several of his teammates and their wives were meeting for dinner.

Tyler wouldn't be here tonight. Marcus smiled to himself as he slipped his wallet in his front pocket and headed inside. Monday was the big ask. Sami had no idea, at least that was Tyler's hope. His plan was perfect. Last night the two of them had hung out late, talking on Marcus's back porch. Tyler had shared his exact plans.

Marcus had listened to every word of his friend's excitement. But he wasn't perfectly focused. Not with his feet on the deck where he and Mary Catherine had danced that long-ago night. Every glimpse of the stars made him think of her. Maybe it always would.

The Hotel Bel-Air was well known for many reasons, but particularly because of the Wolfgang Puck restaurant, tucked away off the main lobby. The place was a favorite for celebrities and athletes looking for a more private dinner.

He checked in with the hostess and she led him to the table. Halfway there, at the back, Marcus spotted Dayne Matthews, an actor and director well known in Hollywood. Dayne was a Dodgers fan, and he and his wife, Katy, had come to the first home game a month ago.

They had joined Marcus and Tyler and several other players for devotions before the game. Marcus had a feeling he and Dayne would be good friends in time. He walked to their table and patted Dayne on the shoulder. "Hey!"

"Marcus." Dayne grinned and rose to his feet. The two shook hands as Katy stood and joined them. "We were just talking about how much fun we had at that game."

"Come to another one." Marcus hugged Katy. "You two are always welcome."

"I'll check the schedule." Dayne put his arm around his wife. "I think I told you we're here doing prep for a film. Shooting it in Indiana, but still a few more weeks of work here."

"I always wanted to be in a movie." Marcus chuckled. "I'll have to audition one of these days."

"Listen." Dayne laughed. "Consider yourself in. I'll find a place for you."

They chatted for another minute before Marcus bid his new friends farewell. "Text me. Let's get together soon! We have home games the end of next week."

"I'll do it." Dayne waved, and his wife did the same.

Such nice people, Marcus thought. *Mary Catherine would love them.* It took him another ten seconds before he corrected himself. Mary Catherine would never meet them. Because Marcus would never see her again—at least if Mary Catherine had her way.

He reached the small back room where the Dodgers group was gathered. Four players and their wives. And one of the wives had brought a friend. A single girl about the same age as Marcus. His teammate had hinted this might happen. It was fine.

Marcus would play the part for a night.

The evening was great. Good friends, interesting small talk. The single girl sat across from Marcus and asked a dozen questions about his life, his past, his love of baseball, his love of Los Angeles.

A couple of times Marcus had to remind himself he wasn't on the field or in the clubhouse being interviewed. At the end of the night he shook the woman's hand and thanked everyone for inviting him. He needed to get home. Things to do.

Which wasn't quite honest.

Sure, he had laundry and an episode of *Storm Chasers* to watch. He would probably read the last email he sent to Mary

Catherine one more time—looking for reasons why she would've avoided answering him. Again. But the truth was, he couldn't handle another ten minutes with the single girl. She was nice and witty, friendly, and connected to his world.

But she wasn't Mary Catherine.

She never would be.

SAMI HOPED TO MAKE IT to each of the Dodgers home games this year. There were eighty-one of them, so she might miss a few. But the best part was that Tyler could sit with her—unless he was needed in the bullpen, overseeing warm-ups for a pitching change.

Otherwise, he did his work with the pitchers during the week, and on game days he and Sami had the best seats in the house. From there he would study his athletes, making notes on future coaching decisions and adjustments.

Sami loved baseball.

But probably not enough to travel to away games, something Tyler completely understood. She used those nights to work on projects for the Youth Center. Sometimes she hung out during open gym or took a few of the teen girls to dinner.

This week, though, the Youth Center was quiet and her apartment even quieter. She missed Mary Catherine so much, she practically hated going home. So when Tyler invited her to fly up to San Francisco for the two-game stand against the Giants, Sami was thrilled.

Tyler had to get there early for a team practice. Now it was four o'clock and she was just stepping off the plane at the

San Francisco International Airport. She spotted him as soon as she reached baggage claim. He looked like the boy she'd fallen in love with back in high school. Tall and blond, tan and athletic.

And he was holding a bouquet of red roses.

She hurried to him, drawn by his familiar smile and the love in his eyes. When the Dodgers had back-to-back road trips, they might go a few weeks without seeing each other. But recently, they'd spent more time together. Biking on Santa Monica Beach, having picnics on the grassy knoll in front of Pepperdine University.

Sami couldn't imagine her life without him.

They hugged and Tyler handed her the flowers. "You look beautiful."

"Mmm, thanks." She smelled the roses. "You spoil me."

His eyes held hers. "You make it easy."

Once Sami had her bag they headed for the ball field. It was supposed to be chilly tonight, so she grabbed her jacket but left the flowers and bag in his rental car. An hour later, after warm-ups, Tyler joined her to watch the game. Marcus was pitching today and from the first inning it was an easy win for the Dodgers. Tyler was only called down to the field once in the fourth inning to help Marcus with an adjustment. After that he put his arm around her. "I have a feeling this is going to be a good night."

Sami loved being with Tyler. It was easy to forget they'd ever been apart. She smiled up at him. "It already is." The early evening breeze was cool off the bay. Sami was glad for her jacket. "I'm with you . . . and we're winning!"

"By six runs." Tyler laughed. "I'll take it." He lowered his arm and took hold of her hand instead. "What do you hear from Mary Catherine?"

"Not a lot." Sami thought about her friend's last email, almost a week ago now. "She's working all day, every day with the kids. There're a few new full-time volunteers—so that helps." Sami paused. "She loves it, she keeps saying that. But she never talks about herself, whether she's lonely or anxious. It's not like talking to her in person."

"She's not one to complain, whatever's happening." Tyler kept his eyes on the pitching mound. "Marcus is on fire tonight."

"Like always." Sami studied their friend. "Does he talk about her?"

"Not as much." Tyler sighed. "The shutdown when he flew to Nashville to see her was the last straw. You can't force someone to care for you. That's what he says when Mary Catherine's name comes up."

"So sad." Sami leaned forward, her eyes still on Marcus. "I know she cares. He does, too."

"Yeah." Tyler paused. "He talked about her again Friday night. Some of the guys tried to set him up, nothing serious. When he came home he said the girl was great. She just wasn't Mary Catherine."

Sami let that settle in her heart for a minute. "I keep thinking when she comes back from Uganda . . . maybe the two of them . . ." She sat up straight and looked at Tyler again. "I don't know."

"Marcus is afraid she might stay in Africa." He shook his head. "She literally gave him no hope."

"Poor guy. The whole thing doesn't make sense." In her

last three emails to her friend, Sami had asked about Mary Catherine's heart and her health. It was the one question she never answered. Another reason Sami was starting to feel concerned.

Marcus struck out the side as they headed into the top of the eighth inning. The Dodgers' lead hadn't changed. Her conversation with Tyler drifted to the Youth Center and the success of Sami's teen mentor program.

Sami felt the familiar joy when it came to the girls. "These kids are really opening up. They're asking about God and what it looks like to live for Him." She thought about the changes in the girls. "God's blessing it beyond my imagination." She hesitated. "All except Lexy."

"Still?" Tyler looked disappointed. Lexy was important to him, too. "I've been praying for her."

"She needs it. One of the girls said she saw Lexy hanging out with the new gang leader." Sami looked at Tyler. "I think she'd come to the group if Mary Catherine were there. But the rest of us . . . she doesn't feel connected. Not to anyone but the gang."

"Her story isn't over yet." Tyler pulled Sami close, slipping his arm around her shoulders again.

"True. God loves that girl . . . I know that much. He loves them all." Sami snuggled in close to Tyler. Being in his arms made the rest of the world's troubles fall away.

After the Dodgers won, Sami expected a group of them might go to dinner. She still hadn't checked into her hotel room, but that could come later. Instead, after they congratulated Marcus and the team, Tyler pulled her aside.

"You ready?" His eyes sparkled in the stadium lights.

"For dinner?" Sami wasn't sure what he meant. He almost looked nervous, the way he had when they first got back together a year ago.

"For whatever comes next." He grinned and pulled her into a hug. As he eased back he looked intently at her. "Are you ready, Sami?"

Chills ran down her arms. What was he talking about? Why the mystery? She gave him the answer that filled her heart. "If I'm with you, I'm ready. Whatever it is."

"Come on." He took her hand. "I have a feeling we'll remember this night forever."

She grinned. "Am I supposed to guess?"

He laughed. "Just trust me."

Sami had no idea what was ahead, but as they walked to his rental car she could feel Tyler's excitement, which only added to hers.

Nights like this Sami could hardly believe the miracle God had worked to bring them together again. Not just in Tyler's life, but in hers. She remembered a few years ago when she wished she was more like Mary Catherine. Finding adventure in every day, seizing life, and creating reasons to laugh. Now she had it. That's how Tyler made her feel.

Whatever tonight held, Sami could hardly wait.

10

MARY CATHERINE WAS HAVING the time of her life—especially today.

Mondays were the one day each week when Mary Catherine introduced the children at the orphanage to new music. It was her favorite day, not because she was particularly gifted at singing or teaching songs. But because she loved watching the children's faces light up.

Music spoke to their young souls the way it spoke to Mary Catherine. Whatever trouble she faced, praising God through song lifted the darkness. Hope and joy could breathe again when they sang to the Lord.

Twenty-two little faces stared up at her from their desks. "Are we ready for a new song?"

The kids clapped their hands, their eyes bright with excitement. "Yes!" They spoke all at once. "Please, Miss Kat."

Mary Catherine laughed. The children ranged in age from two to twelve. Her name was difficult for some of the younger

kids, so she'd found something that worked for all of them—
Miss Kat. She loved how it sounded with their beautiful ac-
cents. English was an official language of the people in
Uganda. Still, with their lilt Mary Catherine sometimes had to
work to understand them.

"Okay, today it's a song with letters. Does anyone know
how to spell the word 'Bible'?" She pulled a stool up to the
front of the room. Sitting while teaching was one way she
could conserve energy.

A thin, long-legged girl in the back row raised her hand.
She was a smart child, maybe ten years old, one of the first
admitted to the orphanage. Her parents had both died of
AIDS and she was losing a battle with starvation when she
was brought in. Now she was making progress toward health.

"Bacia, go ahead." Mary Catherine smiled at the girl.
"Spell Bible for us."

Bacia stood, her head high, shoulders back. "B-i-b-l-e.
Bible." She smiled, proud and confident. "That is how it is
spelled, Miss Kat."

Where the child had learned to spell, Mary Catherine had
no idea. She clapped and motioned for the rest of the kids to
join in. "That's wonderful, Bacia. Very good." Some of the kids
cheered, others stood and danced around their desks, clap-
ping their approval.

These children had absolutely nothing. Not even a family.
Yet they longed for reasons to celebrate. As if God had knit
the need for joy into the fabric of every child. It was one more
reason Mary Catherine loved what she was doing. She had
the privilege of fostering happiness in each of these children.

For the next half hour Mary Catherine taught the children

the first Sunday school song she could remember ever learning. After that, most of the kids could sing along with her. "The B-i-b-l-e . . . that's the book for me! I stand alone on the word of God. The B-i-b-l-e!"

After singing the song with her students a dozen times through, Mary Catherine was suddenly desperate to catch her breath. One of the volunteer teachers must've seen the look on her face. She stepped up and waved her hands at the kids. "Time for recess. Everyone outside!"

The orphanage sat on a newly formed compound. There were three small huts for the workers—one for Mary Catherine, two for the local women who helped with everything from bathing to fixing meals.

The fourth and largest structure was the orphanage itself. It was one story, like most of the buildings in Uganda. One wing was filled with a sleeping area—row after row of bunk beds and two bathrooms. Another wing was the dining hall and kitchen. And the school and play area made up the third wing. In the middle was a gathering space for relaxing and reading. A living room of sorts.

Mary Catherine walked outside and leaned against the wall of the orphanage. *Breathe,* she told herself. *You're fine. Relax and breathe.* She had been in Uganda for seven weeks and for the most part she tried not to think about her health. Still, days like this when she couldn't catch her breath, when she needed safety pins to hold her skirt up because of her weight loss, she knew the truth.

She was getting worse.

She tried to ignore it, she had even taught herself how to slow her pounding heart, how to get oxygen into her blood

even when her lungs felt like they were filled with syrup.
Which is what she did now, and her next breath came a little
easier. Mary Catherine made her way across the playground to
her personal hut. The little dwelling contained a small bathroom and two cots. God was providing for her, and the love in
her heart for the children was worth every risk to her health.
Helping these kids was a dream come true, no doubt. He
would protect her. She believed that no matter how hard it
was to breathe.

Today was exciting for another reason. A missionary from
London was joining them today, someone intent on living here
at least a year. She'd stay with Mary Catherine.

The woman's name was Ember.

Mary Catherine sat on her cot and let her body find its
way back to normal. She had thirty minutes until class re-
sumed. She peered out the single window and admired the
block wall surrounding the facility. A group of men from town
had finished the work just yesterday. The wall was ten feet
high with razor wire. One way to make sure the kids were as
safe as possible.

Despite the wall, the place didn't feel closed in. The orphanage owned two acres, so there was plenty of space for the
kids to play. Janie Omer had worked with churches in Tennes-
see, California, and London to create a stream of funding that
had provided for the facility. There was talk of the group opening a second one not too far from here.

The orphanages would work together, teaching the children and giving them more of a community.

Mary Catherine closed her eyes and smiled. *Marcus
should be running that one, right, Lord?* She unplugged her

laptop from the generator on the floor. The orphanage had electricity, but it didn't work all the time. The generator was more reliable.

She opened the computer to her email and easily found the last letter from Marcus. He had sent it a few days after she arrived. Mary Catherine had read it so often she practically knew it by heart. Even so, she let her eyes wander over the text. Somehow reading his words made her breathe better.

He had that effect on her.

Dear Mary Catherine,

I guess in some ways I'm still recovering from seeing you. I know I took you by surprise and I'm sorry for that. Not just showing up like that, but the things I said. One minute you're headed to security for a trip to Africa. The next you're sitting next to me and I'm talking about wanting to marry you.

Probably not the way I should've handled it.

I don't know. I guess it was just something I needed to say. I was worried about you . . . and I kept thinking how I've told you I want to be with you and that I'll wait for you and that I want to be more than friends. But you haven't known me that long. I didn't want you to think I saw you as just another girl.

You could never be that.

Mary Catherine blinked away tears, the way she always did when she reached that part. The letter made her feel like Marcus was right here, sitting beside her on the thin cot, looking into her eyes. She waited till she could see clearly before finding the spot where she left off.

The truth is, I really do want to marry you. I think we'd be amazing, and in no time you'd forget about not being the marrying type.

But that isn't how you feel, and I respect you.

That's why I'm writing. After today I won't email you or text you . . . I won't show up running the orphanage next door. You've asked me to understand, and after a few days of praying about it, I can tell you this: I will never understand, but I will respect you.

If you want me to leave you alone, I will.

I don't know how long it'll take before I stop thinking about you. It's hard to imagine. Every time I drive by the beach . . . every bicyclist I pass on my drive to the stadium . . . every night when I step out onto my back deck.

Anyway, enough. I'll pray for you, and if for any reason you change your mind, you know where to reach me.

I love you, Mary Catherine. And I still don't believe you.

Love, Marcus

She still hadn't written back. Mary Catherine hated the fact, but what else could she do? If she responded, and if she were honest, she'd have to tell him that he was right. She hadn't been telling the truth about herself. Of course she was the marrying type. She just never thought she'd find someone like Marcus, someone real and deep and loyal. A man who shared her faith.

If she wrote to him, her letter would have to admit that and then tell him the rest of the truth. How she missed him every day and longed to see him again. How she replayed the scene in the airport every few hours and how it was one of the highlights of her entire life.

"Mary Catherine. Come, please!" Someone was yelling her name.

She closed her computer and hurried toward the orphanage. Her breathing was better, but she needed to be careful. If she moved too quickly, she would send herself into another crisis. The children still had another fifteen minutes of recess, but as soon as she stepped into the living room of the orphanage she saw the reason she'd been called.

One of the local women who helped with meals was holding a newborn baby. The infant was cradled in blankets, but he or she looked severely malnourished. Mary Catherine felt her heart melt as she approached. "Boy or girl?"

"Boy." The woman had clearly been crying. "His mama is dead. No daddy." She peered at the baby's face. "He is ours now." The woman held the child to Mary Catherine. "You hold him?"

"Yes." Mary Catherine took the baby gently in her arms and moved to the nearest rocking chair. The local women returned to the kitchen to work on lunch. Cradling the sleeping infant in her arms, Mary Catherine set the rocker in motion. The woman returned with a warmed bottle of milk, and then disappeared back to the kitchen again.

The baby had been asleep, but now he opened his eyes. As if he could sense there was food for him. Finally. Mary Catherine slid the bottle into his mouth and immediately he began gulping down the milk. *Poor baby.* Mary Catherine looked into his eyes. He wasn't a fussy infant, like some she'd seen. This baby probably already knew there was no point in crying. His needs weren't going to be met right away. Maybe not at all.

At least until now.

"It's okay, baby." She ran her thumb along his brow and over his delicate brown skin. *This is how our baby might've looked,* she thought. *If I had a healthy heart. If I could say yes to Marcus Dillinger.* Two emotions competed for her attention. A very great love for this little one, concern for his future and his survival. And at the same time an unfathomable joy.

Because though she would never rock a baby of her own, at least she had this.

No matter what happened from here, no matter how many months she had left to live, this baby and others here at the orphanage were the only ones she would ever cradle or feed. No little ones would ever call her Mama except the toddlers running around on the playground outside. Sure, the older kids called her Miss Kat. But the little ones called her Mama. It was another reason she loved being here, loved seeing this dream come true. She wasn't only a teacher and a worker here in Uganda.

She was a mother.

When Mary Catherine was done feeding him, she handed him back to the local woman. Lunch was over for the students also. Time to get back in the classroom. She was headed to the closet for the math workbooks when she practically ran into a pale-skinned woman with red-gold hair like her own.

"Sorry." Mary Catherine stepped back. "Are you . . . ?"

"Ember." The woman reached out her hand. "Yes. I just got in."

"Wonderful." Mary Catherine looked out the nearest window. There wasn't a car in sight, and already the gate to the facility was closed and locked again. Ember's driver must've left quickly. "Welcome." She shook the woman's hand, and then gave her a hug. "We'll be sharing a hut. Might as well be friends."

"Exactly." Ember laughed. "Everyone says you're the best thing to happen to this village."

Her London accent was as pretty as her face. And her eyes . . . a mix of blue and green and hazel. Mary Catherine hadn't seen anything like them. "Do you have bags?"

"Yes. By the door." She looked over her shoulder. "I'll get them later. I don't want to interfere with the schedule."

Mary Catherine nodded. What was it about the woman? She seemed different, somehow. Maybe because she was European. "Follow me. You can meet the children." She smiled at Ember. "We're doing math next."

"I prefer art." Ember grinned. "But there's no art without math. At least that's what I've heard."

For a moment Mary Catherine stopped and stared at Ember. "Have you noticed . . . ?"

"We look alike?" She laughed again, and the sound was as carefree as a summer breeze. "Absolutely. The man who drove me from the airport said that. Asked if we were sisters."

"Yes." Mary Catherine hesitated. "The kids will probably think so, too."

They grabbed the stacks of workbooks and took them to the classroom. The children were back in their seats, giggling and talking. The minute Mary Catherine and Ember walked into the room, they stopped and stared. Bacia was the first to say something. She pointed. "Miss Kat . . . your sister?"

Mary Catherine shared a look with Ember and allowed a quick laugh. "No, dear. Ember is our newest teacher. She'll work with me in the classroom."

"But she is your sister, yes?" Bacia clearly spoke for the other children, all of whom looked delighted and confused at the same time. Bacia pointed again. "She has your hair."

It took five minutes for the conversation to let up.

They couldn't delay math any longer, so Mary Catherine launched into a lesson on addition and subtraction. The children had already studied both subjects. Now they were ready to combine the ideas. Another hour flew by and only then did Mary Catherine realize she was struggling to breathe. Again.

Ember seemed to notice before anyone else. She came alongside Mary Catherine. "Step outside." She nodded, her expression capable. "I have this."

Not until Mary Catherine was back outside, leaning against the same wall, forcing herself to relax did a question occur to her. Was her struggle to breathe that obvious? Already the new teacher seemed to notice. The reality made Mary Catherine relax a little quicker this time.

She had a feeling Ember was going to become a very good friend.

11

~~~

TYLER HAD ASKED SAMI to bring a nice outfit for dinner. So after the game, the two of them changed clothes, and Tyler took Sami to the Mark Hopkins Hotel at 1 Nob Hill—a spot he'd scouted last time he was here. They rode the elevator to the nineteenth floor and he led her to a secluded restaurant called Top of the Mark. The maître d' was expecting them.

"A special night, Mr. Ames. Miss." The maître d' grinned.

"Yes, it is." Tyler smiled at Sami. He loved her so much.

"Very well." The man nodded. Then in no particular rush, he took them to their table alongside a floor-to-ceiling window with panoramic views of the San Francisco Bay. He handed them their menus. "Enjoy."

So far the night was like something Tyler's heart had scripted the first time he and Sami walked on the beach, after they'd found each other again. Back then he had dreamed that one day they might have a night like this.

And now it was playing out just as he had prayed it might.

They ate filet mignon and grilled salmon and after the waiter cleared their plates they laughed about how young they'd been when Tyler first knocked on her grandparents' door—just a ten-minute drive from here. "I thought you lived in a palace." Tyler reached across the table and took her hands. "And you were the princess."

She eased her fingers around his. "You were the best thing about that summer." Her eyes lit up. "Cutest boy I'd ever seen."

"I definitely couldn't focus on my summer league games." He angled his head, seeing all the way to her soul. "Knowing you were back at your grandparents' house."

A comfortable quiet filled the space between them, but never once did they look away. Tyler thought about his mistakes, the decision to pass up the UCLA scholarship and ride out a few terrible seasons in the minor leagues. He had walked out of her life and become someone he didn't recognize.

Not until he was homeless, out of baseball, and working at the retirement center in Florida did Tyler see Sami again. And then he was too embarrassed to really talk to her. If it hadn't been for dear old Virginia and her words about forgiveness and grace, Tyler might never have believed he could have a second chance.

He looked out the window. *Only You could've done this, God . . . given me this girl again after all the heartache I put her through.*

"Tyler." She giggled. "So serious."

"Sorry." He turned to her and found his smile again. "I

guess I still can't believe I'm here with you. That you're really mine."

Her expression became deeper. "God moved heaven and Earth to make it happen." She smiled. "At least it feels that way."

"It does." He paid the bill and then took her hand again. "You ready?"

"What?" She laughed. "There's more?"

"Definitely." He stood and helped her to her feet. "I want to take you somewhere."

She looked out the window. "You just did." Her eyes found his. "This place is amazing. I've never been anywhere like it."

"Me, either." He paused. "Still . . . " He held her hand as they started walking toward the exit. "I have a feeling our next stop will be your favorite."

"As long as I'm with you." Sami stayed close by his side while the valet found Tyler's rental car. "This has already been the best night ever."

Tyler smiled, anything to hide his racing heart. He sure hoped it was her best night ever. He had a lot riding on the next few hours. Not just the success of the night.

But his entire future.

AFTER THE ROSES at the airport and the intimate dinner on Nob Hill, Sami had no idea how Tyler could top the evening. It was just after ten o'clock as they set out and after a few minutes she knew where they were headed.

When he pulled into the driveway of her grandparents'

Bay Area house, Sami drew a quick breath and turned to him. "What's this?"

"They're not here. I called them." He grinned, thankful she couldn't see the way his knees trembled. "They said it was okay if we stopped by."

"I can't believe this." Sami let the reality wash over her.

The last time she and Tyler were here they were seventeen, with an ocean of uncertainty ahead. Sami had lived with her grandparents since she was five, the year her parents died in a motorcycle accident. Her grandpa had been part owner of the Giants for many years, so he and Sami's grandma owned a house here and a second one in the San Fernando Valley.

Not far from where Tyler had been a star high school baseball pitcher.

But they never would've met at all if it weren't for that San Francisco summer. That year her grandparents signed up to host a summer league baseball player. Tyler was assigned to them.

The night was getting later. They parked and Tyler hurried around to open her door. He helped her out and then slowly took her in his arms. "I had to bring you here." The moon shone in her eyes. "Where it all began."

They hugged for a long time and then together they faced the stunning house. "So many memories." Sami breathed in the smell of the fir trees that surrounded her grandparents' estate. The place was beautiful. Sami had almost forgotten how much so. "You planned this?"

Tyler shrugged. His voice held a sense of mischief and anticipation. "Maybe." He bent down and picked up a small piece of paper from the ground. Only as soon as he held it to her in the palm of his hand, Sami could see she was wrong. It wasn't paper.

It was a rose petal. She looked down and saw something she had missed until now. A path of rose petals formed a walkway from where they stood to somewhere behind the house. Her heart skipped a beat. "Tyler . . . what is this?"

He smiled, watching her, like he was lost in her eyes. "Let's follow it and see."

Whatever was happening, Tyler had planned this all day. "You weren't at a meeting this morning."

"Not for long, anyway." He chuckled and slipped his fingers between hers. "Follow me."

On a path of white rose petals? Sami felt giddy, her heart racing. Where was all this leading? She was wearing her nicest heels, but she wasn't worried. The path was paved. They set out along the flowers. "This must've taken you all day." She looked up at him as they walked.

"You're worth it." He gave her hand a gentle squeeze.

They followed the petals around the house to a small table covered in lace and topped with five pillar candles—the setting was beautiful.

In the flickering soft glow, Sami could easily see a photo book at the center of the table. On the cover, the picture Sami kept in her memory at all times.

A picture of Tyler and her, seventeen and in love.

Her grandmother had taken the photo right here on the front porch of this very house. It was the afternoon Tyler said goodbye and returned home. Sami had kept that picture on the desk near her bed until Tyler's second year in the minors.

When she had no choice but to take it down.

Even then the photograph had stayed in her heart, where it would always stay. And now it was on the cover of this photo book. She felt the sting of tears and at the same time she laughed, too amazed to speak until now. Sami turned to him. "You made this for me?"

"Open it." Tyler put his arm around her and together they looked through the pictures. On each page, Tyler had written a message telling her how he felt about the photograph and the time it represented.

There was Sami in the stands at one of his high school baseball games and Tyler had written, *You were always there, win or lose. No one ever believed in me more.*

And then a picture of him at her choir concert. *I never saw anyone but you that night, never heard any voice but yours. The songs seemed like they were for me alone.* And there they were at the beach and bowling with friends. *You made everyone feel special and included. You have that gift, Sami. Every time we're with friends it's like the best time ever. Because of you.*

There were a few pictures from a day at Disneyland. *Talk about a magical day! I remember sitting behind you on the Matterhorn and thinking how that roller coaster was nothing to the thrill I felt just being with you.*

And then there was a photo that still made Sami ache to look at it—the picture taken when Tyler was getting on the bus headed for his first week in the minor leagues. *Worst day of my life. I never should've left you. If I had it to do over again, I never would have.*

On the next page Tyler had written "2010–2014" at the top. There were no pictures. And of course. Those were the years when she thought she'd never see Tyler again, when he had walked away from her and his family and made choices that nearly destroyed him. Over that time period Tyler had simply written her a message. Long and detailed. She glanced over it, her eyes skipping to the last line. *I'll always be sorry.*

"You can read it later." He ran his hand along her arm. "It's getting cold."

"Okay." She was about to hug him again, thank him for the unbelievable gift, when he nodded toward the back of the house. The path of rose petals continued to a ladder anchored to the house. The sides were adorned with white satin bows.

This time Sami gasped. "Tyler . . . what in the world?"

"Looks like we need to go up on the roof."

She might as well have been seventeen again. Sami started that way but stopped. "My shoes . . ."

"Hmmm." Tyler's eyes were full of secrets. He bent down and from a box near the ladder he pulled out a pair of her old running shoes. "These might work."

"You have them?" She laughed again. "I've been missing those!"

"I had to take them when you weren't looking. Last time I stopped by to pick you up and you weren't quite ready." He feigned an innocent look. "They were right there near the front door. What's a guy to do?"

"Tyler, I can't believe this. Seriously." She slid off her heels, set them in the box, and put the tennis shoes on. "You thought of everything."

He guided her up the ladder until they were sitting side by side on the roof. The exact same place where they'd sat that summer so many years ago.

She turned to him. "I remember everything about that night."

"The last time we were up here." He looked at her. "Me, too."

"The stars were so bright. This far away from the bay and the city lights." She stared at the sky. "Like they are tonight."

"Exactly." He ran his fingers through her hair. "We had our first kiss up here that night."

Sami smiled. "You asked me to be your girlfriend." Her laugh mixed with the cool night breeze. "Crazy . . . I couldn't say anything but yes." She grinned at him. "I think I loved you from the first day I met you." She leaned her head on his shoulder. "You were the only one who ever called me Sami. A name I still love, by the way."

"Your dark hair and pretty face." Tyler put his hand alongside her cheek. "You looked like a Sami. The only girl who ever took my breath away."

"You don't know how often I replayed that night in my head." She looked all the way to his soul. "I was sure I'd never love another boy again."

"It was the beginning of the best year of my life." Tyler took hold of her hand, his eyes still on hers. "Until this one."

"For me, too."

Tyler seemed nervous. She could hear him breathing harder. Sami brought his hand to her face and warmed it on her cheek. "That's why you brought me up here?" Sami loved this side of Tyler, the one capable of pulling off the most romantic night ever. "So we could remember the last time we did this?"

"Well." He shifted so he could see her better. "See, the

thing is, the first time I asked you to be my girlfriend it was right here on this exact spot. And you said yes, right?"

"Right." Her heart was racing again. "It's still yes."

"Okay, so." Tyler released her hand and dug around in the pocket of his jacket.

Sami had her hands over her mouth as soon as he pulled out the small white satin box. "Tyler . . ."

"I figured there really wasn't any better place to ask you the only question that matters now." He opened the box, his hands trembling.

Sami felt tears on her cheeks before she could stop them. This was really happening, he was pulling out a ring. Here on the roof where she had first fallen in love with him.

Inside the box was a stunning solitaire diamond. The exact ring she'd admired before in magazines. He took the ring and set the box aside. Then in a move that looked a bit precarious on the slanted rooftop, he shifted his body so he could bend down on one knee. With all the love they'd need to last a lifetime, he looked in her eyes and held out the ring. "Sami . . . would you marry me? Would you let me spend the rest of my life loving you?"

"Tyler, please." She took his hands and eased him back to the spot beside her. "You can't fall off the roof."

"Good point." He situated himself so he could see her. "You . . . didn't answer."

This time she framed his face with her hands. "Yes!" She giggled, but the sound was more cry than laugh. "Yes, Tyler Ames. I'll marry you!"

"Really?" He kissed her and then pulled her into his arms. He held her for several seconds. Then he cupped his hands around his mouth and shouted to the heavens. "God, You did it! She said yes!"

LATER THAT NIGHT back at the hotel, Tyler had one final surprise for her. After she checked into her room and dropped off her bag, he walked with her to a banquet hall on the second floor. And there, gathered and waiting, were her grandparents and several of her UCLA friends. His teammates and his parents, too.

Tyler held Sami's hand up high over their heads. "She said yes!"

Everyone clapped and cheered. Marcus was one of the first to congratulate them. "So happy for you two." He hugged them both. Sami wouldn't say anything, but she could tell from the look in Marcus's eyes that tonight was a little hard for him.

After all, it hadn't been two months since he'd been turned down by his one true love.

Still, the atmosphere was happy and full of celebration, the perfect coda to the best night of her life. Everyone admired her new ring and they talked about dates. Sami wanted a December wedding—and Tyler was all for it. Right at the start of his break from baseball.

The proposal, the party, all of it was perfect. There was just one person missing, the one person who should've been there. Without her, Sami would never have reached out to Tyler Ames again. The person who had missed it all for the chance to live in Africa.

Her best friend, Mary Catherine.

12

THERE WAS ONLY ONE PLACE Marcus wanted to go on his day off. One place where he could talk to God and think about Mary Catherine. Two more months had gone by without a single word from her.

Marcus drove to Santa Monica Beach early that morning, parked across the street at the Georgian Hotel. He found a spot on the hotel's front porch and ordered coffee. For an hour he answered emails. His manager had several offers for him, endorsement deals, projects he might want to take part in.

On the porch of the Georgian, the morning sun lighting up the blue sky, none of it felt daunting. He worked faster knowing the beach was waiting for him. When he finished, he crossed Ocean Avenue, walked over the footbridge and across the stretch of sand to his spot near the shore.

Their spot.

He spread out his towel, sat down, and leaned back on his hands. For a few minutes he let the wind off the water wash

over him, as if by sitting here he could go back in time and figure out how to never let her go. He breathed in, filling his
lungs until the stress of the last four months lifted from his
soul—the wins and losses, the slump he was currently in, and
the missing her.

All of it.

Okay, God . . . I'm here. He squinted, looking to the distant horizon. *Do You see me?* The question was rhetorical.
Kind of. Of course God could see him. God had been with
him these past four months. The Bible said it in Romans, and
he believed it.

Marcus knew without a doubt that Jesus was with him.

But today wasn't about belief or doubts. Marcus wanted
to experience God's presence, feel the Lord walking on the
beach beside him. Sense His whispered comfort that one
day . . . no matter how far off . . . he might finally find a way to
get Mary Catherine out of his heart.

Marcus pulled one knee up and exhaled. Tyler and Sami
had joined him for dinner last night and the conversation
turned to the wedding. Plans were coming along. Tyler had
asked Marcus to be the best man and Sami hoped Mary
Catherine would be back from Uganda in time to be the maid
of honor.

Hearing Mary Catherine's name had left Marcus no
choice but to at least ask. He anchored his elbows on his
knees and peered at Sami in the twilight. "You've heard from
her?"

"I have." She had looked sad. "You haven't?"

"No." He hadn't let the reality linger. "How is she? What'd
she say?"

Sami had done her best to share the details. Mary Catherine was teaching every day and loving it. She had a new friend, a woman who helped in the classroom. "And I guess she's staying at least a few months longer. Through mid-November. Apparently until another teacher can take her place."

"Hmm." He had stood up and paced to the railing. For a while he'd just let the truth of it sink in. Tyler and Sami stayed quiet, too.

"I asked her about the wedding, and she thinks she might be back in time." Sami sounded discouraged. "I got the sense she couldn't make any promises."

Marcus had raised his brows and shook his head. "She must be liking it. She told me she might never come back."

"I can't believe that." Tyler tried to sound hopeful. "That girl loves LA."

"And she loves all of us." Sami had stood and moved to Marcus. She put her arm around his shoulders. "For what it's worth, she does love you. I know it."

He had looked from Sami to Tyler and back again. "Then why? Why did she cut me out of her life?"

No one had any answers, and eventually the conversation had shifted back to baseball. But the details about Mary Catherine stayed with him. Even still. She was staying another two months? Did that mean she was going to stay there? Forever?

Marcus lay flat on his back and stared at the pale blue sky. Why couldn't he forget about her? She'd been very clear. She wasn't interested. Not in dating. Not in marriage. She clearly had no interest—she hadn't even stayed in touch.

So why was he lying here on the beach by himself on his

day off, thinking about her? He closed his eyes and let the sun melt through him. The reason was the same now as it had ever been: He felt something with her. She felt it, too. She'd told him that much.

They laughed at the same things and shared a love for God and people. There were times when they already felt like a couple—when they held hands and hugged, when they kissed. But then she'd pull away. Again.

He wanted to do more than mourn the past today. Maybe he'd take a hike in the Santa Monica Mountains. Push himself to the top of a cliff so he could see to the other side. Maybe he'd find the answers there.

The sun was higher in the sky now, and even at ten in the morning the day figured to be hot. Marcus sat up and watched the ocean. The sameness of the tide, the buildup, the cresting waves, the crashing surf. All of it felt like a picture of his life.

Get up, run two miles, stretch for half an hour, stick to his low-carb, high-fat, moderate-protein eating plan. Get to the stadium and wait for his name to be called. One in five games he'd get to throw—usually for a complete game. Another game, another three hundred pitches. Back home just to do it all over again.

He sighed and shook off the despair.

Why was he thinking like this? There wasn't an ounce of truth to those thoughts. He ran the Youth Center, he and Tyler read the Bible together nearly every morning at the clubhouse. His life had purpose and meaning, and even though it was routine, it was the routine he'd dreamed about since he was a little boy. His life had everything he could ask for from God.

Except for Mary Catherine.

Marcus stood and collected his towel. *God, I'm sorry. I don't mean to complain.* He shaded his eyes and looked out over the water. This was the place where he'd been baptized, where he'd dedicated his life to the Lord. The place where Mary Catherine loved to ride the waves and where she'd seen an entire school of dolphins once.

But today the water was just . . . water.

He breathed in and straightened to his full height. *I don't want to ask for a sign, God . . . some proof that You see me.* He hesitated. *But right now, well . . . yeah, it would sure be nice. Just to know You're here.*

Seconds passed, and then one minute, and two. Marcus was about to turn around and leave when something in the near waves caught his eye. Again he shaded his brow and suddenly he could see it. A school of dolphins, just like the one Mary Catherine had talked about. They stayed in one area, making dolphin sounds one to another and playing in the waves. A chill came over Marcus. He stood there, unmoving, unable to look away, and as he did his feet no longer felt planted in ordinary sand but on holy ground.

Thank You, Father. Marcus had never felt so small. *You see me and You care. I always believed that. But this . . . this is something I'll never forget.*

And like that, a whisper resonated in Marcus's soul. *My son, I love you. I have plans for you, plans to give you a hope and a future.*

He had read those words in the Bible, in Jeremiah 29:11. But here, now, he knew the whisper came from God Almighty.

Slowly Marcus fell to his knees. He brought his hands to his face, overcome by the absolute goodness of God. He had needed this, the reminder that God was in control.

Even where Mary Catherine was concerned.

After a few minutes the dolphins swam away. Marcus stood, collected his things, and headed across the beach toward his car.

He could not control Mary Catherine. If she didn't want to respond to his email from four months ago, so be it. If he couldn't see her, he could at least pray for her. For her health and safety and for her to stay close to God.

While he was at it, he'd pray that Mary Catherine would make it back in time for the wedding. And if she did, that she would see things differently between the two of them. Yes, that's what he would pray for. And he would believe in dramatic, miraculous results. After all, God was the great miracle worker.

The dolphins were proof of that.

BECK WAS STILL SAVORING the way God had answered Marcus, still amazed that the Father loved mankind enough to sometimes give a sign. The way He had today. But even as the dolphins swam away, Beck felt the presence of evil. Just ahead of where Marcus was walking back to his car.

Instantly Jag was at his side. "Let's go."

The two moved at lightning speed to their places on either side of Marcus. The darkness ahead was marked by hissing and a blur of evil activity. Something was about to take place. "Help us, Father . . . we need You," Jag cried out. "Jesus be with us."

At the name of Jesus, the demons shrieked. The cloud of darkness dispersed, but it didn't disappear. The enemy was definitely up to something. Beck and Jag remained next to Marcus, scanning the distance, ready to defend and protect him, whatever the battle ahead.

"There!" Jag pointed. "Headed for Marcus!"

A quarter mile down the road a teenager was driving toward them, his attention entirely on his phone.

"Texting." Jag kept his eyes on the young driver.

"He has no idea." Beck could see it all now. The teen's car weaved in and out of his lane, but despite the honking from other motorists he stayed focused on his phone. He was closer now, half a block away.

Marcus reached the crosswalk at Ocean Avenue. Beck felt the presence of evil again. "Jesus . . . help us. We need You." He called the words out loud for all of the spiritual realm to hear. More shrieking. In the distance, the darkness swirled and swelled, the enemy's soldiers hissing, ready for the kill.

The battle was under way.

"We have to stop him." Jag's voice was intense. Demons clung to the top of the teen's car, and inside one of them had his claws on the wheel.

Beck understood. Wherever Marcus was—on the sidewalk or in the intersection—the car was headed his way. "I've got this." There was no time to wait.

"Be careful." Jag knew what Beck was about to do. It was necessary.

Marcus stepped into the intersection and began to cross the street.

In the blink of an eye, Beck entered the car. The demons left instantly, unable to stay in the presence of light.

The car was headed straight for Marcus, right through the red light.

"Stop!" Beck shouted to the teen. "Pay attention!"

Startled, the teen looked up. All at once he threw his phone to the floor of his car and slammed on his brakes. He stopped inches from Marcus. The baseball player looked shocked, suddenly aware of the danger he'd been in.

By then Beck was no longer in the car.

As Beck returned to Jag's side, they both watched the teen drive slowly away. "Praise to Jesus!" Beck and Jag joined voices, thanking God, worshipping the Savior. Because in the name of Jesus, in this battle, victory was theirs. The mission would live another day.

And so would Marcus Dillinger.

EMBER WAS DESPERATE for an answer. Mary Catherine was sicker every day, and though the two of them worked right alongside each other, Ember hadn't yet found a way to send her home.

Mary Catherine was out of breath more frequently and there weren't enough safety pins in the supply closet to keep the girl's skirt from falling off. No question she was losing more weight, getting sicker.

It was early on the second Monday of July. Ember and

Mary Catherine were scheduled for a meeting before the children joined them, a chance to look over the curriculum for the week. Ember was already in the classroom when Mary Catherine walked in.

She looked weak, her skin grayish white. So slight and ethereal she might've been an angel herself. "Good morning." She managed a smile. "Sorry I'm late." She sat down in the nearest chair. "I couldn't wake up."

"It's okay." They didn't have long before the children joined them. She would share her concerns with Mary Catherine after class.

Today Ember watched while Mary Catherine led. The subject was storytelling. Ember enjoyed watching her teach— especially today. Mary Catherine was the rarest type of human. She loved God and people, but on top of that she loved life. Every breath, every moment. Even heart failure couldn't dim that.

She used her arms to explain the size of the dolphins she swam with once. "When you tell a story, you want to describe what you see and hear and smell and feel." Mary Catherine was growing winded. But she was too caught up in the lesson to take a break.

The teaching moment was no longer fun. Mary Catherine was in danger every time she got like this. Ember closed her eyes for a few seconds. *Father, get her out of here. Please . . . she won't listen to me.*

When she'd told them every last detail, Mary Catherine leaned against one of the desks. "I like to say a storyteller gets to live life twice. What do you think that means?"

One little boy raised his hand. "You live it first in the

water with the dolphins. Then you live it when you tell the story to someone."

Mary Catherine's entire face lit up. "Exactly!"

Ember watched, taking it all in, feeling an ache in her own heart. Mary Catherine had so much to offer. But not if she didn't get back to Los Angeles soon.

When the kids took their recess break, Ember asked whether the two of them could sit and talk. Every movement seemed to be an effort for Mary Catherine. Ember prayed silently as they took adjacent desks. "I'm worried about you, maybe you need to go home for a while. Get things checked out."

Mary Catherine slowly caught her breath. She seemed distant, lost in thought. "It wouldn't help." She took a slow breath and smiled at Ember. "Besides . . . I already made a commitment to stay another two months. Through November. When the other teacher gets here."

"Oh." Ember tried to hide her alarm. "Well, you could always go home and see a doctor. Then come back. After you're well."

"My health . . ." The topic seemed to shut Mary Catherine down. "It's complicated." She rested her forearms on the desk. "I'm fine. Really."

Panic stirred the desperation in Ember's heart. "At least think about it." Ember reached out and took Mary Catherine's hand. "Whatever it is, you're getting worse. You know that, right?"

Mary Catherine gave Ember's hand a gentle squeeze. Then she stood and faced the open doorway. "I'm going to join the kids." She smiled back at Ember. "There's no greater joy than watching children at recess." She hesitated, her eyes on the boys and girls at play. "No one has to tell children to be excited about life. They were born that way."

"True." Ember walked outside with Mary Catherine.

Ember could do nothing but watch. Mary Catherine pushed a few of the smaller children on the swings. Their giggles filled the summer air. Mary Catherine was clearly determined to live every day to the fullest. But one simple truth weighed on Ember every moment.

If Mary Catherine didn't get home soon, she wouldn't only get sicker.

She would die.

13

Jag CALLED THE URGENT MEETING. They met in Uganda, on the bank of the Nile River. Together they sat in plain sight of a pride of lions and in earshot of a herd of elephants. They waited only for Aspyn, who was finishing an assignment in Arizona at the baseball training facility.

"Serene." Jag looked around. The African plains were so different from Los Angeles. "Every animal, every tree. So little distraction. The Father's fingerprints are everywhere."

"As they are in Los Angeles." Beck raised his brow. "Humans just need to look harder."

"Yes." Ember smiled. "Mary Catherine's beach is one of the Lord's greatest creations."

There was a tension among them, an awareness. The mission was in grave danger.

Aspyn arrived, breathless. "Sorry. Protecting Tyler from an enemy attack." She smiled. "He is fine now."

Never had Jag worked on a mission like this, where they

were in charge of not one but four humans. Four lives that needed constant guarding and protecting—not only from physical danger but from emotional setbacks.

Jag spoke first. "Ember, if you could update us on Mary Catherine's condition."

She nodded. "Every day she seems a bit thinner, her skin more pale." Ember furrowed her brow, clearly troubled. "She struggles to breathe from even the slightest exertion."

Beck clasped his hands and stared at the dark red soil. "I was afraid this would happen."

"There's no way to tell exactly how damaged her heart is, or how much time we have." Jag sat on the highest part of an outcropping of rocks. He narrowed his eyes. "We need a plan. If we don't get Mary Catherine back to Los Angeles, the mission will . . ." He didn't want to finish the sentence.

Aspyn whispered the words instead. "Will be lost."

For a while they were quiet, the breeze off the river gentle on their skin. In the distance an elephant trumpeted and the sound shook the ground. Jag broke the silence. *Help us, Father . . . we don't know what to do.* He drew a long breath. "Let's pray. For God to give us an idea of what we can do next."

They sat that way, each of them lost in prayer, waiting, listening for the Father's wisdom. For His leading. Finally, after a long time, Beck gasped. He stood, pacing along the top of the rock surface where he'd been sitting. "I have an idea!"

Jag loved Beck's enthusiasm. He had less experience in Angels Walking mission work, but he was fervent and determined. He worked with a passion few angels would ever know. Jag nodded. "Tell us."

"I visited the office of Dr. Cohen a few days ago." He stopped and made eye contact with the others. "I was looking for ideas, anything that might help us. And there on the table in the waiting room was a brochure. It was about a device called a left ventricular assist device. Doctors know it as an LVAD." He paused. "Basically it's a mechanical heart. It does the work while a patient like Mary Catherine waits for a transplant."

He furrowed his forehead. "But I'm not sure it applies to Mary Catherine's situation."

"Her doctor would know." Ember's eyes filled with hope. "Is that what you're thinking, Beck?"

"Exactly." An intensity filled Beck's voice. "Maybe we could prompt Dr. Cohen to email Mary Catherine. Tell her she should come home sooner for the LVAD."

Aspyn shook her head. "It doesn't add up. The doctor would've told her before."

"Maybe she wasn't a candidate for it back then." Beck continued. "She might be now."

Ember had been quiet, listening. "I think Beck's right." She nodded. "That would make sense."

Jag thought for a moment. Beck might be on to something. "I like it." He paused. "Either way, the doctor needs to tell Mary Catherine about the possibility. If it is a possibility."

After a minute, Jag looked at the others. "Beck and I will form a plan for Dr. Cohen." He held up his hand. "Ember . . . Aspyn . . . God's power be with you. Until we meet again."

"Until then." Ember nodded to Aspyn and the two hugged. Then in an instant they disappeared, each to her own place.

When they were gone, Jag turned to Beck. "We'll do this together. The doctor needs to email Mary Catherine right away."

They talked a while longer about logistics, but even as their plan became clear, Jag began to doubt. They would need more than an email to turn things around. The enemy was working overtime. The stakes were high—for both sides.

And the entire mission hung on the very frail heart of Mary Catherine Clark.

MARY CATHERINE WAS SITTING at the lunch table, waiting for Ember. It was the first week of the month, the day when the two of them were supposed to walk to the nearest village for supplies. When the children were outside and the orphanage was quieter than usual, Mary Catherine could hear the constant wheeze, proof of the liquid gathering in her heart and lungs. Even so, she would go into town for supplies today.

She wasn't giving up.

Ember brought her lunch to the table, and the look on her face told Mary Catherine her friend didn't want her to make the trip. She waited until Ember was nearly finished with her meal before bringing it up. "I'm going with you." She took a sip of water. Most of her lunch remained untouched on her plate. "I like the walk."

"Mary Catherine." Ember looked straight at her, almost as if she could see through her. "You're sick. You should stay here."

"I can't." Mary Catherine was going. She'd already made

up her mind. "For me, it's about finding life in the moment." She hesitated, steadying her breathing. "I need to get out." She remembered to smile. "It'll make me feel better. Really. I'll be okay."

"I don't like it." It was the strongest Ember had sounded since she'd arrived at the orphanage. "But if you must go, let's leave now. So we can take our time."

Mary Catherine stood. "I'll get my bag."

Like on every other day of her life, Mary Catherine was convinced that taking risks would work out in the end. But this time she couldn't deny the strange uneasiness pushing on her shoulders, sending anxiety through her veins.

The sensation was new to Mary Catherine. Something that had come up every few days lately. The feeling was fear. Mary Catherine went to grab her bag and as she did she lifted her eyes to the vast African sky. *Father, I'm not afraid. I refuse it. Let me make this trip, please. Let me get through another day without being relegated to the sidelines.*

Be still and know that I am God, my daughter . . . be still.

Be still? God, is that really You? I've always felt You calling me to live.

Trust me, Mary Catherine.

The voice resonated inside her. As it did, a Scripture came to mind, something her father had taught her when she was a little girl. It was from Ecclesiastes, chapter three. With God there was a time for everything, and a season for every activity under heaven.

Mary Catherine let the verse settle, easing the rough edges of her soul. A time for everything.

Maybe even a time for being still.

Fine. She would be still after the walk to town. *I will, Lord. I promise. I'll rest after that for sure.*

As she prayed, she felt the fear lift a little. She needed new surroundings and the feel of the path beneath her feet. The sensation of her legs moving beneath her. Yes, the trip was a good idea. She would rest later.

If they took the walk slowly, everything would be just fine.

THEY WERE HALFWAY to the village when two men came into view, walking toward them on the path. Mary Catherine instantly felt goose bumps on her arms and legs. A sick feeling seized her stomach. Something wasn't right with the men, the way they were looking at Mary Catherine and Ember.

Next to her, she felt Ember tense up, too. "They aren't from around here." She kept her voice to a whisper. "Stay by me."

Mary Catherine felt her heart pound against her chest. The men moved toward them. They were tall and buff, but it was their eyes that struck terror in her. A terror she'd never felt before. The closer they came, the more Mary Catherine watched their eyes.

Dark and hateful. Like they were bent on murder.

Ember stopped when the men were just ten feet away. She held up her hand and in a language Mary Catherine didn't recognize, Ember spoke with a bold authority.

Mary Catherine recognized only one word the entire time Ember spoke.

The name of Jesus.

The men raised their voices and shouted at Ember. The

larger of the two glared at Mary Catherine and then at Ember. He gestured and shouted something again.

Ember's voice grew passionate. Mary Catherine had no idea what she was saying or even what language she was speaking. But then again—the name. "Jesus!" Ember took a step forward. As she did, the men stepped back.

This time they yelled louder. Their eyes blazed with hatred. They took turns gesturing at her and shouting at her, but Ember was unwavering. Every time she said the name of Jesus, the men took another step back. Until finally they headed off the path and into the brush.

Ember's face was pale, and her eyes held a concern Mary Catherine had never seen before. "They're gone." Ember started walking and motioned for Mary Catherine to follow. "We're fine."

As they passed, Mary Catherine peered in the direction the men had turned. But there was no sign of them. For a moment, she stopped and blinked a few times. The grass wasn't that tall. She looked back at Ember. "Where did they go?"

"Where they came from." Ember looked at her. "How are you feeling?"

"Better." They kept walking. "Now that they're gone." She studied Ember. "How did you know their language?"

"I've seen them before." Ember looked angry.

Mary Catherine kept up despite the wheezing in her chest. "I thought you said they weren't from around here."

"They're not." Ember paused. "I've seen them on other mission trips." She looked over her shoulder and then back at Mary Catherine. "They're bad guys."

"I sensed that."

Ember hesitated and then slowly a smile lifted her lips. "I'm not surprised."

The entire trip there and back, Mary Catherine kept telling herself the same thing. The walk felt wonderful, the exercise was doing her heart good. She was bound to feel better after having an adventure. Even watching Ember stand up to the men had made the afternoon memorable.

Especially the power in the name of Jesus.

Not until they were back at the orphanage and in their huts, turning in for the night, did Mary Catherine consider how she really felt. Her legs and arms ached and her lungs hurt with every breath. There was a time when she would've thought those healthy signs, proof she'd lived the day to the fullest or worked out in a way that made her feel alive.

But this was different. The feeling wasn't a good kind of tired. It was more like a flu, the sort of aching that usually meant a fever was coming on. Which would be especially dangerous in her case. And suddenly, Mary Catherine couldn't shake the memories of Marcus. The way he made her feel safe and loved.

She'd been wrong not to respond to him. And suddenly as the hours went by she wanted nothing more than to reply to his email. As if by doing so she could pretend he was here beside her. And that everything was going to be okay.

Mary Catherine waited until Ember was in bed. Then she did something she hadn't done in too long. She pulled her laptop from her bag, plugged it into the generator, found the last email from Marcus, and read it. Every word made the aching in her bones a little less. When she reached the last line she was convinced. She'd waited long enough.

She opened a new email and began to type.

Dear Marcus,

I can't believe I've waited this long to write to you . . .

The words came slowly. Her body protesting even the slightest effort. But that didn't matter. She would write to Marcus no matter how long it took.

She managed a full breath and kept typing.

It's not because I haven't thought about you. You must know that. I think about you all the time. Really. But I want you to find your way, meet new people. Go on dates and fall in . . .

Mary Catherine stopped typing. She sat up, too sad and weary to write another word. That wasn't what she wanted. For Marcus to fall in love with someone else. How could she send him an email saying something she didn't mean at all?

She closed her eyes and tried with all her strength to stop the tears, to stave off the flood of sorrow that welled up in the broken places of her heart. She missed Marcus so much. If she tried, if she really focused, she could smell his cologne, feel his arm against hers, hear the smoothness of his voice.

The tears forced their way down her cheeks and she put her hand over her mouth. She didn't want to wake Ember, didn't want her friend to see her crying.

But it was too late.

Mary Catherine felt Ember's hand on her shoulder. She was out of her bed, standing behind her. "Talk to me, Mary Catherine. What is it?"

She opened her eyes and shut her laptop. She slipped it back in her bag. She didn't want to talk about Marcus. He was a part of her past. No email could make his presence real at this point. She turned to face Ember. "I guess . . ." A sob caught in her voice. She covered her mouth again until she had more composure. "I . . . I don't feel good."

"Okay." Ember's voice spoke peace. "Then maybe it's time. Write to someone back in Los Angeles. Tell them you're coming home to get well."

To get well? The words only doubled Mary Catherine's sadness. She felt like she would never get well. "Thank you, Ember. You've been so kind." She wiped her eyes and nodded. "I'll let someone know."

"Okay." Ember looked satisfied. "Can I pray for you?"

Mary Catherine was so touched. God had known exactly whom to bring for this season of her life. And yes, she was still grateful she'd come to Africa. She loved teaching the children, loved reading to them and hearing their dreams. Loved when they called her Mama. They were the family she'd never have, and that made it all worth it. But tomorrow she would do something she should've done much sooner.

She'd write to Dr. Cohen and tell him the truth.

14

Lㄸxʏ sᴀᴛ ᴀᴛ ʜᴇʀ ɢʀᴀɴᴅᴍᴏᴛʜᴇʀ'ꜱ kitchen table and stared at the cell phone in her trembling hands. Then, like she'd done a dozen times in the past few months, she dialed Mary Catherine's number.

One ring, two. After the fourth ring the call went to voice mail. Again. "Umm, hey . . . it's me. Lexy. I'm not doing too good, so maybe when you get back, you could call me. Okay? See ya."

She hung up and tossed her cell phone on the table. Mary Catherine said she'd be there. She promised. So why wasn't she calling her back? Lexy cursed under her breath. *Figures. Girl talks all about God and answered prayers. But where is she now? Now that I need her?*

A few times she even considered going to the Youth Center and talking to Sami. She would know how to reach Mary Catherine. Sami had called a bunch of times. But Lexy didn't know Sami the same way.

A cold fear ran through her. What if something had happened to Mary Catherine? She had talked about going to Africa, but that was more like a dream. Not something she would've done, right?

Either way she was going with Ramon tonight, a date she couldn't cancel. Not even if Mary Catherine were here in person. Ramon was the new leader of the West Knights. He chose her. Sure, she knew better. She had promised Mary Catherine she would do everything she could to get out of the gang.

But really, who was she kidding?

She stood and went to the top drawer of her grandmother's buffet table. There at the back corner was the letter from her mother. The one she'd given Lexy the day she toured the prison. First time Lexy had seen her mother since she was eight years old.

Last Time In Program. Lexy rolled her eyes. *A day in prison couldn't get you out of a gang.* Especially her. Lexy had been with the leader of the West Knights before. So it was only right that the new leader would claim her as his own.

She took the letter and sat back down at the table. She opened it and tried to read it again, the way she had tried to read it three times since that afternoon. Her reading was better, but she still couldn't piece all the words together. Her eyes ran over the lines of letters and words. A few phrases made sense.

Sitting here and missing you. That's because her mama wrote the letter from her prison cell. She had a janitor help her write the words. A little further down she read a bit more. *The right way is with God, baby.*

Again Lexy rolled her eyes. God hadn't helped her mama make the right choices. He hadn't stopped Lexy from going back to the gang. A little further down she read more. *You and me when you were six years old* . . . That was the saddest part of the letter, where her mama remembered a picture of Lexy at six years old. Her first day of kindergarten.

After that Lexy skipped to the end. She could read the last line. This time she read the words out loud. *"I love you always. Every day. Even from here."* There was a catch in Lexy's voice. *"Love, your mama."*

Anger rushed at her. Where was her mother now? If she cared, she wouldn't have gotten into drugs in the first place. She would've loved Lexy enough to stay clean. She would've learned to read so she could teach her little girl.

No, her mama didn't love her. The letter was a bunch of lies. She thought about ripping it in half and throwing it in the trash. But instead she folded it up and put it back in the top drawer. Because sometimes it felt good to pretend she had a mama who really did love her.

But the truth? The truth was her mama didn't love her and neither did Mary Catherine. Even her grandma didn't seem to care anymore. She was always asleep—usually by eight o'clock. About the time Lexy left the house to hang with the West Knights.

She heard the sound of an engine out front. Her hands began to tremble again. Ramon was rough with her—rougher than any guy she'd been with. Much as it suited her to date the leader of the gang, much as it meant she was the prettiest girl in the West Knights, that didn't change the truth.

Lexy was afraid of Ramon.

Tonight she and Ramon were having a special hangout. To celebrate a drug buy Ramon had taken part in. He had told her tonight would be better than their other dates. More special. Ramon had a little more cash. Tonight they'd get dinner at a drive-thru and then they'd finish their time together someplace romantic.

A hotel room.

THEIR NIGHT WAS GOING BETTER than Lexy imagined. Ramon had only cussed at her a couple of times, and when they stopped for beer he bought her a plastic rose. Tossed it on her lap when he got behind the wheel.

"Only the best for you, Lex." He grinned at her. "Here." He handed her a beer. "Drink it."

Most nights Lexy didn't drink. But Ramon wanted this to be a celebration. Lexy popped the top and downed half of it. "Thanks." She smiled.

"You're really pretty, you know that?" Ramon crooked his finger and used it to lift her chin. "You got a perfect face."

The compliment made Lexy feel special. Like a princess. She smiled and batted her eyelashes at him. "You're perfect, too."

He narrowed his eyes. "Just don't ever make me mad." He brushed his knuckles against her cheek. "You wouldn't look so great then."

Lexy laughed. Mostly because she didn't know what else to do. Ramon was serious. He'd kill one of his own boys if there was a reason. Everyone knew it. They ate at Taco Bell and drove to the hotel. It wasn't too fancy. Less than forty bucks a night. Lexy saw the sign as they pulled up in front of the room. Ramon left to pay and get the key. When he got back he opened the car door and leaned in.

"You know what you are?" Ramon smiled at her. "You're a slut, Lexy Jones." He laughed. "Tonight you're gonna prove it."

She had no idea what that meant. Prove it? By now he couldn't doubt the fact that she belonged to him. But if he wanted her to prove it . . . "Is that a challenge?"

"Better believe it." He nodded at her door. "Get out. Time's wasting."

He already had the key to the room. She followed him to the door and even before he unlocked it, he pressed her against the wall and kissed her. "That's a good girl. You want me, right?"

Lexy's teeth began to chatter. "Of course." His kiss was rough, a little too wet. She didn't dare wipe her mouth. "I'm all yours, Ramon."

His smile faded. "Like I said . . . you're about to prove it."

Ramon opened the door and closed it behind them. He never even turned on the light. Two hours later when he took her home, he wasn't nearly as kind.

She started to roll down the window. Just for a little fresh air. But he grabbed her arm. "Leave it up." He shouted at her. "Or get out."

Lexy blocked out his words and the way he said them, she ignored the bruise probably starting on her arm. "I can roll down the window if I want." She lifted her face, defiant. "What's the big deal?"

He jerked the wheel of the car and almost hopped the

curb. The whole car lurched forward as he hit the brakes. "Get out!" He shoved her. "You cross me, you get out and walk."

"Fine." She held up her hands. She was instantly scared to death, but she wouldn't show it. Ramon hated weakness. "I'll leave it up. Forget about the fresh air."

Ramon gripped the wheel, his knuckles locked in place. He mumbled a bunch of cuss words at her. When he pulled up in front of her grandmother's house he came to a sudden stop again. "Go."

Once she was out of the car, Lexy stood there, shivering.

She hated how she felt and she hated how the night had ended. But there was one thing that mattered more than her bruised arm and broken heart: getting inside the house before her grandma woke up. Because whatever Ramon did to her, however he treated her, one thing was certain.

Her grandmother could never find out.

15

IT WAS THE TENTH OF SEPTEMBER and the Dodgers were on the road in the play-offs. Later that night Sami planned to go to the game with Tyler. But today she was in Santa Monica with two of her UCLA friends—Nichole and Megan—looking for a wedding dress.

They started with coffee and a conversation about Sami's wedding plans. Now it was time to focus on the matter at hand. They walked along Santa Monica Boulevard to Fourth Street and several wedding dress boutiques.

Along the way they saw a woman walking two small dogs—one of them dressed as a bride, the other as a groom. The girls slowed, watching the trio until they turned left, out of sight. Even before that Sami's friends began to laugh, and Sami joined them. She shook her head. "That has to be a sign, right?"

They kept walking, still laughing, and after four hours and three boutiques, Sami found the perfect white dress. It was simple and shirred at the top, with a cascade of white taffeta and satin layers for the skirt. The back formed a pretty train.

In every way it was perfect.

But the trip made Sami miss Mary Catherine. That night after Marcus pitched a shutout game to give the Dodgers a 2–0 lead in the division series, and after she and Tyler and Marcus hung out at his house for another few hours, Sami made herself a cup of chai tea and thought about Lexy.

Sami's friends had stayed committed to the Youth Center, attending each week and mentoring the girls. Many of the teens were coming around, talking more openly, asking for advice and even for prayer. But not Lexy.

However many times Sami had called the girl, no matter how often she had left a message, she never heard back. She was worried Lexy was caught up in her old way of life.

Sami sat at the kitchen table and opened her laptop. She usually waited until now to check her email. Especially with Mary Catherine gone and Tyler out of town. Email was one way to pass the lonely nights.

The last letter from Mary Catherine came a week ago and it was super brief. Just an update on the kids at the orphanage and what they were learning. A quick story about two shady guys and how the volunteer, Ember, had spoken in their language and made the guys leave.

Mary Catherine asked about Sami, of course, and Tyler and the wedding plans. But like always she said nothing about herself or her health. Nothing about Marcus. Sami had written to her twice since then, but she'd gotten nothing in return.

Enough. Sami was worried about her friend. She couldn't

shake the fact that something was wrong. Why else would Mary Catherine ignore the question about her health? Every time she asked it?

Sami opened a new letter and began to write.

Dear Mary Catherine,

I'm sitting here late this Saturday night wondering about you. Worried about you, really. The Dodgers won tonight— Marcus pitched the game of his life. He misses you—which I know you didn't ask about. But he does. It's obvious to anyone who knows him.

The thing is, I always tell you the happy things going on here and you tell me the happy things you're doing there. But I have this really awful feeling tonight that you're not being fully honest. That something else is going on and you just don't want to tell me.

I've asked God to protect you, and I know He is. But how is your health, Mary Catherine? How come you don't talk about your heart? I know you need surgery—you told me you need a valve transplant one of these days. But when? How will you know?

Please tell me I'm worrying for nothing. Tell me your heart feels perfect and you're better than ever. All I know is I can't shake this feeling, and I hate it.

Oh, and something else. I picked out my wedding dress today. You should've been there. I think you'd love it. But tonight I'm not thinking about my dress. I'm thinking about you and whether everything is okay. Because I can't get around this feeling.

So please . . . write to me and tell me you're okay. Or tell me the truth. Whatever the truth is. Love you and miss you, Sami

The letter was more abrupt than anything Sami had written before. She needed to get Mary Catherine's attention, needed to know that everything was okay. Otherwise why hadn't she written back?

Sami read it one more time, then she hit the send button. Before she could change her mind.

NORMALLY AFTER PITCHING a complete game, Marcus could feel the ache in his arm for three days. But that Monday morning—their day off—the pain in his bicep and shoulder was nothing to the hurt in his heart.

Yesterday, Mary Catherine had finally written to him. But the letter was brief and impersonal. He took his coffee to his back porch and stared at the treetops in the neighborhood below his. The dense clouds and cool temperatures this September morning suited his mood.

Marcus pulled out his phone and read the email once more.

> Hi, Marcus, it's me. I know, you're probably wondering why I didn't write sooner, but you know me. Always running. I guess I finally figured it couldn't hurt to drop you a note and tell you how much I'm loving it here. The teaching and the children—all of it is exactly what I needed. I really do belong here—just like I told you. Because of that, I committed to staying another two months. Through November at least, when another teacher will arrive to replace me. The kids need someone, and I really want to stay.

By now I'm sure you're dominating the play-offs. I follow you on Twitter, so I know you've been playing some of your best baseball.

Anyway, I'm sorry so much time has passed. I think of you still.

Love, Mary Catherine

Marcus slipped his phone back in the pocket of his jeans and exhaled hard. Every memory of Mary Catherine was filled with depth and beauty. She was like no other girl he knew. Yet it was like someone else had written the entire letter. Factual, breezy. Nothing she wouldn't have said to an acquaintance.

All except the last line.

I think of you still . . . Marcus closed his eyes. *Lord, I'm so frustrated. What is it with that girl? And why won't she let me see what she's really feeling? Why is she keeping her distance?*

He waited, but there was no answer, nothing audible. Instead he felt the slightest sense of fear. A panic, almost. Or maybe it was just the not knowing that was clouding his mind. For a minute he let himself sit in the anxiety, just live in it. *What is it, God? Is something wrong with her?*

A verse came to mind, one he had read last night as part of his devotions. It was from Proverbs 4:23—*Above all else, guard your heart, for it is the wellspring of life.* He thought hard about the message there. *Guard your heart* . . . The words were pure wisdom. Especially after the way Mary Catherine had treated him.

But he had the feeling they applied to Mary Catherine, too. He stood and walked to the balcony railing. Was that what Mary Catherine was doing? Guarding her heart? Was she keeping something from him as a way of preserving her own peace of mind?

Or was there some other meaning he was supposed to take from the verse?

Marcus peered into the cloudy sky. It reminded him of Mary Catherine. He could study her and look deeply in her direction, but always there was this layer of clouds he could never quite see through.

What am I supposed to do, God? How can I help her?

My son, go to her. Go to Africa.

Marcus took a step back. The voice was clear and powerful, audible. Or at least it seemed that way. *Lord?* A cold feeling ran down his arms. *You . . . you want me to go to her?* He dropped slowly to the nearest chair. *I already tried that. She doesn't want to see me.*

Listen to me, my son. Trust me.

Again the voice! Marcus jumped up and looked around. It took a few seconds before he could settle down enough to sit. Was the voice really God's? What sense did it make? Why would God want him to go to Africa? Marcus rubbed the back of his neck and tried to make sense of the voice. It was too clear to ignore.

But if he went to Africa, Mary Catherine would think he was crazy. What possible purpose could there be in taking a trip like that? She'd already made herself very clear. Mary Catherine had moved on without him. She wanted him to do the same.

But then . . . if God wanted him to go to Africa, maybe there was a different reason. A reason Marcus didn't know about yet. He thought about booking a flight but stopped himself. Flights could wait—since the idea of going seemed ludicrous. But there was something he could do. Just in case.

Marcus checked his schedule. He and Tyler had talked about getting dinner later since Sami had a teen moms meeting at the Youth Center. But between now and then he was completely open. He walked back into the house even before the idea was fully formed. An hour later he was at the reception desk of the clinic in Santa Monica.

"I remember you!" The woman was the same one who had helped Mary Catherine six months ago. "How can I help?"

Marcus didn't hesitate. "I'd like shots. Everything I need for Uganda."

The woman smiled. "You'll be visiting?"

"Maybe." He grinned. The woman clearly didn't know he was a pitcher for the Dodgers. Which suited Marcus just fine.

"All right." The receptionist opened a door and found a clipboard with a few sheets of paperwork. "Have a seat in the waiting room and fill these out. I'll call you back in a few minutes."

On the drive here Marcus had done the math. Even if they won the World Series again—which wasn't likely—he could be in Africa soon enough. Six weeks tops—if God really wanted him to make the trip. Either way, Marcus would wait to be sure. He wouldn't go to Uganda without absolute certainty that the trip was God's idea. If this was the Lord's plan, Marcus needed more than the voice he'd heard earlier.

He needed a sign.

❦

MARY CATHERINE COULD sense Ember's growing concern.

When the kids were dismissed for lunch, Ember walked up and put her hand on Mary Catherine's shoulder. "You need help." Ember searched Mary Catherine's eyes. "Did you ever email someone?" She hesitated, intently serious. "I've prayed about this. God told me you are very sick."

God had told her? Mary Catherine hung her head and did her best to hold back the tears. *If You told her, Lord, then maybe it's finally time for me to tell her.* She lifted her eyes to Ember's again. "Can we go talk somewhere?" She pressed her fingertips to her eyes and tried to stay strong. "I have something to tell you."

"Of course." Ember didn't look surprised. She followed Mary Catherine to a pair of chairs on the back porch of the orphanage. From their seats they could see the children playing a raucous game of tag.

Never stop playing, she wanted to tell them. For a long while Mary Catherine simply watched the children. Finally she spoke to Ember in a way that allowed a new level of depth. "I did email my doctor." She shook her head. "He never responded."

"What?" Ember sounded outraged. "That's terrible."

"I know." Her doctor should've seen the email and responded by now. He must not have read it. Which was strange, since he had asked her to stay in touch. Maybe talking to the doctor simply didn't matter at this point. She sighed. "Getting medical help . . . it might not make a difference."

Ember shook her head, clearly confused. "A doctor could see what's wrong. Maybe he would have you fly home so they could run tests."

Mary Catherine nodded, distracted. Lately she had experienced moments of peace like never before. A sense of deep contentment would come over her as if she and God were the only ones in the room.

This was one of those times.

After a minute, Mary Catherine turned again to Ember. "I know why I'm sick." She paused, and the wheeze in her chest was loud enough for both of them to hear. "My heart is failing—something I was born with."

As soon as the words were out, Mary Catherine felt a weight lift from her. She should've told Ember a long time ago, but at least she'd done it now. Her honesty brought a rush of relief.

Across from her, Ember's eyes flashed with concern. "If your heart is failing, then you should definitely go home, right? So you can get help?"

"That's just it." Mary Catherine could feel the peace in her eyes. "I need a heart transplant but that could take months." She allowed a weak smile. "Ember, most heart patients die waiting."

Ember stood and folded her arms. She looked out at the play yard for a long time before turning again to Mary Catherine. "You have to go home if you're going to receive a heart. Isn't that true?"

"My doctor told me it wouldn't matter. Being home wouldn't put me at the top of the list."

"But you're sicker now. That could change things." A sigh

came from Ember. "Your doctor couldn't possibly have wanted you here."

"No." Mary Catherine hesitated. As long as she was being honest she might as well be up front with this, too. "He didn't want me to leave."

Ember looked like she might cry. She returned to her seat and stared at Mary Catherine. "Don't you want to live?"

"Of course." Fresh tears sprang to Mary Catherine's eyes. She coughed a few times. "That's why I'm here. If I didn't come now, I might never have another chance."

A hot wind danced through the dusty grounds, and in the distance storm clouds gathered. Mary Catherine could feel the tension from her friend.

Ember waited before speaking again. "I understand. I really do." But her eyes said she wasn't ready to give up. "But if you get home and get your transplant, you can come back whenever you want."

Ember was right, of course. "I guess I'm not much of a sidelines person." She struggled to take a full breath. "I figured if I have six months to live, I'd rather spend them here. Where I always dreamed of living. Rather than waiting back home only to die without ever . . ." She looked out at the children again. "Without ever knowing this."

Ember looked at her. "I get that." She reached for Mary Catherine's hand and gave it a slight squeeze. "But write to your doctor again. Keep an open mind. Please." She paused. "Your doctor might think of something new, another way to help you. I'm going to pray for that."

"Okay." They stood and walked toward the lunchroom.

Mary Catherine struggled beneath a blanket of exhaustion. "Thank you, Ember. For caring."

"What can I do? To help you breathe better?"

Mary Catherine smiled. "Pray. God's brought me this far."

Lunch was chicken and rice, and Mary Catherine was able to eat more than usual. Proof that she felt better having Ember know the truth. Less anxiety in her gut. After lunch she spent half an hour in her hut, resting on her bed and talking to God. Yes, He'd gotten her through to this point, and He would get her through as long as He wanted her here on Earth.

And Mary Catherine had a sense that she wouldn't be here long. Even so, she felt comforted by peace and contentment, an assurance that knew no boundaries. Her faith was not dependent on circumstances or illness or ever seeing Marcus again.

It was anchored in Jesus. So why was she constantly avoiding telling her friends the truth about her heart? Mary Catherine knew the reason. She didn't want the people she loved most trying to talk her out of being here.

Mary Catherine put her hand to her chest and felt the beating of her heart. It still *seemed* strong, but she knew it wasn't. Once a long time ago she had worked out with a trainer at the Santa Monica gym. He led her to a bench press and at first she had rattled off a quick ten reps. Then the trainer put more weight on either end of the bar. When she tried to lift it, the bar settled on her chest. She had choked and gasped for breath, making terrible sounds until the trainer rushed in to help her. The ordeal was terrifying.

Which was how she felt constantly now.

The wheezing, the pressure on her chest, it was part of the process. Her fear wouldn't get the best of her, though. Mary Catherine reached for her Bible and opened it to Philippians, chapter 1. This was Paul's letter to the church at Philippi. The Scripture that had brought Mary Catherine so much hope lately. In this book, Paul was near death and in prison. Yet he wasn't afraid. He was filled with the same kind of peace that kept Mary Catherine company lately.

She looked at verse twenty-one; the words Paul had written spoke to her very soul. *For me to live is Christ, to die is gain.* That was it, exactly how Mary Catherine felt. Yes, if her heart stopped beating soon she would miss Sami and Tyler and every wonderful moment she might've shared with Marcus. But here, her life was about Christ in a simpler, more pure way. Serving Him, relying on Him, making Him known to the children. Children who needed her. And if she died?

Well, then, that would be gain.

Mary Catherine couldn't see it any other way.

16

Sami didn't turn on the TV at the Youth Center until the teen meeting was finished, just in time to watch the Dodgers miss a return to the World Series. The Dodgers and Reds had been tied, three games each. Marcus was pitching a shutout, but the Reds' ace hitter caught the outside edge of a fastball and sent it over the fence for a walk-off home run.

And that was that.

Sami turned the TV off and gathered her things. She wasn't glad for the loss, but it wasn't the worst news. The team still had a successful season, and now she and Tyler could finalize their wedding plans.

A few security guards and volunteers were still finishing up at the center, but most everyone had gone home. Sami was about to leave when she heard someone out in the hallway. She turned just as Aspyn walked into the room.

"Sami! I caught you!" Aspyn was a local volunteer. She

hadn't been around as much lately. "One of the neighbors told me I could find you here." She walked in and took one of the seats in the front row. "Can you talk?"

"Umm." Sami was supposed to talk with Tyler later. She checked the clock on the wall. "I have another meeting." She didn't want to seem uninterested. "I haven't seen you in a while. What's up?"

Aspyn took a deep breath and shook her head. "So much. I've been helping with another ministry. But today, I had this feeling I needed to stop by. Maybe hear about the teen program. How's it working out?"

Sami wasn't getting out of here anytime soon. She kept her phone in her hand in case Tyler called, took a seat near Aspyn, and gave her a quick rundown on the teen mentor program. "We don't have Mary Catherine. She went to Africa." Sami felt the familiar uneasiness, the anxiety that was worse every time she thought about her friend. Once again, Mary Catherine had responded to her last email, but without any of the answers she had asked for.

Concern shone in Aspyn's eyes. "I heard about that. I was hoping she'd stay here. There's so much to do."

The conversation bounced from Mary Catherine to the teen mentor program to the progress the Youth Center had made. Tyler called midway through the talk, and Sami held up her phone. "Let me get this. Just for a minute."

Aspyn sat back. "Take your time." Clearly she wasn't going anywhere.

Sami answered the call and told Tyler she was sorry about the loss. She'd call him back. Then she turned to Aspyn again. "Where was I?"

"The teen program. How it's working without Mary Catherine."

"Right." Sami tried to sum up the work they'd been doing, and how her friends from UCLA were helping out. "As for the local girls, they're making progress, definitely."

"Glad to hear it." Aspyn looked thoughtful. "It's still a battle, though."

Sami agreed, but she really wanted to get going. Wednesdays were her longest days, and she couldn't wait to talk to Tyler. She stood and held her hand out to Aspyn. "I'm glad you came by. We've missed you around here."

"I've been around." Aspyn remained seated. "Just busy. Speaking of which, one of the women said you're engaged! I want to hear all about it!"

There had to be a better time to catch up. Tyler would be wondering if everything was okay—especially this late at night. Sami was about to suggest she and Aspyn schedule a lunch date next week when she heard someone running down the hall. Sami turned just as Lexy appeared.

"I . . . I thought I'd miss you!" The girl was shaking. Her eyes were wide and she held her arm close to her body. Like it was injured. She cast a suspicious look at Aspyn. "I need to talk. Just to you."

Aspyn didn't need to be asked twice. She was already on her feet and headed for the door. "I was just leaving." She waved at Sami. "We'll catch up later."

Lexy entered the room and waited for Aspyn to go. When they were alone, the girl sank to the nearest chair. "I'm in trouble. I need Mary Catherine!" Lexy started to cry. "Please, help me. I'm so afraid."

"Mary Catherine is in Uganda." Sami sat down. Tyler would understand if she was late. "Lexy, what happened, honey? Tell me everything."

"I . . . I wasn't going to come. I need Mary Catherine." She covered her face with her good hand and wept for a full minute. Then she seemed to gather some sort of desperate strength. She held her arm. Her attention remained focused on the ground. "I told God I'd try one time. Just once." She sniffed. "I'd come here and if I couldn't find Mary Catherine . . . or . . . or someone who would listen, then I'd never believe in Him again."

Sami thought about Aspyn's visit. If she hadn't stopped by, Sami would've been gone. "Well, I'm here." Sami silently thanked God. "What happened to your arm?"

"I think it's broken." Her words came in fits and starts, tangled up with the sobs wracking her small frame. "Ramon . . . my boyfriend . . . he beat me up."

Sami hid her anger. "What happened?"

Still Lexy wouldn't make eye contact. But after a while she lifted her head and looked straight at Sami. "I'm pregnant."

Sami felt herself reeling. Lexy was just seventeen. Sami stood and took the seat closest to the girl. Without saying a word, Sami put her arm around Lexy's shoulders. Sami had no idea how long they stayed like that. Five minutes, maybe more. Until Lexy stopped sobbing and was able to really talk.

"It's my fault, I know it." Lexy hung her head. Her eyes were swollen, her nose stuffy. She looked like a lost child.

"Is Ramon mad about the baby?" Sami was still trying to get her mind around the crushing reality. "Is that why he hurt you?"

"Yes." Lexy sniffed again. "He said I should've used something. He was mad so he twisted my arm."

"Lexy . . ." Sami clenched her jaw. Ramon should be locked up for this. "I'm so sorry. Can you move it?"

Lexy shrugged. "Not really." She took a slow breath and told Sami a story she couldn't begin to grasp. How six weeks ago—after Ramon had claimed her as his girl—he had taken her to a hotel room to celebrate a drug deal.

"I found out yesterday that I was pregnant. And . . . Ramon told me it was my fault. I should've been on the pill. That sort of thing." Fresh tears glistened in Lexy's eyes. "I'm having an abortion tomorrow. I already called the clinic."

Sami wasn't sure where to begin. *God, please give me the words.* If Lexy went back onto the streets tonight, Sami might never see her again. "I have an idea."

"Don't try to talk me out of it." Lexy's eyes flashed, dark and full of despair. "I can't have a baby. I just can't."

"Let's go have your arm looked at. You can stay with me at my apartment tonight. Call your grandma and see if that's okay."

The idea seemed to make Lexy nervous. "Ramon told me not to tell anyone." She touched her damaged arm. "About this. Otherwise . . . he'll kill me. He said so."

"Either way your arm needs to be checked. In case it's broken."

Lexy nodded, her expression distant. "Yeah. Okay." Alarm sounded in her voice. "But don't mention Ramon. Not at all."

They stopped at an urgent care in Santa Monica, closer to Sami's apartment. Forty minutes later, they had the X-ray results. Thankfully, the girl's arm was only sprained, not broken.

While the doctor was working on Lexy, Sami excused herself and found the nurse. In hushed tones she explained that Lexy's boyfriend had beaten her up. Sami gave the woman Ramon's name and his gang affiliation. The woman looked as angry as Sami felt. "I'll get this to the police."

Sami couldn't worry about whether the report would make Ramon angry. If she needed to, she would keep Lexy with her until the danger passed. Sami paid the bill. Lexy didn't have insurance and her grandmother had no money. Not that she would ever tell her grandmother the truth about her injury.

Half an hour later they were at Sami's apartment. Lexy's grandma had said she could stay as long as she wanted. Anything to get her away from the West Knights. And Sami called Tyler to explain the situation. They both agreed to postpone their conversation until after tonight. So Sami could talk to Lexy privately. Sami heated up chicken and broccoli for the two of them, and after they ate Sami found her laptop.

She'd been praying all night about how she should approach the subject, and only one answer came to mind: with love.

"Come here, Lexy. I want to show you something." Sami patted the seat next to her on the sofa. She pulled up an adoption website, then she angled herself so Lexy could see. "Let's talk about your baby. There are couples everywhere who can't have children, so—"

"No! I'm getting the abortion." Defiance darkened Lexy's eyes. "The clinic said it was tissue."

Sami closed the adoption website. A sick feeling welled up in her. The recent news about Planned Parenthood disgusted her on every level. Now this statement by someone at the clinic. Sami steadied herself. "Would you look at some pictures?"

Lexy's curiosity must've gotten the better of her. She acted uninterested, but she gave a slight shrug of her good shoulder. "Of what?"

Sami closed the adoption website and pulled up photos of unborn babies at various stages of gestation. "Have you looked at pictures of babies before they're born? Like in health class?"

A sad chuckle came from the girl. "They teach us how to use a condom. But Ramon doesn't like them. So I guess that was a waste."

Another level of heartache. How were these kids supposed to find their way out of the cycle of gangs and kids having kids if the only sex education they were taught was proper use of a condom? She was thankful for one of her friends who taught health at a private school in LA. There, she had the right to teach abstinence to the teens.

Sami shut her laptop. "Let's start with what the Bible says about babies. Could we do that?"

"The Bible says something about that?"

"It does." Sami found her Bible in her bedroom, brought it back to the sofa, and turned to Psalm 139:13-16. She read the verses about God knitting a baby together in a mother's womb and how God, from the beginning of time, ordained every day for every child.

Lexy's eyes grew wide. She looked shocked at the truth. "So the cells dividing . . . that's really God knitting a baby together?"

"Yes. That's how He planned it. Every cell, everything about the baby is in God's hands." She shut the Bible and looked at Lexy. "How many weeks are you?"

"Weeks?"

Sami didn't want to rush the moment. Clearly Lexy knew nothing about the experience she was caught up in. "How long since you might've gotten pregnant? How many weeks?"

She thought for a moment. "Maybe six."

"Okay." Sami opened her laptop again. "Let's look at those pictures. An unborn baby at six weeks." She found several ultrasound images and showed them to Lexy.

The girl's mouth hung open. She pointed at the screen. "So that's the baby's head? Already?"

"Yes." Sami passed the laptop to Lexy. "Go back a page. You can see babies at all the stages right up until they're born."

For several minutes Lexy looked at the pictures.

"Science matches up with what God teaches." Sami took her time. "Can you see that?"

Lexy's tears were back. She shut the computer and hung her head. One at a time her tears dropped onto her worn jeans. She put her hand over her lower stomach. "My trouble's with Ramon. It isn't the baby's fault. I don't know what to do." She lifted her eyes to Sami. "Ramon . . . he'll kill me if . . . if I don't get the abortion."

"What if you could get away from him?" Sami was going out of her comfort zone, but why not? What was life if you couldn't help someone else?

"What do you mean?" She brushed her tears off her cheeks. "I don't want a baby, Sami. I can't."

Again Sami took the laptop from Lexy. She pulled up the adoption website again. "See this?" She turned the computer so the girl could see it. "There's a listing of couples here, all of them looking for a baby."

"Why?" Lexy looked confused again. Never mind her age, she knew almost nothing about childbearing—even this.

"Usually because they can't have children. They've tried, but it just hasn't happened. So they're a husband and wife looking for a baby to love. They have a home and a way to support the child. Now they can only hope and pray for a baby." Sami felt a sense of calm come over her.

"Through adoption."

"Yes." She could see Lexy listening. The truth was sinking in. "What a beautiful gift for your baby. The gift of life not just once, but twice."

A light dawned in Lexy's eyes. "First by not having an abortion . . . and then by giving the child to a family who wants a baby."

"Right." Sami gathered her thoughts. Once she made this offer there would be no turning back. Usually she would take more time for something like this. Which meant the offer would only work if Mary Catherine was on board, too.

But Sami knew Mary Catherine would be completely willing. "What if I ask Mary Catherine about you living here until you have the baby. First with me until I get married and move in with Tyler in December. And then with her, after she gets back." The idea took root at a different level. It made sense in so many ways.

"You think Mary Catherine would let me?" Lexy looked shocked.

"I do." As long as Mary Catherine didn't decide to live in Uganda. Sami's mind raced. "You'd be safe from Ramon . . . and the baby would be safe. And after that . . . we could see what doors God opens."

It took only a minute for Lexy to start crying in earnest. Not the fearful, desperate sobs from earlier that night at the Youth Center. But the tears of someone who maybe—for the first time in her life—could see a way out.

"So this . . . this is where Mary Catherine lived? Here with you?" Lexy looked around, seeming suddenly aware of her surroundings in a different way.

"It is." Sami knew for sure that Mary Catherine would agree with this decision. "She'd be so glad you were here." Sami smiled. "If you move in, she might come back sooner."

"Really?" Lexy squinted at Sami, as if she didn't dare believe this was even happening. "You'd do this? Let me live here?"

Sami's mind raced. There were still many details to think through. "There'd be rules. You'd have to stay with me—when I go to the Youth Center, you'd have to go, too. And when school starts"—Sami thought for a moment—"you'd have to take online classes. So you can keep working toward your high school diploma."

"I'd do that." Lexy looked worried again. "At the Youth Center . . . what if Ramon finds out?"

"We'll be careful. I have a feeling he'll move on." She waited for Lexy's reaction. "Would that be okay?"

"Yes." She nodded, looking more like a twelve-year-old. "I never want to see him again."

Sami could only hope the guy would be arrested before the end of the week. That way he'd be nowhere near Lexy.

Long after Lexy had gone to bed in Mary Catherine's room, Sami stayed up praying about the situation. What had she gotten herself into? She called Tyler and he agreed that on the surface the idea was crazy.

"But you saved a life tonight, Sami." He was clearly proud of her. "And you know Mary Catherine will be all for it. If she gets home in time."

"I thought about that." Sami paced her living room, her cell phone pressed to her ear. "Like, what happens to Lexy if Mary Catherine stays another year?"

There was a long pause on the other end. "Sami." Tyler's voice held a smile. "You know the answer. She'll stay with us."

Sami stopped cold. "Really? You'd do that?"

"Yes." Tyler chuckled. "Life isn't about us or our comfort. It's about rolling up your sleeves and getting dirty. As long as it means showing Jesus to another person."

They talked about other options, too. Coach Wayne and his family might be open to having Lexy at some point. Sami felt better after talking to Tyler. People helped each other. That's what Jesus called them to do. If in faith she took Lexy in, then somehow—by the grace of God—it would work out.

Sami was convinced.

JAG WAS READY to take drastic measures. They had no choice. He and Beck had found their way into Dr. Cohen's office twice already. One time they left the brochure for the LVAD on his desk, and the next visit near his computer. Both times Dr. Cohen came into his office, saw the brochure, and set it aside. He made no connection whatsoever to Mary Catherine.

Beck had done more research. Mary Catherine seemed to be a perfect candidate for an LVAD device. So why hadn't her doctor considered it? He must not have known how sick she'd gotten in Africa. The device was known as a bridge to transport, a way of buying time. They had to help Dr. Cohen understand just how little time was left.

Today they were ready to take things to another level. Angels didn't always take action first. Often they liked to incite it, create an opportunity for humans to get the work done. Sometimes, though, they had to use desperate means.

Like tonight.

Beck was dressed as a security guard, Jag a doctor. Beck kept watch near the front door while Jag moved through the doors to Dr. Cohen's office. The office was armed with security cameras. Jag wasn't terribly worried if he was caught on camera.

If someone checked the security footage they'd simply see a blur of very bright light. Nothing more. Even so, Jag worked quickly. He looked for Mary Catherine's last email, the one where she admitted her failing health. But it wasn't there.

This could explain why Mary Catherine hadn't heard back from her doctor. Jag made a note to talk to Ember about the email later. Still he had work to do here. He found an earlier email from Mary Catherine.

Then he hit reply.

Dear Mary Catherine,

It's been six months since I last saw you, and in that time I haven't heard from you at all. I hope this means you are feeling well and not exerting yourself too much.

I wanted to discuss an idea with you. Depending on how you're feeling, whether your symptoms are worsening or not, you may be a perfect candidate for a left ventricular assist device (LVAD). The LVAD is basically a mechanical heart. It can buy you time—years in some cases—while you wait for a heart transplant.

I want to run tests and do a full work-up on your condition. Depending on your symptoms and the results of your tests, I'd like to get you prepped and ready for this operation right away. I think this could save your life, Mary Catherine, so my orders are for you to come to the office as soon as possible. Please take this very seriously.

Sincerely,

Dr. Gerald Cohen

Jag read the letter one more time. He hit send and was logging off the computer when someone flipped on the lights in the next room. It was Dr. Cohen's nurse, Sally Hudson. Jag straightened, mustering his best official-business expression.

The woman entered the office and screamed. "What . . . who are you?"

Help me, Father . . . Jag slid his hands in his pockets and smiled, cool and collected. Then he held out his hand. "I'm Dr. Jay Agate. Medical intern from USC."

The woman narrowed her blue eyes, doubtful. But after a few seconds in Jag's presence an unearthly peace seemed to wash over her. Jag watched her relax and eventually she shook his hand. "Dr. Cohen . . . he didn't tell me you'd be here."

"I needed to submit some paperwork." He nodded to her and started to leave. But before he got to the door, he turned around. The Lord was giving him words. "Sally, God sees the good you do. The way you love Him and your family." Jag smiled. "Keep up the good work."

Sally Hudson's mouth hung open. She blinked back tears and started to talk. But by then Jag was gone. He left the office and then stepped into the hall, where he disappeared. He found Beck out front and the two of them hurried off.

A warm feeling spread through Jag as they made their way. Angels were God's army. They could protect and rescue, yes. But sometimes they offered words of hope and encouragement, messages from God.

He loved those times. The look on Sally Hudson's face was something he would treasure long after this mission was over.

Now if only they could get Mary Catherine home. Heaven's angel armies had joined forces to pray for her to book the flight back to LA, and Jag was grateful. They needed all the help they could get.

Otherwise all of mankind would lose.

17

THE FEVER WOKE MARY CATHERINE up an hour before daybreak and she knew immediately what was happening. She'd waited too long. Her entire body ached and she couldn't stop shivering. Her breaths were fast, too fast. Short and raspy. And the pressure was worse than before. Like someone was sitting on her chest.

And only then, in that desperate moment, did she remember something from yesterday. A truth Mary Catherine had denied until then.

She wanted to live.

The difference was something Ember had said. They'd had the conversation just yesterday during recess. Ember sat next to her on the edge of the playground. "Mary Catherine, if a person jumps off a bridge, that isn't God's plan. Right?"

"Of course not." Mary Catherine hadn't been sure what Ember was leading up to.

"Okay." Ember leveled her gaze straight at her. "If you don't try to get help, how is your situation any different?"

Accepting death was one thing. If an early death was God's will, then so be it. But giving up too soon couldn't possibly be God's will. If God would let her live, then she wanted to live.

Desperately.

She felt delirious, too hot to move or think or act. But suddenly she was overcome by an intense desire to get home. *God, what have I done? I'm so sorry. I should've gone home sooner. Help me, please.* She used all her energy to roll onto her side.

As she did, she spotted her laptop. *Sami. God, this is all my fault. Why didn't I tell her the truth?* Her laptop might as well have been an ocean away. But somehow Mary Catherine found a way out of her bed and across the hut to her computer. She sank to the dirt floor and glanced at Ember.

Her friend was still asleep.

Mary Catherine's teeth chattered, and she wondered if her fever might be even higher now than ten minutes ago. *Help me, Father . . . I made a mistake. Please . . .*

She opened her laptop, and before she could find Sami's email, she saw one from her doctor. She opened it and scanned through it. Something about a mechanical heart, a device that could save her life. *Too late,* she thought. *God, I need a miracle. I can't get home like this.* She closed the email and found the last one from Sami.

Mary Catherine hit reply and started writing.

Dear Sami,

I should've sent this letter much sooner. Please . . . forgive me.

A wave of nausea crashed through her. Every keystroke, every movement was an effort. The ground rocked, shifted. Dizziness engulfed her. If only she could make it through this email. She doubled her focus and kept typing.

> I'm very sick. I found out right before Uganda that I don't need a new valve. I need a heart. My doctor said I might not have long to live if a donor isn't found. I know you're probably frustrated by this. I should've told you. Maybe I shouldn't have come here at all.
>
> But you know me, Sami. I have to live life. I didn't want to sit in my apartment too sick to walk to the beach just to wait for death. I couldn't do it.

The sound of her chattering teeth grew louder. Why was she so cold? Like ice was running through her veins. Mary Catherine could hardly keep her eyes open. *Come on, Mary Catherine, you can do this. God, help me.* She positioned her hands on the keyboard and forced herself to move.

> The thing is, I don't want to die. I want to fight this thing so I can live. I want to see you get married and I want to tell Marcus how much I miss him. My doctor said he can give me a mechanical heart, but I have to find a way home. Only I don't think I can, I feel so sick. Can you help me, Sami?

She was losing consciousness, falling over onto the floor, and there was nothing more she could do. Nothing she could say. *I'm so sorry, God . . . I waited too long. I don't think You meant for it to end this way.* She pictured heaven and how wonderful it would feel. This was the end, then. It had to be.

She closed her eyes and let it come.

❧

EMBER WAS AWAKE the entire time, but she couldn't intervene. Not while Mary Catherine was still typing. The letter needed to come from her. But now there wasn't a moment to lose.

Father, go before us . . . please keep her alive. Ember wasn't a doctor. But she was skilled in lifesaving. It was one of the reasons she had been chosen by the team to take on this part of the mission.

In a rush, she took Mary Catherine's laptop, hit send on the email, and put the computer aside. Then, using a strength specific to angels, Ember carried Mary Catherine into the orphanage. She needed to be near water and food, blankets and medical supplies.

The girl was burning up—so hot Ember felt a new level of dreaded fear. She carefully pushed through the doors, laid Mary Catherine down on a couch in the living room, and then ran to the kitchen. Ember knew exactly where the pills were. She immediately found several medications in the supply cupboard.

For weeks she'd been dreading this moment and ready for it all at the same time. She filled a glass with water and hurried back to Mary Catherine. "Come on, sit up for me." Ember's voice was gentle. She helped Mary Catherine to a sitting position.

Then by some miracle of God, Ember was able to get the pills down Mary Catherine's throat. Pain relievers and a megadose of antibiotics. Whatever infection was attacking her, it would have trouble standing up to these pills.

She found a cool cloth and ran it over Mary Catherine's forehead and along her arms. *Father, she is Yours. All of heaven knows the plans You have for her. Please, bring down the fever, let her wake up. Please, God.*

For two hours Ember stayed at Mary Catherine's side, praying for her, giving her sips of water, using the cloth to cool her. And finally at just after seven o'clock Mary Catherine opened her eyes.

"What . . . happened?" She was drenched in sweat. "Why am I here?"

"I brought you." Ember helped Mary Catherine sit up. "I think your fever broke."

"I . . . don't feel good." Mary Catherine closed her eyes. And just like that she began shivering once more. Twenty minutes later she was burning up again.

Ember wouldn't give up, not while Mary Catherine was still breathing. She gave Mary Catherine another medication for lowering her fever. And a dose of probiotics—to strengthen her immune system. Ember could feel all the prayers of heaven surrounding the orphanage with light and power.

Even so, Ember wondered if it would be enough. This was Earth, after all. Every day mankind encountered new losses, fresh battle scars. The sad truth was something Ember had to consider.

Not all missions succeed.

DESPITE LEXY'S PROTESTS, Sami took her to church that Sunday morning.

It was the girl's fourth day living at the apartment, and already Sami could tell the journey wouldn't be easy. Lexy was terrified that Ramon would find her, moody over the changes in her daily routine, and frustrated by the rules. But yesterday seemed to be a breakthrough. Lexy found Sami in the kitchen and started helping—all on her own, without being asked.

After a while she looked up. "I'm sorry. I've been a jerk."

Sami smiled at the girl and kept washing the sink. "Thank you. I appreciate that."

"I'm just scared. You know?" She found a towel and began drying the places on the counter where Sami had washed. "Everything is changing so fast."

"It is." Sami had waves of doubts since asking Lexy to stay. But every time, God reassured her that this was the right thing to do. Through a Bible verse about not growing weary in doing good, and her conversation with Tyler the other night— when he told her he'd never loved her more than now, seeing her help Lexy.

Today Sami planned to get Lexy set up with online school. She waited until they were done cleaning the apartment and then Sami found her computer.

She had heard of a program that might work for Lexy. It was through Liberty University Online, and it was interactive—allowing for better communication between students and teachers. Sami was about to look into it when she saw she had new email.

Sami checked her in-box and noticed the message was

from Mary Catherine. Sami's heart skipped a beat, and again the familiar sense of fear and concern came over her.

She opened the email and began to read.

From the beginning, Sami was shocked. Mary Catherine needed a heart transplant? She hadn't wanted to sit in the apartment and wait so she went to Africa . . . even knowing she might not have long to live? Sami was too afraid to be mad at her friend.

Reading to the sound of her own racing heart, Sami finished the letter. Bottom line, Mary Catherine desperately needed to come home, but she was very sick. Too sick to travel. Sami carried her laptop to her room and shut the door.

Immediately she called Marcus.

He answered on the third ring. "Hey. What's up?"

"Marcus . . . it's Mary Catherine." Sami's words all ran together. "She's in trouble."

"In what way?" Instantly Marcus sounded frantic. "Sami, tell me everything."

Sami rattled off the details of the email, including how Mary Catherine had asked for help, saying she had to find a way home. Just then, Sami remembered something. She had the number for Janie Omer—the coordinator for Mary Catherine's trip to Africa. She promised to forward everything to Marcus, starting with the email.

"I'll need an address, maybe the name of the nearest airport." Strength filled Marcus's voice, like he was ready to take charge of the situation.

"What are you going to do?"

Marcus didn't hesitate. "I'm going to go get her."

18

MARCUS WAS TOO WORRIED to be angry at Mary Catherine. He called the airline as soon as he got off the phone with Sami, and ten minutes later he had a flight out later that afternoon. Los Angeles to Amsterdam to Nairobi to Entebbe. Uganda was eleven hours ahead of Los Angeles, so he would arrive in Entebbe tomorrow night.

His flight left in three hours. Too much time. He packed a single leather backpack with a change of clothes and a few toiletries. What about Mary Catherine? He went to his pantry and searched the shelves. She would be dehydrated and weak, no doubt. He found a few individual packets of a hydration drink and a small container of ketogenic protein powder.

The last thing Mary Catherine needed was refined carbs. They were bad enough for healthy people—let alone someone fighting an illness or inflammation. He threw the packets into his backpack.

Before he left his house, Tyler and Sami stopped by and

prayed with him. "Call us, please. When you know anything." Sami hugged him after the prayer. "Tell her we love her, okay?"

"I will." He hugged Tyler last. "I haven't told anyone . . . but I knew God wanted me to go to her. Fly to Africa. I got the shots a while ago." He shook his head. "The idea seemed crazy." He paused, still trying to comprehend what was happening. "I asked God for a sign. If He really wanted me to go."

"You got your answer." Tyler took a step back and put his arm around Sami.

"Yeah." Marcus opened his car door. "Pray, please. The whole time. It sounds like she's going to need a miracle."

They all agreed about that much.

Not until he was headed to the airport did he let the reality of the situation hit him. All this time she'd been deathly sick. All this time. Of course everything made sense now.

This was why she hadn't wanted a relationship. It was the reason she never wrote back and ran from him as soon as she felt herself falling. She hadn't wanted to be a burden—not to him or Sami. Probably not even to her parents.

The whole thing was so sad. She could've spared herself this crisis, and all the months of heartache, if only she'd been honest. If she had trusted him with her darkest secret. *Mary Catherine, I'm coming for you. Hold on, baby. Please, God, let her hold on.*

Marcus gripped the steering wheel and flexed the muscles in his jaw. Did she really think he would run if he knew the truth? Did she honestly think she'd be a burden to him? If he'd known from the beginning they would've prayed for an answer and together with God's help they would've found it.

He couldn't wait to see her, to take her in his arms and

tell her enough. Enough hiding and pretending and lying. From now on she had to be honest. If he wanted to date a girl with a sick heart, that was his decision. It wasn't up to her to run from him because she was worried about how he might react. Or how he might suffer.

Covering up her health had only hurt both of them.

Marcus stepped on the gas and got to the airport in record time. The entire flight to Amsterdam, he replayed every wonderful time they'd been together. She always had an answer, a reason why she didn't want to date. Everything made perfect sense now. She wasn't ready for a relationship. She wasn't looking for love. She wasn't the marrying type. She didn't want the house in the suburbs or the white picket fence.

Marcus closed his eyes and thought about the last time he saw her. Hadn't he known she was lying? He had even told her so, right to her face. And even still Mary Catherine simply wouldn't tell him the truth.

He tapped his foot. If only the plane could fly faster. *Father, I never would've left her. You know that. And now . . . please keep her alive, Lord.*

Marcus felt a sense of peace in response. He couldn't wonder about her reasons all the way to Africa. Mary Catherine cared about him—he was sure of that much. And suddenly he remembered other things that she'd said. How she'd choose him if she were going to choose any man, and how she couldn't just be his friend. *If I was going to love someone . . . it would be you.* Those were her words. He would remember them forever.

She had loved him all this time.

He took a quick breath and exhaled slowly. He needed to

relax. More than that, he needed to pray. God was with him, Marcus could feel His presence. And something else. It made him hold on to hope: The Lord had prompted him to get shots at just the right time. Otherwise he couldn't take this trip without the risk of getting sick.

They had rough turbulence landing in Amsterdam, but Marcus wasn't concerned. He was on a mission, and he believed with everything in him that God would assign him angels to get him to the orphanage in Uganda, if that's what it took.

He slept on the flight from Amsterdam to Nairobi, and prayed from Nairobi to Entebbe. By then he'd practically memorized Mary Catherine's email to Sami. He read it on his phone every hour or so, searching for clues. How sick was she? And why was she finally telling them the truth? Did someone in Africa change her mind?

With so many flights, the odds were high that Marcus would experience a delay. But that didn't happen until they landed in Entebbe. Another plane was in their spot, so for ten minutes Marcus and the other passengers sat on the tarmac.

Father, she needs me . . . please get this plane to the gate. Whatever it takes.

A few minutes later the plane began to move. As they deplaned Marcus saw a few mechanics talking, walking away from the gate. Marcus made eye contact with one of the men and he stopped for half a second. There was something familiar about him. Where had he seen the guy before?

Marcus let the thought go.

He hurried through the small airport, boarded a shuttle bus out front, and took it to a car rental agency a mile away.

He'd talked to Janie on the layover from Amsterdam to Nairobi. The drive to the orphanage would take an hour and he'd definitely need a Jeep. Some of the roads weren't passable any other way.

Marcus was first off the bus. He ran into the building and up to the man behind the counter. "I need a Jeep. As quickly as I can get it." *Help her hold on, God . . . Please, help her.* He was almost there, almost to her side.

But the man shook his head. "Sorry. I rented my last Jeep an hour ago."

This couldn't be happening. Marcus felt the blood drain from his face. "When will you have another one?"

"One day. Maybe three days." The man pointed to a laminated piece of paper with other, smaller vehicles. "This may help?"

Marcus shook his head. "No, thank you." He walked to the window and stared at the sky. He would walk to her if it took that. But he couldn't carry her all the way back to the airport from the orphanage. It was a thirty-mile, difficult drive.

"I'm desperate, God." Marcus whispered the prayer against the filmy glass. "I need a Jeep. Please, Lord . . . I don't know what else to do."

Marcus was used to being in control. He didn't drink or do drugs, and he always knew what pitch to throw. Lately he'd even been memorizing Scripture so he'd always have the right verse at the right time. But here, he was completely out of options.

He needed a Jeep.

Mary Catherine's life depended on it.

BECK FOUND THE broken-down Jeep next to a Dumpster behind the rental agency. With supernatural speed and dexterity, Beck fixed the old Jeep in a few minutes and drove it to the back door of the office.

Beck wore coveralls, the type used by most mechanics. Same ones he wore earlier at the airport. He stuffed a grease rag in one of his pockets and with a brisk pace he walked through the back door of the office, holding the keys.

The man behind the counter spun around, surprised.

"Got a Jeep ready. Heard you had a customer looking?" Beck spotted Marcus over by the window.

"What?" At the sound of Beck's message, Marcus hurried back to the counter. Again Beck and Marcus made eye contact. Beck expected Marcus might recognize him, especially after the brief encounter at the airport. But Marcus was too distracted. Too anxious to get in the Jeep and drive to Mary Catherine.

The man behind the counter was still confused. He took the keys from Beck and then furrowed his brow. "What Jeep is this?"

"The one out back. Behind the garage."

Disbelief played out on the man's face. He shook his head. "That car was broken. We planned to sell it for parts."

"It works." Beck took a step back.

"Who are you? I have never seen you before." The man behind the counter looked borderline angry. "You pulling a joke on me, man?"

"This isn't a joke." Beck stayed calm. "I used the transcode vector and fixed the one out back." He nodded to Marcus. "I think the customer's in a hurry."

The man finally gave up trying to make sense of the situation. As soon as he shifted his attention to Marcus, Beck slipped out the back and disappeared.

Mary Catherine still might not make it. There were no guarantees, as Ember had reminded them. But at least now Marcus had a Jeep. A way to get to the orphanage in a hurry.

And a way to get Mary Catherine out.

19

BY THE TIME MARCUS pulled up to the orphanage gate, he felt like he'd been driving for a week. The road was worse than Janie described. He had to drive through streams and deep holes and areas that looked too narrow to cross.

But none of that mattered. He was here.

He used the gate code to enter the compound, and once he was parked, he ran into the building. A redheaded girl with pale skin was waiting for him. If he didn't know better he would've thought she was Mary Catherine's sister.

The woman held out her hand. "Marcus." She nodded. "I'm Ember. Follow me."

Marcus could sense the woman's urgency. The two of them walked through a kitchen to a living area, and there on the couch was Mary Catherine. She was asleep, covered with a blanket. Even before he reached her Marcus could see how much weight she'd lost. Her skin looked gray and she was shivering.

"She's cold?" The afternoon was blazing hot outside, and not much cooler inside.

"She has a high fever." Ember took a wet cloth from a bowl of water on a nearby table. She wrung it out and handed it to Marcus. "Use this. It helps keep her body cool."

"But she's already cold." Marcus felt desperate. Panic choked him, and he struggled to focus. Mary Catherine looked like she was barely clinging to life.

"Feel her head." Ember stood by, waiting.

Marcus put his hand on her forehead. Ember was right. Mary Catherine was burning up. His stomach felt sick. He knew she was bad off, but he had no idea she was this sick. He turned to Ember again. "I know about her heart . . . but what else?"

"She has an infection. It's throughout her body." Ember looked at Mary Catherine. "I gave her more medication half an hour ago. Her fever should break, at least for a while. She'll wake up then." Ember paused. "The local hospital isn't equipped for something this serious. So I took care of her here."

Marcus felt the sweat on his own forehead. Adrenaline flooded his body. "I need to get her home."

"Yes." Ember's voice was kind but laced with deep concern. "As soon as possible."

Marcus had pictured simply getting Mary Catherine and hurrying back to the airport. This newest revelation, seeing her this way, was devastating.

He took the damp cloth and knelt by Mary Catherine's side. He laid it gently across her forehead and then he ran his hands along her arms. The heat from her skin was unlike anything he'd felt before. He removed the cloth and dipped it in the cool water again, wrung it out, and ran it over her arms before placing it back on her forehead. Anything to stop her intense shivering.

"Hey." He brought his face close to hers. "Mary Catherine, it's me. Marcus. I'm taking you home."

A weak moan came from her and she turned slightly onto her side, facing him. The wheezing she made with every breath sounded terrible. How was she getting any oxygen into her system if her lungs were that sick?

"Mary Catherine." He kissed her cheek. "Can you hear me?"

Like she was coming out of a coma, Mary Catherine blinked a few times and opened her eyes just a bit. She looked at him and after a few seconds, as she gradually woke up, she gasped. "Marcus." Just saying his name seemed to take all her strength. Her eyes closed again. "You're here."

"I am." He flipped the cloth so the cooler side would be against her skin. "I came as soon as I heard about your heart." He had a dozen questions for her, but they would have to wait. The only thing that mattered now was getting her out of here. "I'm taking you home."

Mary Catherine managed a slight nod. "Okay."

"You're going to get better." Marcus ran his thumb along her burning cheek. "The medicine is working."

Another weak nod, and over the next ten minutes, Mary Catherine stopped shivering. Her breathing still sounded awful, but Marcus was pretty sure her temperature was dropping. He looked over his shoulder at Ember. She was still there a few feet away, her hands outstretched, eyes closed.

Praying, no doubt.

Marcus was grateful. He needed a miracle if he was going to get Mary Catherine home in this condition. Ten minutes passed, then another ten. Moment by moment, Mary Catherine's fever left and she gathered strength. Marcus found some water and mixed in the hydration packet he'd brought from home.

He helped Mary Catherine sit up. "I have something for you."

Now that she was up, she looked more like herself. Too thin and pale, still very sick, but better than when she was asleep on the couch. Her eyes met his and in an instant Marcus could see straight into her soul. "I missed you." He whispered the words as he held the cup to her lips.

She took some of the liquid, her eyes never leaving his. "I'm sorry. I . . . should've . . ."

"Shhh." He brushed her hair back from her face and kissed her forehead. "It doesn't matter now. I'm here."

Her eyes glistened with tears and her chin quivered. But she didn't cry. It took all her energy to get the drink down— which she did, one sip at a time. Along the way he could almost feel her gaining strength.

Ember left the room and when she returned she handed Marcus a bag of pill bottles. "She needs these every three hours. Two of each kind." She motioned to the glass Mary Catherine was finishing. "And as much of that as you can get down her. The protein drink, too."

Marcus looked long at Ember. "How did you know I brought protein powder?"

For a split second Ember looked nervous. Then she

smiled. "I saw them in your backpack. When you got the hydration powder."

"Oh." Marcus blinked a few times. That didn't actually seem possible from where Ember had been standing. But it didn't matter. He nodded at the woman. "Thank you. For everything." He had no idea where Ember had come from or how God had provided just the right person for this ordeal, but he was beyond grateful.

"Marcus." Mary Catherine was more alert now. "Thank you . . . for coming here."

"I told you I would." He smiled at her. "I'll build my orphanage on the other side of that gate."

The lightest bit of laughter came from her. "Build it back in LA."

"Right." Marcus looked around. "Where is your suitcase?"

"By the door." Ember pointed to a tall blue suitcase. "She came with four bags, but mostly filled with supplies for the children. That's all she's taking back."

Marcus stared at the suitcase. He could've sworn it wasn't there before. But again he had no time to debate the fact. He searched Mary Catherine's eyes and put his hand alongside her face. "You ready?"

"Yes." She still looked frail and sick, but there was a strength in her eyes that hadn't been there before. "I can do this."

Marcus made her a quick protein drink, ran her suitcase and the bag of pills to the car, and came back for her. She made an effort to stand, but then fell back against the couch. Marcus bent down and picked her up. "Just rest, okay?" He spoke straight into her eyes. "I've got this."

Ember followed him outside and after he had Mary Catherine buckled into the passenger seat, he shook her hand again. "This wouldn't be possible without you."

"Of course. It's part of the job." Ember walked to Mary Catherine's side of the Jeep. "Believe, Mary Catherine. God is working in this. He's going ahead of you." Ember put her hand on Mary Catherine's shoulder. "I'll keep praying."

"I need your contact information." Mary Catherine attempted to find her laptop but Ember stopped her.

"I'll email you. Just rest. I'll see you again. I promise."

Marcus had no time to waste. The last flight out today was scheduled to leave in two hours. He waved once more to Ember, handed Mary Catherine the protein shake. The gate opened automatically as he pulled up and the moment he was clear he took off. "Let me know if I need to slow down."

The Jeep kicked up dust and rocks as they sped away. It had a soft top but no windows, so Mary Catherine would be shielded from most of the dust, but not all of it. Marcus tried not to worry about the fact. They needed to make the flight.

"Marcus." Mary Catherine reached for him. "Hold my hand. Please."

It was the single best moment he'd had since he heard the news about her heart. He took gentle hold of her fingers and brought them to his lips. "I won't ever let go."

"Okay." She smiled, her eyelids heavy. "Me, either."

He kept his eyes on the dangerous road, but every few minutes he caught a glimpse of her. She finished her drink and fell asleep. Marcus felt her hand in his as keenly as his own heartbeat. *Lord, give her strength. Let her survive this trip, please. And let us make this flight.* If they missed it, the next plane out wouldn't be until tomorrow morning. Marcus had a terrible feeling that tomorrow wouldn't only be worse for Mary Catherine.

It might be too late.

ASPYN STEPPED OUT of the restroom at the Entebbe Airport in a pilot's uniform. She carried a thick packet of paperwork, her expression stern. She had no room for error. None at all.

With crisp steps and a practiced confidence, Aspyn walked to the gate where Flight 2933 from Entebbe to Nairobi was in the final stages of its pre-flight check. Marcus was still twenty minutes away at least.

"Can I help you?" A gate attendant looked at Aspyn.

She ignored the woman and walked straight to the boarding door. With a flick of her badge, the door opened.

"Hold on!" The gate attendant, a wiry man with what seemed like years of experience, ran up to her. "You need clearance!"

Aspyn released a loud breath. She turned and held up her badge for the man to see. "I'm the captain of this plane."

The man wrinkled his face, baffled. "No, you're not. The captain and first officer are already on board."

"That's impossible." Aspyn handed the man her paperwork. "See? Flight 2933. That's my name." She gave him an impatient smile. "Someone's made a mistake somewhere."

This time the man took her paperwork and scanned the top page. He reached for his wall radio and asked the other pilots to return to the gate. "There's some kind of mix-up. I need to see your orders again."

Thank you, God, it's working. Ember stayed in character. Confident. Certain. Biding her time until the confusion could be cleared up and she could get to her spot in the cockpit.

It took five minutes for the pilots to exit the plane and join the group at the gate. By then the attendant had called management. Three officials from the airline were almost to the gate. "We need to figure this out." The attendant looked nervous. Like he fully expected to lose his job if he didn't sort through the paperwork and make the right decision.

One of the pilots looked at Aspyn. "Who are you?"

She smiled in a way that was just short of condescending. "I've worked for this airline for three years. You and I shared a flight my first month with the company." It was true. But that was a different mission.

The management team arrived. One at a time they asked to see Aspyn's credentials. Confused by the mix-up, they checked the credentials of the other two pilots as well.

"This is ridiculous. We were supposed to push back ten minutes ago." The taller of the two pilots rolled his eyes. "We were assigned this flight." He pointed to Aspyn. "I've never seen her before."

"Her paperwork checks out." The leader of the management team lined the counter with papers from all three pilots. "We need to understand what happened."

"Would someone call the main office?" The shorter pilot was frustrated, too. "If she's a pilot, she's never flown with us."

"Yes, I have." Aspyn remained calm. "The gentlemen don't

remember. It was three years ago." Aspyn reached for her papers and in the process she knocked down all three stacks. The papers mixed together as they fell to the floor.

"Perfect." The taller pilot raised his hands and let them fall to his side. "We'll never get out of here at this rate."

Another five minutes passed while the group picked up the paperwork and sorted it back into three stacks once more. "I apologize." Aspyn looked at the faces in the group. She was running out of ways to stall. "I'm as frustrated as the rest of you." She held up her flight orders. "Clearly I'm the captain of this plane."

Out of the corner of her eye she spotted movement. She glanced over and felt overwhelmed by gratitude. It was Marcus, running through the concourse, pushing Mary Catherine in a wheelchair.

She nodded to the other pilots. "Let's line up our orders. Something must be wrong with one of them."

"Yes, we need to see them all together." The leader of the management team nodded, terse. He turned to his peers. "Every line needs to be matched up until we find the mistake."

Aspyn watched as a different gate attendant helped Marcus and Mary Catherine board the plane. At the same time she pulled a piece of paper from lower in her stack of documents. "Wait a minute." She slapped the page on the counter. "I'm wrong. Flight 2933 is next week. I'm a few gates down today."

The men surrounding her remained speechless. "Let me see that." The main manager reached for Aspyn's documents. "I'm sure today's date was on the Flight 2933 orders."

"Hold on!" Aspyn grabbed her paperwork before the man could take hold of it. "I better check in at the other gate. I need to follow protocol. I don't usually fly that flight."

Aspyn was gone before the men could figure out what she'd actually said or what it meant. When she turned the corner she stepped into a restroom, dropped the paperwork into the nearest trashcan, and vanished.

Mary Catherine was one step closer to making it home alive.

MARCUS PRAYED EVERY HOUR of the journey. Twice Mary Catherine's fever returned but not until they were en route to Amsterdam. He used the medicines Ember had given him to bring it back down again.

A good thing. Someone with a fever coming from Africa would never be allowed to fly. Along the way he explained a number of times that Mary Catherine didn't have an illness. She was headed home for a heart transplant. They needed desperately to make it back to Los Angeles.

In Amsterdam they were delayed due to mechanical difficulties. But like before, in a matter of minutes, someone fixed the plane. Marcus used the time to call Dr. Cohen and explain the situation. The doctor promised to meet them at the hospital as soon as they arrived.

During the layover, once in a while Mary Catherine was strong enough to sit up on her own, strong enough to talk to him about Uganda and the children and how she was glad she'd gone.

"They called me mama." Her eyes shone, despite her weariness. "It was the best time of my life, Marcus."

He held her hand. "I'm glad." He just wished she would've told him about her heart before she left. Maybe she could've spent half the time there and come home sooner. Marcus kept his thoughts to himself. Those days were behind them. All that mattered was getting her to the doctor.

Mary Catherine was quiet for a long while. She lay her head on his shoulder, her hand still in his. After several minutes she looked at him again. "I should've waited. Gone to Africa later." They were minutes from boarding the plane in Amsterdam. She looked right at him. "All of this . . . it's my fault. I should've waited."

"You?" He chuckled, relieved that she was well enough to talk. "You aren't happy unless you're falling from an airplane or darting on a bike through LA traffic at some crazy speed." He kissed her forehead. "You never would've waited for Africa, Mary Catherine. You had to go."

Her smile was so sad. "True. Maybe that's why I didn't tell you. So you wouldn't talk me out of it."

"No." He ran his hand along her cheek. "That's not why."

She looked down; her eyes seemed fixed on a spot in the distance. As if she was lost in those long-ago days before she left. After a while she looked at him again. Tears welled in her eyes. "I didn't want you to get hurt." She blinked and two tears rolled onto her pale cheeks. "That's why."

"I know." He kissed her fingers. "But I can handle the situation with your heart. Nothing . . . could ever hurt as much as watching you leave."

She squeezed her eyes shut, clearly fighting her sorrow.

When she looked at him again she couldn't speak. Instead she mouthed two words, the same two words she'd said every hour since he'd come for her. "I'm sorry."

"It's okay. I'm here now. You're here." Marcus cradled her to himself. "Rest. We can talk later."

She slept until they boarded the plane, and again for most of the flight to Los Angeles. On Tuesday night at seven thirty they landed at LAX, and thirty minutes later he pulled up at the emergency room entrance to Cedars-Sinai hospital. They took her back immediately to where Dr. Cohen was waiting.

Marcus watched them wheel her away. "You have friends in the waiting room," a nurse told him. "Stay with them. We'll come get you when she's stable."

His head pounding, arms and legs heavy with exhaustion, Marcus found Sami and Tyler. The three of them hugged and Marcus explained what little he knew. Mary Catherine was with Dr. Cohen. They were working to save her life.

"We need to pray." Tyler put his arms around Sami and Marcus and the three of them took turns begging God to bring healing to Mary Catherine. When they finished praying, her parents arrived. Sami had called them as soon as she received Mary Catherine's email.

Sami introduced the older couple to Tyler and Marcus. Mary Catherine's father shook Marcus's hand first. "You rescued our girl." His voice broke. "How can we ever thank you?"

"It was my privilege." Marcus took a deep breath, still weary from the trip. "I went for her as soon as I heard."

They talked for a minute about the urgent trip, and then together the five of them settled in to wait for news. One hour became two, and Marcus thought about her parents. He doubted they had any idea why he had gone to Africa or how strongly he felt for Mary Catherine.

Finally Marcus approached Mary Catherine's parents. "Mr. and Mrs. Clark . . . could I talk to you in the hall, please?"

Her parents followed him to a private place in the hallway. Marcus wasn't sure if this was the time, but he had to explain his presence. He was hardly just their daughter's friend. "Has Mary Catherine told you about me?"

Mr. Clark smiled. "Everyone knows you, Marcus." He patted Marcus on the shoulder. "You're quite an impressive athlete." A smile lifted the corners of his lined face. "Our daughter has talked about your Youth Center. Very impressive, young man."

"Thank you." Marcus smiled. Clearly these people had no idea of the depth of his feelings for Mary Catherine. Of course, before this the two of them had never been officially an item.

Marcus cleared his throat and looked at the Clarks one at a time. "Ma'am . . . sir . . . I'm in love with your daughter. I have been for a while now." He hesitated, searching for the right words. "There's no one like her. I believe God brought us together and . . ." The weight of the situation settled on him. Marcus blinked back tears. "I believe she'll get through this. And when she does . . ." A tear slid down his cheek and he wiped it with the back of his hand. "When she does, I'd like to marry her." He pinched the bridge of his nose, trying to find control. "I'm sorry. It's been a long few days."

Mary Catherine's mother put her hand on Marcus's arm. "That's wonderful, Marcus." She looked at her husband. "We couldn't be more thrilled."

Her encouragement seemed to breathe strength into him. Marcus smiled. "Good." He looked at each of them. "I'd like to ask for your blessing."

Mr. Clark smiled, and for the moment the gravity of Mary Catherine's health seemed to lift. "Son, you have our blessing. Absolutely."

"Thank you." Marcus exhaled. "That means so much." He went to shake Mr. Clark's hand again, but this time the man held out his arms. The two embraced, and then Marcus hugged Mary Catherine's mother.

Marcus told the two of them a little of the history between him and Mary Catherine. And then after a while the three of them returned to the waiting room with the others. Tyler and Sami both smiled at him—as if they had guessed about the conversation in the hall.

He returned the smile and together they settled in to wait for news. Another hour passed. Marcus had no idea what they were doing to her or whether it was helping. Most of the time he stayed quiet, praying silently, asking God that Mary Catherine might have another chance at life. At the three-hour mark he closed his eyes and covered his face. *I love her, Father . . . this world needs her light. Please let her live.*

Finally, ten minutes later, Dr. Cohen joined them. His expression looked dire. "She's very sick." He shook his head. "I have to be honest . . . I'm not sure if we can save her." He explained that they'd started her on several medications intended to take pressure off her failing heart and saturated lungs. In addition she was now on a breathing tube. They'd done X-rays and a CAT scan. The details weren't nearly as impactful as the last thing Dr. Cohen said before leaving the room.

"I'll say one thing. If Mary Catherine wins this battle it won't be because of anything I do." He paused, his expression serious. "It'll be nothing short of a miracle."

Somehow, the doctor's words made Marcus feel better. Everything was going to be okay. *Please, God, let it be okay. Let her live, Lord. Please.* If they needed a miracle, Marcus had to believe they would get one. Because God was clearly already working miracles for Mary Catherine.

Otherwise she would've lost this battle days ago.

20

M ARY CATHERINE KNEW SHE was alive and not in heaven, because the first thing she saw when she opened her eyes was Marcus Dillinger.

"Hey." He moved closer, his hand on her arm. "There they are. Those beautiful eyes."

She tried to move, but she couldn't. Where was she? What was happening? Her eyes darted around the room and suddenly she understood. She was in a hospital bed, attached to a number of machines. Worst of all she had a tube in her mouth. She wanted to talk, wanted to ask him where she was and how she had gotten here, but it was impossible.

Marcus seemed to understand. "It's okay. You're in Los Angeles at Cedars-Sinai. Intensive Care Unit. We've been here two days."

Mary Catherine felt her eyes grow wide. Two days? She shook her head, confused, her eyes locked on his.

"I went to the orphanage and brought you home." He searched her face. "Do you remember that?"

She thought for a moment. Yes, she remembered. He had carried her to a Jeep and taken her to the airport. And then another airport and another. The details were hazy, but she remembered. He had stayed beside her the whole time.

"Your parents are here. They flew in an hour before we did." He smiled. "They're in the waiting room. I'll get them in a few minutes."

Her parents were here, too? She felt terrible that they'd found out the news like this, in the middle of a crisis. She blinked back tears. But at least they were here. She would see them again, after all.

Mary Catherine touched the tube in her mouth and the one in her arm. Again she cast a questioning look at Marcus.

"They're helping you breathe." He looked concerned. "You could barely take in oxygen when we got here." He looked her over. "You're on several medications. Something to take fluid off your heart and lungs. I'm not sure of the rest." He ran his thumb along her brow. "Your fever's been down for a full day."

Her fever. *I was burning up. I couldn't stop shivering.* Suddenly Mary Catherine remembered how it all happened. She woke up sick on Sunday morning and tried to send an email to Sami. Before she could put any more of the pieces together, Dr. Cohen entered the room.

"You're awake!"

"She woke up ten minutes ago." Marcus took hold of Mary Catherine's hand and leaned back in his chair. "She wants to talk, but she can't. The tube in her mouth."

Mary Catherine nodded.

"Very well." Dr. Cohen checked a few of the machines. "She's only on a very partial assist. Let's take her off the breathing tube and see how she does. Her fluid's way down, so that should help."

He called for a nurse and the two of them worked to remove the tube from Mary Catherine's mouth. When they were finished, Dr. Cohen stood beside her; he seemed to study the rise and fall of her chest. "How do you feel?"

Mary Catherine coughed a few times. Her throat felt like sandpaper from the tube. Marcus helped her take a few sips of water and she coughed again. But after that she found a scratchy voice. "Better."

"I'll bet." Dr. Cohen took hold of her bedrail and stared down at her. "We pulled volumes of water off your heart. More than I've ever seen on a patient who lives through it." He lowered his brow. "I'll never understand how you survived the trip home. Each flight puts pressure on the heart as it is. But in your condition?" He shook his head. "You must have someone watching out for you."

Marcus grinned. "Dr. Cohen said I'm your bodyguard." He looked from the doctor back to Mary Catherine. "I told him God needed more than a bodyguard to get you home. He must've given you a whole team of angels."

"I like that. A whole team of angels." Mary Catherine's voice still sounded weak. But she wasn't wheezing. That alone made her feel like she could walk out of the hospital without any help. "My breathing's so much better. It's amazing."

"I'm glad." He sighed and pulled a clipboard from the counter behind him. "The reality is you're very sick, Mary

Catherine. Your heart is finished. You need an immediate heart transplant. I moved you to the critical list. Even so it could be months . . . or not at all."

Mary Catherine nodded. None of this was a surprise, but it still hurt. Hearing the reality that her heart had given up.

"So what happened?" Dr. Cohen looked from her chart back to her. "What made you realize you needed to get home?"

"The fever, most of all. You told me that was a danger sign." Mary Catherine was glad for Marcus's hand in hers. He gave her strength without saying a word.

"It's a very bad sign." Dr. Cohen looked over her chart. "Your heart's not only very sick, it's infected. Another reason it's time."

"But"—it was the first time Marcus had interjected—"you said there wasn't a heart available."

Dr. Cohen nodded. He looked at Mary Catherine a long time, the way a father might look at his troublesome daughter. "I have a question for you, Mary Catherine."

"Yes, sir?" She was nervous, wondering where this was headed.

"Do you want to live?" He crossed his arms. "When you went to Uganda, basically against my orders, I wasn't sure."

"You weren't sure?" She felt her heart beat harder. She squeezed Marcus's hand, her attention still on the doctor. "Yes, of course I want to live. I just . . . Uganda was a dream for me."

"Okay, then." Dr. Cohen exhaled. "I'm glad to hear that. Because you have to want to live if you're going to fight the battle ahead."

"I'm ready." She felt terrible. Was that how she'd come across to Dr. Cohen? Like she didn't want to live? It was the exact opposite. She'd gone to Africa because she *did* want to live.

She focused on the doctor. *Help me listen, Lord. I'm ready to fight for my life. Really, I am.*

"Here's what I'd like to do." Dr. Cohen pulled a brochure from Mary Catherine's file. "This is a different kind of heart transplant. A mechanical one. I believe it could save your life." Dr. Cohen handed her the brochure. "Take a look. It's called a left ventricular assist device."

"The LVAD!" Mary Catherine remembered now. "You wrote me an email about it, telling me to come home and get to your office to be tested. In case I was now a candidate for the LVAD."

For a moment no one spoke.

"I never sent an email." Dr. Cohen's brow knit together. "I haven't told you about it until just now. Someone must really want you to get better, because this brochure kept showing up. And even though I've known about the LVAD all along, you were never a good candidate because diabetics don't do well with this device. Now, though, your blood sugar is fully normal. That's the only reason it could work."

"You did email me." Mary Catherine could easily find his letter on her laptop. "You told me the LVAD could possibly work in my situation. That it could buy me eight years or ten even."

"Mary Catherine." The doctor looked beyond confused. "I didn't send you an email."

"I'll show you later." She didn't want to argue. How else would she know about the device? "So you think I'm a candidate for it now?"

"I do. Now that your fever is gone, we can operate first thing in the morning. The situation is . . . dire, Mary Catherine. I can't express that enough."

She handed the brochure to Marcus and kept her attention on Dr. Cohen. "Can you tell me more about it? How it works?"

"Definitely." Dr. Cohen explained that the device was like an artificial heart. It would piggyback on a person's failing heart and take over the work of the left ventricle. Then it would continue to work until a donor heart could be found. "Some people have lived nearly normal lives for eight or ten years on an LVAD. On rare occasions we've even seen a heart recover completely. So that the need for a transplant is eliminated."

Mary Catherine felt stronger just listening to the man. "What does it look like?"

"Well." Dr. Cohen used his hands to show the size of a small apple. "It's not very large and it runs on a battery. You'll have a driveline from the device through your chest wall. The wire will run from the exit site on your chest to the battery pack, which you'll have to wear all the time." He paused. "The pack has to be charged while you sleep, so you'll need to be near an electrical outlet for at least ten hours each day."

Not ideal, Mary Catherine thought. *But doable.* "What about the rest of the time?"

"Again, you can live a fairly normal life. We have LVAD patients who exercise and ride bikes. The only thing you really can't do is get pregnant or swim. You can't get the exit site wet. A nurse will teach you how to shower so it stays dry."

No swimming. Mary Catherine blinked back the sting of tears.

"It's okay." Marcus's whisper was only loud enough for her to hear. He gave her hand a soft squeeze. She pictured herself in the waves off Santa Monica Beach, swimming with the dolphins. "No swimming . . . ever?"

"Not until you get a transplant—or the device is removed. That could be a while."

Mary Catherine nodded. And the other . . . she couldn't get pregnant. That was fine. But it raised a question she hadn't thought about before. "I shouldn't get pregnant while I'm using the LVAD. I get that, but what about later? After I have the transplant?"

Dr. Cohen nodded. "It's a little more complicated, but we've had much success with women having normal pregnancies and deliveries after a heart transplant."

A surge of hope ran through Mary Catherine's veins. "And I'll stay on the list the whole time?"

"You will. Like I said, in rare cases a person is actually healed while using an LVAD. It's something we don't quite understand yet. It could happen—though I wouldn't count on it."

"Okay, then. That's all I need to know." She swallowed, wincing at the pain in her throat. "I'm ready." Mary Catherine smiled at Marcus and then back at Dr. Cohen. "Let's get this done."

Days ago, Mary Catherine was certain she'd be in heaven in a matter of hours. She couldn't breathe or walk or do anything to stop the way her body ached. Today she could breathe without wheezing, and she'd just been given something she hadn't thought she'd have again.

Hope.

Francesca Battistelli's song came to mind, the one she

loved so much. The song was called "Hundred More Years" and it talked about living life to the fullest, holding on to precious moments. Even as a person longed for a hundred more years of this wonderful life. Suddenly the song didn't just apply to regular people, people without defective hearts.

It applied to her.

MARY CATHERINE SLEPT much of the day, but every time she woke Marcus was there, right beside her. Holding her hand or watching her, making sure she was okay. Other times her parents were in the room, one on either side of her bed.

The first time Mary Catherine saw her mother, she began to cry. Her mom was at her side immediately. "Shhh." She kissed Mary Catherine's cheek. "Don't cry. We're not upset."

"I'm sorry." She looked to her dad also. "I should've told you."

Her dad took her hand. "Honey, we love you so much. All that matters is you're home. And you're getting help."

Tears slid down Mary Catherine's face. "Thank you." She felt tired again, her eyes barely able to stay open. "I love you both."

After that, she slept most of the afternoon. Before dinner, her parents, Sami, and Tyler came to visit.

It was the first time Mary Catherine had sat up in bed all day. Normally a patient in ICU could only have one visitor at a time. But because of Mary Catherine's surgery in the morning, Dr. Cohen had made an exception. Sami's eyes welled up the moment they saw each other.

"You crazy girl, keeping all this a secret." Sami came to

Mary Catherine's side and hugged her, careful not to disturb the wires and IV tubes. "Thank God you're here."

"Because of Marcus." She looked at him, still amazed. Then she remembered the letter to Sami. Her eyes found her friend again. "So you got my email? The one where I told you about my heart?"

"And that you wanted to come home." Sami's concern flashed in her eyes. "I called Marcus right away." She looked at Marcus and back to Mary Catherine. "Three hours later, he was on a plane."

"I was so sick. I remember writing the email." She hesitated, thinking about that early morning. "I feel like I passed out before I sent it."

Marcus stood at her side. He took her hand in his again. "Maybe Ember sent it. She said she got you from your bed to the main building."

Mary Catherine tried to imagine how that was possible. Ember didn't look strong enough to carry her. "I'll have to call and thank her. As soon as I'm better."

"I'm just glad you're here. However it all happened." Tyler stepped up. "We want you up there with us when we get married."

Tears blurred Mary Catherine's eyes. She hadn't thought she'd ever see these two again. And now here they were talking about the wedding. Like she was any other normal, healthy girl.

"I have so much to tell you." Sami ran her hand over Mary Catherine's arm. "Lexy is living with me now."

"What?" Mary Catherine wanted to jump from the bed. "That's wonderful." She hesitated. "It is wonderful, right?"

Sami gave a quick version of what happened. "I told her she could stay until she had the baby. You and I would talk about things after that."

"Of course." The news about Lexy being pregnant was tough to take. "Poor girl."

Mary Catherine wondered if things might've turned out differently if she'd stayed. Suddenly she remembered Aspyn, one of the volunteers, telling her she should consider making this her mission field. But Mary Catherine hadn't listened. By going to Africa, she'd done what she wanted to do, what she had dreamed of doing. And she had loved every minute of her time with the children. But had she even listened to the wisdom of people she trusted? Godly people? Had she followed the Lord's leading? Or just her own?

The regret was hard on her.

A nurse came in with more medicine. It was time for visitors to leave. Sami smiled, but she wiped away a few tears as she gave Mary Catherine another hug. "We'll be praying for you. Everything will be fine. I believe that."

Mary Catherine nodded. "Me, too. Love you."

"Love you, too."

When they were gone, Marcus slid his chair closer and sat beside her again. "Are you afraid? About tomorrow?"

"No." The peace Mary Catherine had felt before getting so sick was back again. "God brought me halfway around the world so I could have this surgery. He'll see me through it."

"He will." Marcus lowered the bedrail that separated them. Once it was down he moved his chair even closer. "I don't know what I would've done if . . ." He paused, searching her eyes. "I can't lose you."

She kept her eyes on his. *How could I have run from him?* A man who would rescue her from Africa to prove how much he cared? She touched his shoulder, his cheek. "I asked God to give me this."

Marcus searched her eyes. "This?"

"You." She felt at home with him. "The chance to be with you in person . . . and tell you I was wrong."

He looked relieved. "I couldn't stop thinking about you." His eyes grew a shade darker, more troubled than before. "Even after our time at the airport that day. Before you left."

"I figured you'd hate me forever." She slid a little closer to him. It was still hard to believe she was back home, alive. And he was here with her. "I'm so sorry."

"I told you back then." Marcus allowed the slightest smile. "I didn't believe you."

Mary Catherine didn't have to think about what to say next. She was tired of sidestepping the truth. Again she put her hand alongside his face. "You were right."

It took Marcus a moment to understand what she was saying. He sat up a little straighter and studied her, as if he couldn't quite believe what she was saying. "Meaning . . ."

"Meaning you were right." A quiet giggle came from her. "Of course I'm the marrying type." Her smile faded. "I just didn't think I'd live long enough."

"Mary Catherine." He kissed her hand, his eyes locked on hers. "People never know how long they have. Less time doesn't mean less life." He held her hand to his cheek. "You of all people should know that."

She nodded. "I do now."

Marcus leaned his forearms on her bed and brought his face as close as he could to hers. "This might be a strange time to ask." He looked around. "I mean, if I had it my way we'd be on some windswept beach and there'd be dolphins playing in the surf."

She laughed, her heart suddenly giddy. She had no idea where he was going with this, but she loved how it felt to be this close to him.

"Since we can't have that . . . and since it looks like you'll be in here awhile, let me tell you again what I told you at the airport." He smoothed his hand over her hair and down her arm, his eyes still holding hers. "I've talked to your parents." A depth of emotion seemed to come over him. He had to work to find his voice. "I have their blessing."

"Marcus?" Her mind raced, disbelief and the most beautiful joy colliding around her.

"Mary Catherine, I want to marry you." He searched her eyes. "As soon as you're well enough, please . . . would you be my wife?"

This time there were no walls between them, nothing to stop her from really hearing him, from seeing past her obstacles to the heart of the man. The very real man that was Marcus Dillinger. She rolled onto her side and took his hands in hers. "Yes." She looked deep into his eyes and she could see the future they might have together. Whether it was hours or years, she only wanted to be by his side, only wanted to be his wife. As long as God would give them. She laughed even as her tears came. "Yes, I'll marry you."

Marcus looked beyond relieved, as if he'd been holding

his breath waiting for her answer. "You don't know how long I've prayed for this."

They stayed that way, searching each other's eyes, and eventually neither of them was afraid any longer for what tomorrow held. "I can't wait to get out of here." Mary Catherine spoke in a whisper. "I want to be in your arms so badly."

He leaned in and kissed her lips. "I thought I'd spend the rest of my life wondering about you, missing you." He smiled at her. "I could never find someone like you, Mary Catherine. My heart was made for yours."

Her heart. The reminder sent a ripple of doubt through the beautiful moment. "The surgery . . . it'll go fine. It will."

"Yes." His strength was tangible, a physical presence. He kissed her again. "God brought you this far. You'll get through it."

Mary Catherine nodded. She needed to live in that place, believing that God had brought her home for a reason. That she would have a successful surgery and live long enough to marry Marcus. Maybe even have children one day.

A week ago she was sure she'd be in heaven by now. But now God had given her another chance at life, and she wanted it desperately. And though she believed in the best, Mary Catherine knew the statistics. Not everyone survived open-heart surgery. A person's body could reject a mechanical heart the same as a donor heart. She could contract pneumonia or even succumb to infection in the valves.

Every day God gave them would be a gift.

Mary Catherine ran her hand alongside Marcus's face. "When the doctor asked me . . . if I wanted to live . . ."

"The question killed me." He spoke softly, straight to her soul.

"I want to live, Marcus." She felt a rush of sadness. "If I would've died in Africa . . . I can't think about it."

He searched her eyes. "What changed your mind? About coming home?" He took hold of her hand again. "What made you want to fight for your life?"

Mary Catherine looked toward the window. She was back at the orphanage again, dust on her shoes, the hot air all around her. "It was Ember." She blinked and looked back at Marcus. "She told me it wasn't God's will to give up on life. Not ever."

Relief softened Marcus's eyes. "Thank God for that woman."

"God sent her at just the right time." Mary Catherine closed her eyes. She was tired again, but she still had more to say. She forced her eyes open again. "Marcus?"

"Yes, love."

She didn't want to think about it, didn't want to put words to the possibility. But if this was her last time to see Marcus, she had something to say. "If I don't . . . if something goes wrong tomorrow." She put her hand against his chest, the place over his heart. "Keep me here. Please, Marcus."

His eyes filled and his chin trembled. "You can't think like that."

"I have to." She blinked and a few tears slid down her cheeks. "I always have to. There's no guarantee." Her hand remained. "Please, Marcus."

All her life seemed to hinge on these minutes with him.

He wiped her tears with his fingertip. "As long as I live . . ." He put his hand over hers, the one still on his heart. "You'll be here. With me."

"Thank you." She smiled. Being with him felt so good. "Whatever happens tomorrow . . . I will always be with you. Until we see each other again. However long that takes."

He didn't say anything. He didn't have to. The love in his eyes said it all.

"Okay." She sniffed and the seriousness of the moment lightened. "And I promise the rest of our days I won't be as difficult."

He tilted his head back and laughed. Then he shook his head and kissed her again. "That's good."

For the rest of the evening and into the night, Marcus stayed by her side. They didn't tell anyone about his proposal or their plans to marry. He would tell them tomorrow. For now it was just the two of them, dreaming about a future that until today had not seemed possible.

After tomorrow her heart would no longer beat inside her chest. Instead a machine would keep her alive. There would be no swimming, no escaping the cord that would come from her chest to her battery pack. But she would be alive.

Finally around nine o'clock, he stood. "I want you to sleep."

She couldn't find the words. It hurt just thinking about telling him goodbye.

He reached for her hand. "Let's pray."

"Okay."

And with that Marcus prayed the most beautiful prayer Mary Catherine had ever heard. He asked that God would get her through the surgery and that the mechanical heart would take perfectly, and that the Lord would give them a life to-gether.

And something that gave Mary Catherine a peace that passed understanding.

Marcus asked that God would keep His angels around her until they saw each other again.

21

Lᴇxʏ ʟᴏᴏᴋᴇᴅ ᴏᴜᴛ ᴛʜᴇ apartment window just as the car pulled up. In all her life she had never felt more scared and sick and unsure of what she would even say. This was all still a shock. First the news that Mary Catherine almost died.

Then this.

Just yesterday Sami had gotten news that Lexy's mother was being let out of prison today. Today. With no warning. Her mama's sentence had been cut short a year and now she was free. She was going home to live with Lexy's grandmother. But first she wanted to come here and talk to Lexy.

Sami had picked her up from the bus stop fifteen minutes ago.

Lexy watched her mom step out of the passenger side. Her clothes hung on her and she held just one small plastic bag of things. She looked nothing like the mama who had gone to prison when Lexy was just a little girl. Her eyes were tired and her face and arms were skinny.

Like she was more dead than alive.

Lexy closed her eyes for a moment and held her breath. She wasn't ready for this. Sami would tell her to pray, so she tried. *God, it's me. Lexy. I feel sick, so maybe You could help me get through this. Thanks.*

She stepped back from the window and opened the door. As soon as their eyes connected, her mom looked down for a long while. She seemed embarrassed. Like it might be easier to go back to prison than face Lexy now.

Finally she lifted her head. Her eyes looked a million years old. "Hi, baby girl . . . I'm back."

Lexy didn't speak or move. What was she supposed to say?

Sami followed Lexy's mother into the apartment. She pointed to the couch and chair a few feet away. "Maybe we could all sit down for a bit."

"Yes." Lexy's mom nodded. "Thank you."

Lexy couldn't imagine sitting next to her mom. Like nothing had happened. Lexy took the chair and waited while her mother sat on the sofa. They were facing each other but it felt like there was an ocean between them. Her mom folded her hands neatly on her lap and cleared her throat. "Sami tells me you're . . . pregnant."

Lexy nodded. It took her a minute to look at her mother after that. "Yeah. I am." Lexy had asked Sami to tell her mom about the baby before they got here. It was too awkward for Lexy to do it herself. She stared at her fingers and nodded.

"I'm two months along." She looked at her mother. "Not how you hoped I'd turn out, right?"

"Nothing is how I hoped." Her mom shook her head and then slowly, like water from a breaking pipe, she began to cry. She covered her face with her hands. "I'm sorry, baby girl." Her words were hard to understand through her tears. "I'm so sorry." She held her hand out. "Please . . . can you come sit by me?"

The distance between them felt good. Her mama didn't deserve to sit near her. She was the one who did drugs and got sent to prison for most of Lexy's childhood. She leaned her head back, defiance in her heart. "I wouldn't be like this if you'd been here!" Tears filled her voice before they leaked into her eyes. "You didn't love me enough to be a good mama!"

"I did love you." Her mother's crying was softer now, more painful. "I never wanted the drugs. I'm an addict, baby girl. I couldn't help it."

She could help it. If she loved me enough, she would've stayed clean. The response shouted at her on the inside. But on the outside, Lexy didn't say anything. She put her hand over her flat stomach, over the place where her own little baby was growing.

And for a moment she imagined keeping this child, and how nothing could ever get in the way of her love for her baby. She lifted her eyes to her mother and gradually Lexy saw things differently. At some point her mom must've loved her like this, the way Lexy loved the baby inside her.

Lexy felt her defenses falling like broken glass, dropping in sharp invisible pieces at her feet. Her mother hadn't moved, hadn't taken her hands from her face. But Lexy was seeing a different picture from the one in front of her. Her mama standing next to her before her first day of kindergarten. All of life ahead of them.

She would probably never be close to her mother again, not the way she had felt that long-ago school day. But Lexy wasn't the only one who had suffered. They had both lost. They had missed out on the mother-daughter talks and times together that other little girls and their mothers got to have. She didn't want to lose any more time.

"Mama . . ." Lexy stood and took a step toward her.

Her mother lowered her hands and blinked a few times, her eyes red and swollen. "I'm sorry." Her mom's voice was just a whisper. "I've been sorry every day I've been away." Her face was so sad and lost, it hurt to look at her. She stood and faced Lexy. "I don't know what else to say."

Like a wave crashing on the ocean shore, Lexy's heart broke. She could do nothing to stop herself from rushing into her mother's arms. "Mama!" Lexy clung to her as if she might die if she let go. "I needed you, Mama. I needed you every day." She held on, her voice choked up. "I missed you so much."

Her mother hugged her tight. She kissed the top of Lexy's head the way mamas are supposed to do. "I missed you, too. Every day, baby."

There was no going back, no way to live again the days they'd lost. And yes, Lexy would be a different girl if she'd had her mom. But this was what they had. It was who they were. If she stayed angry at her mama now, then they'd lose this, too. And Lexy couldn't stand the thought of that.

Lexy noticed that Sami had left the room, which was

good. For the first time in a long time she wanted to be alone with her mother. They sat next to each other on the sofa and her mom reached for her. Like when she was very little, Lexy reached out and tucked her hand into her mother's. The feeling was better than Christmas.

She had her mama again. Lexy leaned her head on her mother's shoulder. "Sometimes I want to keep this baby." She paused. "But I won't. I'm giving it up for adoption." She turned slightly and looked into her mom's eyes. "I'm not ready to be a mama."

Her mother brushed the hair from Lexy's eyes. "I understand." She looked sad again, but she nodded. "It's the right thing to do." The look in her eyes changed. "I need to tell you something, baby."

Her mother drew back a bit and looked at her hands for a few seconds. When she looked at Lexy again, her eyes seemed nervous. Her voice, too. "I'm working on a plan for you."

"For me?" Lexy had no idea what her mom meant. "I'm good, Mama. I'm here with Sami . . . away from the gang."

Her mother looked around the apartment living room. "It's real nice here, Lexy. I can see that." She waited. "But Sami's getting married. And your other friend—Mary Catherine— she's sick."

Lexy felt uneasy. The sickness from the pregnancy seemed worse all of a sudden. "I like it here."

"I know." Her mom took hold of both her hands. "Just listen to me, okay?"

So much of her life she hadn't had a mother's advice, a mother's kind words. Lexy pushed her fears to the back of her mind. "Okay."

"All right." Her mom looked like she was holding her breath. "So there was this janitor in prison. The one who helped me write that letter to you. Aspyn. That was her name." Her mom relaxed a little and, a few lines at a time, the story spilled out.

Aspyn had come to visit her again—she didn't work at the prison all the time. Just once in a while. "This time Aspyn wanted to talk about you."

Lexy listened, trying to be patient.

"She asked me if I had a plan for you, a place for you to live so you didn't have to be near the gangs in LA. A way for you to go to college and find a different life." Her mom looked almost dizzy. "So many questions. And I didn't have answers for any of them."

Her mother explained how that's when Aspyn mentioned Lexy's uncle in Texas. "I still got no idea how Aspyn knew I had a brother." She thought for a minute and then focused her attention on Lexy again. "But I do. Your uncle."

Lexy blinked a few times. Then she remembered. "Grandma talks about him sometimes. Her son. The one who escaped the drugs and gangs."

"Yes." Again her mom looked sad. "He's married. Two older kids in college. He and his wife are good people. Christian people."

Where is this going? Lexy released her mom's hands and folded her arms. "The janitor lady knew about him?"

"Yes." Her mom looked confused. "Maybe I told her about him and I just forgot."

Lexy wanted her mom to get to the point. "So why did the janitor bring him up?"

"She asked me if I ever wrote back to my brother." Another sad look came into her mom's eyes. "Your uncle wrote me every month or so. One of the girls always helped me read his letters. But I never . . . I never asked anyone to help me write him back." She looked at her hands again. "What could I say? I was in prison."

Of course. Lexy understood.

"Aspyn said maybe my brother would be willing to take you." Hope flickered in her mother's voice. "Maybe your uncle could give you a new start."

"In Texas?" Lexy wanted to run out the door and keep running. "I don't want to go to Texas, Mama. I like living here."

A few seconds passed and Lexy's mother didn't say anything. Finally she took a slow breath. "Aspyn, the janitor, helped me write to him and ask." She paused. "I haven't heard back."

"Good." Lexy didn't know what to think. Her mom had no right trying to send her off to Texas. After so many years apart, how could her mother know what Lexy needed? "I told you, I like living here."

Her mom nodded. "Maybe we should pray about it. You and me both. Then God can show us what we're supposed to do."

Lexy hated the idea. She didn't want to pray about leaving her new life here, and she certainly didn't want to live halfway across the country in Texas. But every day since she'd moved in with Sami, the two of them had read the Bible together. One thing that stood out was this—God wanted people to be humble. The reason Lexy had gotten pregnant was because she was running her own life. The Bible said when people gave up their old ways and let God run their lives instead, good things would happen.

She gritted her teeth and tried to hear what God might say. Sometimes He actually seemed to talk to her. And just like that she could hear His voice in her soul. *I love you, daughter . . . I have good plans for you. Trust me.*

Lexy looked at her mother and tried not to feel scared or angry. "Okay. I'll pray about it. But as long as my . . . as long as your brother doesn't write back I guess we have the answer."

They sat in quiet and this time Lexy reached for her mom's hand. She couldn't be angry at her mother for trying to help her. The uncle in Texas obviously didn't want anything to do with Lexy or her mom. There was no reason to wreck the time with her mom over this. "Sorry for getting mad."

"I understand." Her mom looked deep at her. "I'm sorry about you being pregnant."

Lexy nodded. "Me, too. I'll never know her. Or him." Her eyes stung because of the sadness. She would miss her first child, and her mom would miss her first grandchild. She put one of her hands over her stomach again.

The missing would last forever.

Sami popped back into the living room. "I'm going to make dinner."

"We'll help." Lexy stood and helped her mom to her feet. Then in a voice just for her mother, Lexy whispered, "Thank you. For coming here." She leaned up and kissed her mom's cheek. "For saying you're sorry."

Her mom dried her eyes again. "Thank you." She kissed Lexy's cheek. "For letting me. All I want is to be your mama again."

They worked with Sami and made chicken salad with tiny pieces of grapes and strawberries and almonds. Sami washed the spinach, spread the dried leaves on three plates, and topped them off with a scoop of the chicken mixture.

The air between Lexy and her mama felt lighter now. Just making dinner together and talking about the beach and Sami's upcoming wedding and Mary Catherine.

Like normal daughters and mamas.

They sat at the table with their salads and Lexy's mother smiled at Sami. "You're teaching my girl about health." She pointed her fork at the salad. "This is the best kind of food. God's food."

"It is." Sami smiled. "We eat too much sugar in this country. My friend Mary Catherine taught me that."

"It's true." Lexy's mom shook her head. "That's one thing I'm looking forward to. Eating better." She put her hand on Lexy's shoulder. "So I can live long enough to be a better mother to this girl."

Sami prayed over the meal, and the subject turned to Mary Catherine. Lexy still wanted to go see her at the hospital. But it was too soon. Lexy turned to Sami. "Is she any better today?"

"She is. Tyler and I were just there at the hospital. The surgery is tomorrow. They had to wait a day to be sure her fever was gone." Sami looked a little worried. "It's a serious operation."

"You told her? About me living here?" Lexy felt sick again. She pushed her fork around her salad.

"I did." Sami's eyes were soft and kind.

"So she's mad at me?" She hated that Mary Catherine knew how bad she'd messed up. She never should've gone back to the gang. "I mean, of course she's mad. I messed up bad." She wasn't sure she wanted to hear what came next.

"Mary Catherine's not mad." Sami stopped eating long enough to look right at Lexy. "She's sorry for you. But she can't wait to see you after the surgery."

Lexy could've cried. Mary Catherine wanted to see her. It was the best news ever. She cleared her throat. "You'll be there tomorrow, right?"

"I will." Sami poured them each a glass of water.

Lexy took a deep breath. "Tell her I can't wait to see her, too." She stared at her plate. *Thank You, God. Please help Mary Catherine get through her operation.* When they were finished eating and doing the dishes, Sami checked the time on her phone. She looked at Lexy's mom. "I need to get you back home."

Her mother nodded. She turned to Lexy. "I got something to say."

Lexy came closer. "Okay."

Her mom took hold of both her hands. "I used to dream about a day like this." Her voice was quiet. "Today . . . was the best day of my life."

Lexy smiled. "For me, too." She slid her arms around her mom's neck and they held each other for a long time. Then she walked her mother to the door. "I'll pray about the Texas thing."

"Thanks."

Lexy could tell they were both sad, she and her mama.

They'd missed so much time together. The losses were still there—no matter how well they'd gotten along for the last hour. But today was something neither of them had expected, and Lexy could only credit God and Sami for bringing it about.

A new beginning.

22

THE LAST FACE SHE SAW before the anesthesia took her was that of her beloved Marcus. He held her hand and stood beside her bed until the last possible moment.

"You'll be okay. I believe that." He bent down and kissed her lips, soft and brief. A team of surgeons and medical personnel stood by, ready for the operation. After today she would have a man-made heart with a dozen serious restrictions.

But she would be alive.

Marcus hadn't left her side for the last two days, while doctors pumped her full of antibiotics and made sure her body was free of infection. Now, in her waning moments before surgery, she savored the feel of Marcus's hand around hers. She felt safe and sure and full of life around him. *God, please . . . give me more days with this man. Give us a life together. Please, Father.* She looked up at Marcus, at his warm, caring brown eyes.

Of all their many goodbyes, this one was the hardest.

"I'm not afraid." She spoke straight to his eyes, to his soul. "Ask everyone to pray."

"I will. You know that." He remembered something. "The Waynes told me to tell you they have their whole church praying."

Mary Catherine nodded slightly. "Good."

"Yes." It didn't matter how many people were waiting for this moment to wrap up. Marcus looked at her as if she were the only person in the room. "I love you."

She refused the tears that rushed to her eyes. "I love you, too."

He had to leave then, and she watched him go. Watched while he held her gaze until the last possible moment. When he was gone, she closed her eyes, ignoring the few tears that slid down her face. She could feel the bed moving as they wheeled her into the operating room.

"Mary Catherine, are you okay?" It was Dr. Cohen.

"Yes." She didn't open her eyes, didn't want to see anything in her mind except the image of Marcus Dillinger.

"We've been over what's about to happen. We'll see you in ten hours or so." He paused. "The medication is going into your IV now. I want you to count out loud, backward from ten, okay?"

Mary Catherine did as she was told. "Ten, nine . . ." *How could I ever have walked away from Marcus?* "Eight . . . seven . . ." *God, I must've been crazy, letting fear of tomorrow keep me from falling in love.* A heaviness settled over her. She couldn't open her eyes if she wanted to. "Six . . ."

Noises began to blur around her and she could feel her body growing warm. It was time. Her failing heart was finished. She remembered Marcus once more, the look in his eyes, the way he told her he'd pray for her and how much he clearly loved her and . . .

Mary Catherine felt her beating human heart for the last time.

And then there was nothing but darkness.

EMBER, ASPYN, JAG, AND BECK—the entire invisible team was present in the surgical theater. All of them praying and moving, making their way between the team of surgeons and doctors and nurses. Every minute was critical here. The angels would make sure nothing was missed, no mistakes were made.

Jag and Beck took turns praying away the enemy—hovering outside the hospital walls. Aspyn prayed over the medical personnel. And Ember stood beside Mary Catherine's bed. She was the one who had spent much of the last year praying for the girl, living with her. Helping her.

This surgery was a crucial part of their mission. And it was personal for Ember.

She watched as the lead surgeon opened Mary Catherine's chest and began to work. Ember had come to care very much for Mary Catherine. Like a sister, maybe. As humans go, Mary Catherine was rare indeed. Filled with hope and grace, love and faith. Nothing was the same at the orphanage without her.

Ember put her hand on Mary Catherine's shoulder. *Father, You know how much this daughter of Eve means to me. Please let her live. Our efforts depend on her.*

The surgeon connected Mary Catherine to a heart-lung machine—which would do the work of breathing and pumping her blood throughout the surgery. Her heart would remain attached to her body when the operation was finished. Blood would still flow through it. But it would not be required to do any of its normal work.

The mechanical piece would fit above it and take over the job of keeping Mary Catherine alive.

There was much to do.

Ember stared at Mary Catherine, at the way her skin looked gray at this point in the surgery. The doctors still had another nine hours of work. *Father, I beg You, please breathe life into Mary Catherine. Only You can give her another chance.*

Ember didn't let up.

She prayed like that with every breath, every minute as the delicate and dangerous operation continued. They had made it this far. Now all of heaven was praying with them. That Mary Catherine would not only survive the surgery.

But that she would have a second chance at living life to the fullest.

THE HOURS FELT LIKE DAYS, and from a chair in the waiting room Marcus tried to grasp everything that had happened. A week ago he believed he'd never see Mary Catherine again. Back then, he had no idea how he'd forget her, he couldn't imagine even trying.

Now he and Mary Catherine were engaged and his fiancé was fighting for her life in an operating room down the hall.

Marcus looked at Mary Catherine's parents, sitting across from him, holding hands, praying quietly. Her mother smiled at him and nodded.

The moment was too intense for small talk.

Marcus buried his face in his hands and prayed again. *Father, if You would put angels around Mary Catherine even this very minute. She needs Your help, Lord. Please . . .*

He heard footsteps in the hallway. He held his breath. At any point he could get another update from Mary Catherine's medical team. Instead Tyler, Sami, and Lexy walked into the room. Together with her parents and him, they were the only people in the waiting room.

He stood and hugged each of them. "Thanks, guys."

Mr. Clark nodded. "Yes, thank you for coming." Tears filled his eyes. He looked at his wife and then back at Marcus and the others. "You all mean so much to our daughter."

"We wouldn't be anywhere else today." Tyler shook hands with Mary Catherine's father.

They all sat down, Marcus next to Mary Catherine's parents, with Tyler on his other side, and Sami and Lexy across from them. Marcus leaned over his knees and folded his hands. "It'll still be a long time."

"What have you heard?" Sami looked nervous.

"She went into surgery around seven this morning. About three hours later a nurse came in. Apparently everything was going as planned."

"That's good, right?" Lexy still sounded nervous.

"It is." Marcus smiled. "It'll be okay."

The girl nodded, clearly troubled. Even so, Marcus could see that the changes in her were remarkable. She spoke with less of the gang dialect and her clothes were more modest. She even walked straighter, like she believed in herself more than before. Getting her out of the inner city and into a daily friendship with Sami seemed to have changed her life. Sami had told him that Lexy was praying constantly about Mary Catherine, terrified about losing her. She almost didn't come today.

The air in the waiting room fell silent. Marcus pictured his conversation with Mary Catherine yesterday, when he'd asked her to marry him. It was a moment he would remember forever.

Suddenly he realized he hadn't told anyone about his proposal. He took a long breath. Nothing about the past week seemed real. This least of all. But he couldn't hold the news in any longer.

"So . . . Mary Catherine and I have an announcement." Marcus grinned at her parents. Mr. Clark winked at him.

Sami's eyes flew open. "No you didn't!"

Lexy waited, confused. "Didn't what?"

Mary Catherine's mother linked arms with her husband. "Let's just say there's going to be two weddings in the near future."

"Yep." Marcus chuckled. "It's true. I asked her to marry me and . . . she said yes!"

"Really!" Tyler just grinned. "I wondered."

"What?!" Lexy stood and danced around in a tight circle. "She loved you all this time! I knew it!"

Across from him, Sami put her fingers to her lips, her eyes

shining with tears. "Marcus . . . I'm so happy for you. Both of you."

Tyler stood and gave him a hearty pat on his back. "No wasted time there."

"That's what I said!" Mr. Clark grinned, his eyes twinkling. "The two of us are thrilled for you, Marcus."

"Thank you." He'd only known Mary Catherine's parents for a few days. But already he loved them. "I told her I wished we could've been at the beach or at a nice dinner. Something more romantic. But I had to ask her."

Marcus told them how the doctor had asked Mary Catherine if she wanted to live and how she had been shocked. "Of course she wanted to live, that's what she told the doctor." His throat felt tight as he remembered the moment. "I asked her as soon as he left the room."

Lexy was still beaming, but she settled down next to Sami. "This is like a movie. I can't believe it!"

Sami shook her head. "She finally admitted what the rest of us have known from the beginning."

"The rest of us?" Tyler looked lost.

"Yes!" Sami allowed a slight laugh. "She's been in love with Marcus since the day they met."

Tyler grinned and elbowed Marcus. "Well . . . let's be honest. Mary Catherine wasn't the only one, huh?"

"Yeah. You could say that." Marcus laughed again. The relief felt wonderful amid all the unbearable waiting.

Gradually the laughter died down. Sami leaned on her knees. "Why did it take her so long to admit it?"

"She kept all this to herself." Mary Catherine's mother shook her head. "Her health. Even you, Marcus."

"One reason." Marcus hated this part. "She thought she was dying. She didn't want to put me—or any of us—through that."

Lexy gasped. "She thought she was dying?" She looked at the others. "I didn't even know she was sick."

"No wonder I was so worried about her." Mrs. Clark leaned against her husband. "We both were."

"None of us knew how sick she was." Sami sat back, her eyes soft. "I knew about her heart condition, but nothing like this." She paused. "She never should have gone to Africa."

"I thought that, too. At first." Marcus felt Mary Catherine's convictions in his own soul. "But going to Africa—for Mary Catherine—*was* like choosing to live." He cast a sad smile toward Sami and then Mary Catherine's parents. "When have you ever known her to give up?"

"True." Sami nodded.

Lexy folded her arms. "I knew she wouldn't leave me unless it was really important."

They talked a while longer, about the Youth Center and the mentor program and finally about Sami and Tyler's wedding. Marcus wasn't sure this was the time to bring it up, but he wanted to see if it was at least possible.

He looked at Tyler. "You're getting married December third, right?"

"Yes." He smiled at Sami. "I wish it was this Saturday."

"We found a place!" Sami looked giddy about the news. "The Ritz-Carlton at Laguna Niguel."

Tyler raised his brow. "Thankfully the owner's a Dodgers fan."

"I went to a wedding there a few years ago." Marcus was impressed. "The place is stunning."

Tyler locked eyes with Sami. "The beach has always been important to us."

There would be no better time than now. Marcus sat up a little straighter. "So here's my question. And be honest. Mary Catherine doesn't know I'm asking you this. It's just an idea." He hesitated, holding his breath. "What would you think of a double wedding? If Mary Catherine is well enough by then?"

As soon as he said the words, he watched Sami and Tyler's eyes light up. Sami was the first to speak. "We'd have practically the same guests." She looked at Tyler. "Should we talk about it later?"

"I love it." Tyler smiled. "Sounds perfect."

Marcus felt the warmth of their friendship come over him like July sunshine. He had never felt more loved. And Sami was right. They really would have a lot of the same guests. And the beach was as special to him and Mary Catherine as it was to Tyler and Sami. "Well, then . . . if Mary Catherine is well enough . . . it would be very special for both of us."

Lexy squealed. "This makes me so happy."

"A double wedding!" Mary Catherine's mother looked at her husband, then back to Marcus. "How beautiful."

"Definitely." Mr. Clark nodded. "Unforgettable!"

They talked about the idea for a while longer and sometime around six o'clock Sami, Tyler, and Lexy went for dinner. Marcus and Mary Catherine's parents stayed. They could hear news about the surgery any minute, and the three of them didn't want to miss it. But as it turned out, there were no updates, even after the others returned with sandwiches for Marcus and Mary Catherine's parents.

Marcus couldn't eat. The longer the time, the more he struggled. What if something had gone wrong? He stood and paced to the far end of the waiting room. *God, please, don't let anything go wrong. Please let this new heart work and let the doctors be amazed at how well things go today.*

Finally, nearly thirteen hours after Marcus had said good-bye to Mary Catherine, Dr. Cohen joined them in the waiting room. His smile was the first thing Marcus saw. Marcus was on his feet immediately. The others, too.

"She came through very well." Dr. Cohen's expression was bright, but the bags under his eyes were proof that the man was drained. "Her heart was very sick. It took longer than we thought." He gave a single shake of his head. "Just when things seemed touch-and-go, we'd make the exact right decision or someone would provide the perfect assistance." He looked one at a time at the faces in the room. "There were times I'd swear we were getting a little divine help in there."

Chills ran along Marcus's arms. "I asked God to send His angels."

"Apparently He did!" Dr. Cohen took a step back toward the door. "I need to get in there. She's got a long road ahead. At least two weeks in the hospital before she can start rehabbing at home."

"Thank you, Doctor." Mr. Clark was on his feet. He shook the man's hand.

Marcus did the same. "Yes. Thank you so much." He barely paused. "When can I see her?" Marcus was ready to follow the doctor back to the recovery room.

"Give us a few hours." Dr. Cohen smiled. "I'll have someone come get you when she's ready."

After the doctor left, Marcus prayed with the group. Sami, Tyler, and Lexy said goodbye and promised to visit tomorrow—as long as Mary Catherine was doing well. Another two hours passed before Marcus was allowed back. He had to wear a mask and a gown before entering her room.

Mary Catherine was so buried in wires and tubes and wrappings, he was afraid to come too close. Her nurse encouraged him. "It's okay. Pull up a chair and sit beside her."

Marcus doubted Mary Catherine would actually wake up. She looked completely drugged. Still, he pulled up a chair and again glanced at the nurse—just to make sure he wasn't sitting too close.

"You're fine." The nurse came up beside him. She took Mary Catherine's temperature and wrote down a few of the numbers from her monitors. "I'd expect her to wake up soon."

The nurse stepped out and Marcus leaned closer. She looked so small, her face beautiful even with her breathing tube and heart monitors attached to every visible part of her body. "Mary Catherine. I'm here." He spoke through the mask and waited, watching her. She showed no signs of life. He hung his head, his hands trembling. *God, she looks awful. Please . . . give me a sign that she's getting better.* If only he could fast-forward the days until she could sit up and look into his eyes again.

He looked up and tried again. "Your new heart is working great." He didn't touch her. "God is healing you."

At first she didn't seem to hear him. But then, gradually,

she began to move her eyes. And finally she blinked them open.

She was clearly medicated, her movements slow. But she looked right at him. The breathing tube prevented her from talking, but that didn't matter. She didn't need to speak. Marcus could read her eyes without a single word.

She was alive and she loved him.

Nothing else mattered.

23

SAMI LOOKED OVER THE DISPLAY of fresh-sliced meat and cheese and the berries she and Tyler had washed and arranged on Marcus's kitchen counter. The whipped cream was freshly beaten and the slivered cinnamon almonds were roasting in the oven.

Everything was just the way Mary Catherine would like it.

After twelve days in the hospital, she'd come home earlier than anyone expected. Her doctor was thrilled at her progress. A week recuperating at home and now she was already able to leave the house.

Today was her first outing.

Marcus was picking up Mary Catherine and her parents at the apartment and taking her out for a surprise. The surprise, of course, was right here at his house. Mary Catherine was going to be shocked to see everyone who was here. Sami and Tyler, Ollie and Rhonda Wayne, and even Lexy. The girl had been staying with the Wayne family since Mary Catherine came home from the hospital. Just to make room for Mr. and Mrs. Clark.

And seeing all of them wasn't the only surprise ahead.

There was another surprise coming tonight at dinner— one Mary Catherine knew nothing about.

Sami could hardly wait.

The whipped cream—organic and grass-fed—had just a pinch of real vanilla and no sugar whatsoever. Sami scooped the fluffy cream into a pretty bowl and set a spoon beside it. She caught a quick lick from the mixing bowl. Like most of God's foods, it didn't need sugar. It was sweet all by itself.

Dr. Cohen agreed with Mary Catherine's high-fat, low-carb diet. New research showed that transplant patients—like most people—were better off avoiding most carbohydrates. Fuel the body with healthy fat, the doctor had told Mary Catherine. Ketosis would provide a better environment for healing.

Sami was proud of her friend. Mary Catherine had been following Dr. Cohen's orders perfectly, and her body had developed no infections. Of course, Mary Catherine already ate a low-carb diet to control type 2 diabetes, but now she was more intentional. Refined and empty carbohydrates caused inflammation, illness, and disease.

Since she wanted to live, Mary Catherine needed to stay away from all of that.

"Rhonda, can you please get the almonds out of the oven?"

Across the room, Rhonda had been working with Lexy, arranging fresh flowers in a pretty vase at the middle of Marcus's kitchen table. "I'm on it." Rhonda ran to the oven and used the mitts to take out the tray of almonds. "They smell great!"

Tyler and Coach Wayne were outside washing down the table and chairs on Marcus's deck. The two of them walked in and grinned at the spread. Tyler gave them a thumbs-up. "Looks like we're ready for an engagement party!"

Marcus had built-in ceiling speakers in most of the main rooms, so Coach Wayne logged on to his kitchen computer and created a playlist with Francesca Battistelli, Matthew West, Colton Dixon, Newsboys, and Kyle Kupecky. All favorites of Mary Catherine's.

Tyler grabbed a broom from the pantry and swept the kitchen. Marcus's housekeeper came once a week, but she'd been on vacation and the house needed sprucing up. Especially because Marcus was spending all his days with Mary Catherine and her parents.

Sami smiled as she thought of how involved Marcus was in Mary Catherine's recovery. Her parents planned to stay another week, and the two of them had been available around the clock. But Marcus was there to help her move from the hospital to the apartment, and he bought groceries whenever she ran out.

Once every hour as long as she was awake, Mary Catherine needed to get up and walk—something she loved. And always it was Marcus leading her around the apartment, making sure she was steady—especially when she tried to push herself a little too hard.

"All we need is lemon water." Sami found two pitchers from one of the cupboards and Rhonda pulled a lemon from the refrigerator. Colton Dixon's "Through All of It" was playing over the speakers. Tyler finished sweeping, put the broom away, and came up behind Sami at the sink.

"This song says it all." Tyler slipped his arms around Sami's waist. "It's my anthem."

"Mmmm." She turned around and put her hands on his shoulders. He was right. The lyrics were perfect. "'I have won . . . I have lost . . .'" Singing wasn't her gift, but with him she wasn't afraid to miss a note.

"'I got it right sometimes, and sometimes I did not.'" Tyler sang the next line and then their voices joined together. He chuckled. "We make a good team."

"We do."

"I second that." Coach Wayne chuckled. "No doubt."

Rhonda smiled as she sliced the lemon. "Definitely a great team."

Lexy came into the kitchen and grabbed a few paper towels. "Relationship goals." She paused, and her smile fell off a little. "You two and Marcus and Mary Catherine. That's what I want one day. A long time from now."

Sami shifted to Tyler's side, her arm around his waist, his arm around her shoulders. She reached for Lexy's hand and gave it a gentle squeeze. "Remember what we talked about?"

"Yes." Lexy's eyes warmed up again. "'Seek first His kingdom and His righteousness . . .'"

Tyler looked straight at Sami. "'And all these things will be given to you.'"

"Yes." Sami smiled at him. "Exactly."

Lexy used paper towels to wipe up the water drops from the fresh flowers. "There. The table looks perfect."

"Everything does." Tyler raised his fist in the air. "Home run!"

Ten minutes later Sami heard a key in the front door, then

the voices of Marcus and Mary Catherine and her parents. It took just a few seconds for them to reach the back of the house, where the party was set up.

As soon as they were in view, Sami and Tyler, the Waynes, and Lexy all shouted, "Surprise!"

Sami watched Mary Catherine stop, hands flying to her mouth. "What's this?" She looked at Marcus and her parents, and then back to the group. "I had no idea!" Mary Catherine seemed genuinely surprised. "This is amazing! Thank you! Y'all are the best!"

Lexy ran to Mary Catherine first. Then each of them took turns giving her a hug. Sami held Mary Catherine tight.

Mary Catherine blinked back tears. "You had this all planned?"

Sami laughed. "We did. You're engaged . . . and you're healthy. Two great reasons to celebrate!"

Marcus put his arm around Mary Catherine and kissed her cheek. "Your parents were in on it, too."

"Oh, yeah?" Mary Catherine grinned at her mom and dad. "Now you're keeping things from *me,* is that it?"

Everyone laughed.

Sami had only dreamed the surprise would go this well. She watched Mary Catherine lean against Marcus and whisper, "Really, though. This is the best surprise ever."

"Everything's ready." Sami reached for Tyler's hand on one side and Lexy's on the other. "Let's pray."

They formed a circle near the food and this time Lexy spoke up. "Can I say it?"

"Absolutely." Mary Catherine looked like she was proud of the girl.

Sami's heart swelled within her. Lexy's bond with Mary Catherine was as strong as ever.

Lexy closed her eyes. "Father, thank You for the food. Thank You for Mary Catherine being healthy enough to join us today. And thank You for this family. We love You, amen."

Her words spoke straight to Sami's heart. They were a family, indeed. Bloodlines and titles weren't the only way people became a family. Faith could do that, too. The fact that Lexy felt so much a part of them even after the life she'd been living . . . well, that was a miracle, too.

As much as Mary Catherine's recovery.

They ate on the back patio, where the sun was still warm even on this late October evening. It wouldn't get chilly until after the sun went down in an hour or so. Marcus and Mary Catherine and her parents sat across from Sami, Tyler, the Waynes, and Lexy. The setting was serene and beautiful—exactly what Mary Catherine seemed to need.

Sami noticed today even more than yesterday how much better Mary Catherine's complexion looked. Her cheeks were pink again, her eyes bright and full of life. The mechanical heart was working brilliantly from everything her doctors had told her. Seeing her so alive was the answer they had all prayed for.

Over dinner Lexy talked about the baby. "I don't know about other moms, but my morning sickness is all day." She rolled up a slice of turkey and a piece of cheese and dipped it into mustard. "This is the only thing that doesn't make me feel sick." She'd been off the streets for a month and definitely the way she talked now was different. Less slang, more communicative. Four weeks ago, Sami had wondered about her decision to take the girl in. It was Lexy's only option, of course. The only way to keep her from having an abortion.

But it had turned out to be so much more than that.

"Have you heard from your mom since you saw her a few weeks ago?" Marcus directed the question to Lexy.

"A few times." Lexy looked at Sami and then Mary Catherine before turning back to Marcus. "She's still trying to arrange something with her brother in Texas. She wants him to take me in after the baby."

"So far Lexy's uncle hasn't contacted her mother. So that's not a strong possibility at this point." Rhonda Wayne put her arm around Lexy and gave her a brief hug. "We've got her, though. Until God shows her what's next."

Whatever the future held for Lexy, none of them were willing to resign her to a life on the streets. She needed this change—that much was obvious. Sami smiled now as Lexy talked about learning how to cook, and loving the Bible. She really was like an entirely new person, with her past fading a little more every day.

Not only that, but Sami thought Lexy looked younger. Maybe because her eyes were softer, her voice kinder. She had no one to be tough around, nothing to prove. She wondered whether Lexy struggled to forget her life on the streets. Sometimes she seemed to slip into a quieter mood and Sami would find her staring out the window.

"I think about Ramon," she'd told Sami and Rhonda a few days ago at the Waynes' house. "He did love me." She looked at Sami, confusion darkening her eyes. "Don't you think?"

And again Sami had to remind the girl exactly how Ramon

had treated her. The bruises and verbal abuse, the threats that he'd kill her. And the way he hadn't respected her.

Lexy had nodded, looking distant. "You're right. I just . . . I wonder, that's all."

Other times, Rhonda had confided that Lexy would wake up in the middle of the night screaming. The first time it happened, Rhonda had been certain someone had broken into the house. Coach Wayne had grabbed a baseball bat and run toward the screaming. But Lexy was alone, tossing and turning, rolling about in the bed. "No!" She'd screamed again. "I don't want to die!"

Gently the Waynes had woken her up and helped her to a sitting position on the edge of the bed. "You were screaming, honey. What were you dreaming about?"

Sami felt sick about the story. Lexy had been out of breath, shaking, her forehead sweaty. She told the Waynes that in her dream Ramon was going to kill her. Sometimes she worried that he might know where to find her.

It had taken the Waynes an hour to calm the girl down. Sami was glad for Lexy's fear of Ramon. Maybe it would keep her from finding a way back to her old life on the days when she was tempted.

The meal was winding down, and Sami looked at Tyler. The two of them exchanged a knowing smile. "Time?" she whispered.

"Definitely." Tyler reached under the table and took her hand in his. "This is going to be fun."

Mary Catherine had been in a conversation with Lexy and Marcus and her parents, but now she turned and gave Sami a questioning look. "What's the whispering about?"

Sami looked at Marcus and Tyler, and then at the other faces around the table. All of them were silent for a moment. Mary Catherine looked at each of them and then back to Marcus. "Someone please tell me what's happening."

"Okay." Sami took the lead. "Tyler and I wanted to ask you something."

Mary Catherine allowed a nervous laugh. "I'm listening."

"So you know that Tyler and I are getting married December third . . . and that we're getting married at the beach."

"Yes." Mary Catherine's expression turned dreamy. "The most beautiful spot for a wedding, ever. Laguna Niguel." She looked at Sami. "Dr. Cohen says I'll be there. Standing at your side."

Sami could hardly contain herself. They had wanted to wait a few weeks to see how Mary Catherine was feeling. And now that she was making such an amazing recovery, there was no reason to wait. "We want you and Marcus to think about having a double wedding with us."

Marcus put his arm around Mary Catherine's shoulders. "Actually . . . it was my idea. These two were great with it. We have the same friends . . . we can share the cost. Plus . . . the beach means so much to us all."

Mary Catherine's eyes filled with tears. "I was thinking it could be months before we got married." She put her hand on Marcus's face. "You're okay with that? So soon?"

"Mary Catherine." Marcus seemed to search her face, her eyes. "I would marry you right now, right here on this back deck if I could."

And like that the plan was set. Mary Catherine thanked Sami and Tyler for sharing their day and in a rush of excitement the group began planning the wedding. Who would attend, what colors they'd use, the dinner menu, and flowers. All the details. Invitations would have to go out at the end of this week, but already Sami had found a company who could rush them.

Good thing. They had only six weeks until the wedding.

No one talked about the obvious, the fact that Mary Catherine was still on the heart transplant list, after all. A mechanical heart could only buy her so much time. The sooner the two of them could be married and sharing their lives together, the better.

The four of them had so much joy and happiness ahead, so many reasons to look forward to the days in front of them. Sami was thrilled for her friend. Mary Catherine's energy seemed particularly high tonight, her eyes as bright as the setting sun.

The fact that they were marrying the men of their dreams, that all of it had worked out, was overwhelming. Moments like this, Sami would catch herself just watching and listening and thanking God. Letting the reality sink into her overflowing heart. She had a feeling when December 3 finally got here, it wouldn't only be their family and friends celebrating with them.

But all of heaven.

MARY CATHERINE LOVED EVERYTHING about this new plan, the one that had unfolded over the most amazing dinner she'd had in a year at least. The conversation was full of hope and promise and arrangements they all easily agreed upon. It was more than Mary Catherine could imagine, more than she had prayed for.

Before the meal was over, Coach Wayne—who was also an ordained minister—even offered to officiate both weddings. Which brought all of them to happy tears.

A few hours later, after everyone else had left, Marcus took Mary Catherine out onto his back deck. She still moved more slowly than she wanted and usually by now she was tired, but not tonight.

They leaned against the railing, facing each other. Marcus took her hands in his and stared into her eyes. "Familiar." He looked at the distant lights of the city and breathed in the sweet autumn air. His eyes reflected the night sky. "Even the stars. Just like our first night here."

"Back then . . . I never dreamed." She shook her head and looked at her engagement ring, the beautiful solitaire diamond surrounded by smaller ones. Marcus had given it to her before they left the hospital. Her eyes felt watery, but only because she was so happy. "I told myself a million times I could never have you, never have the things other people have."

He ran his thumb along her forehead and eased his fingers into her long hair. "Look how wrong you were."

The truth of his words swirled around her and through her. She closed her eyes and rested her forehead against his chest. "Sometimes it all feels like a dream." She looked up at him. "And now the wedding? Getting married at the same time as Sami and Tyler?" She felt like dancing. "How can this be my life?"

"Because. God is just that good." Marcus smiled at her.

No one knew her as well as he did. He believed that. "Are you okay with it? The double wedding?"

"Of course." She loved the way she felt. Every breath was slow and clear. The effort that marked her existence before the surgery was completely gone. "It's not too soon for you?"

"Are you kidding?" He chuckled softly. "I meant what I said, baby. I'd marry you tonight if I could."

Mary Catherine hesitated. For a moment she eased from his embrace and faced the lights off the deck. "Do you remember Dr. Cohen's warning? About the mechanical heart?" She looked over her shoulder at him. "I can't have kids as long as I have it."

"I remember." Marcus didn't blink, didn't look away. "That doesn't bother me."

They hadn't talked about this—not in depth, anyway. "Do you want children? One day?"

Marcus smiled. "I'd love that. We could have kids now or ten years from now." He leaned on the railing, his eyes locked on hers. "God has a plan even for that. Otherwise you wouldn't be here."

Hope like sunbeams shot through her soul. "I had to ask."

"All I want is to marry you and help you get strong and stay healthy. I want to take walks on the beach and watch you work for the studio and I want to make a difference in this world right by your side." He put his arm around her shoulders, their arms touching, the two of them looking out at the valley. "Yes, one day I want to have children with you. But you know what?"

"What?" Mary Catherine loved being with him, safe in his arms.

"I have a feeling children will come along sooner rather than later." He looked at her.

She turned toward him again. "Because God's just that good?"

"Exactly."

24

J AG WASN'T GOING TO give up.

He was a window repairman today, working at the large house of a Texas man who had once worshipped and followed God closely. A man whose recent negligence in attending church and serving people and even responding to a certain letter was only because he was busy and distracted.

Success could do that to a person.

Jag rang the doorbell and waited. This was a key part of the mission.

"Hello?" The man answered the door. Tall and well dressed, he looked confused by Jag's presence. "Can I help you?"

"I'm the window guy." Jag held up a business card. "You wanted a quote. You called our firm."

"Oh . . . right." The man stepped aside and welcomed Jag in. He gestured up into his expansive entryway. "The windows start here and run all through the first two floors. It's been a decade or so. The seal's broken on several of them." He smiled, distracted. "My wife must've called. We keep meaning to get them replaced."

"I'll work up a bid." Jag looked around. "Could take an hour."

"That's fine." The man pointed to an adjacent office. "I'll be in there if you need me."

"Perfect." Jag knew exactly what he had to do. He started upstairs, listing windows and casing sizes until he reached the master bedroom. *Time to make it happen. Please help me, Father.* The letter was tucked beneath a stack of sweats in the man's walk-in closet. Jag took it and slipped it into his pocket.

On his way down the stairs he made a detour to the kitchen. He left the letter in the middle of the counter, in plain sight—where it couldn't possibly be missed. Jag listed the rest of the windows on the form, then he walked to the man's office and knocked on the glass door. The man pushed back from his desk and came to him.

"All finished." Jag held up his clipboard. "Got 'em all. I'll turn this in to our business office and see what estimate we can get you."

"Great."

They walked to the front door. On the way Jag stopped at the cross on the wall near the entrance. Jag knew it was there—he had seen it when he came in. "Nice cross."

At first the man seemed distracted, anxious for Jag to leave. Then he did a double take and his eyes landed on the cross.

Jag knew the history. The cross was a gift for the man's wife a decade ago, when they first moved into this house.

The man nodded at it. "Bought it in Europe."

Jag leaned in, studying the piece. "God likes when His people display reminders of their faith." He turned to the man. "That's in the Bible. Deuteronomy." Jag didn't blink. "One way to remember what's important."

The man hesitated and gave a slight shrug. "I guess so."

"You and your wife believers?" Jag looked straight into the man's eyes.

He was listening now. "Uh . . . yes." He smiled, his eyes kinder. "We believe."

"Jesus is the Way, the Truth, and the Light." Jag smiled. "That's what I always say."

The man looked at the cross again. "It's . . . been a while since we went to church."

"Life gets busy." Jag breathed deep and shook his head. "But I'll tell you, church is a privilege. I know I need it. That weekly reminder that life isn't about me. God wants us to do more than build our own empire." Jag grinned at the man. "That's the adventure of life, right?"

"Yes." The man seemed amazed or overwhelmed. "Well, then . . . I'll be looking for your estimate on the windows."

"You got it." Jag tipped his baseball cap. "Church meets early this week. New service times. Ten o'clock, I believe." Jag waved and then headed out the door. He was halfway down the walkway when he heard the man call after him.

"How do you know when my church meets? I've never seen you—"

Jag turned right and walked past a large section of tall bushes. With a quick look over his shoulder, he disappeared.

LEXY WAS GOING HOME for Thanksgiving.

She hadn't shared a holiday with her mom and grandma together in almost a decade. Besides, she wanted to tell them the news—the decision she'd made just this past week.

Lexy was back at the apartment now, ever since Mary Catherine's parents returned to Nashville. She slept on the pullout couch in the living room and now she needed to clean up her area in a hurry. Mary Catherine and Marcus would take her to her grandmother's house in an hour.

After that a big group of them were having Thanksgiving dinner at Marcus's house. His parents and Tyler's and Sami's grandparents would all join them.

They had invited Lexy and normally she would join them, but today was different. Since she didn't have much time to visit with her mama, she wanted to spend the day at home. Her first visit back since Sami had rescued her two months ago.

Since then, Ramon had tried to contact her a dozen times at least—especially at the beginning. The police had never charged him for beating her up. She hadn't wanted to push the issue. Ramon still scared her. Most of the time anyway. Lately she wondered whether maybe Ramon might be different now. Nicer.

Maybe he was ready to be a father.

Probably not. She knew better than to trust him or text him back. Sami gave her good advice. Don't respond to his texts. Ramon wouldn't know if she was ignoring him or if maybe her phone was lost or broken. Eventually he would give up.

Lexy rolled up her sheets and set them aside. She slid the bed back into the sofa and placed the cushions neatly across the bottom and back. Next she positioned the decorative pillows.

As soon as the couch was back together she grabbed her phone from the table and sat down. She pulled up Ramon's texts and read the last few again.

> Girl, I know you can see these. I'm looking for you. I love you. I never thought you'd run like this. Hit me up.

The text had come in late last night. Hours before she was set to go home. Which meant maybe this was the perfect time to see him again. Just once. She could see whether he'd gotten nicer and whether he'd changed his mind about the baby. Then she could tell him that maybe someday they might have a chance. But for now she needed to make a life for herself. Away from the gang.

Yes, that might be worth a visit. A short visit.

Maybe he would want what she had found. And then he could try to find his way out of the gang, too. And one day, the two of them could be together again.

It was all she could think about ever since she woke up. She read his text once more and then before she could stop herself her fingers began flying over the keys. She was still trying to become a better reader. But she could get by on text.

> Hey, it's me. I'll be at my grandma's for Thanksgiving later today. Maybe you could stop by. We could talk. You choose. I miss you, Bae.

She shouldn't send it. If Sami were sitting beside her, she'd be so mad. Lexy could almost hear Sami and Mary Catherine telling her to put her phone down and forget about Ramon. He wasn't good for her. He had hurt her, abused her.

But hadn't she also hurt him? She left without saying goodbye. They never even had an official breakup. What sort of girlfriend just disappears the way she had? She hadn't told Ramon where she was staying or how come she moved. It was like she had vanished from life altogether.

He deserved at least a final hangout time. And Thanksgiving was one of the best days to meet up.

Everyone was in a good mood on Thanksgiving.

She hit the send button and then slid the phone in the back pocket of her jeans. She was four months along now, but still not showing. She wouldn't have to tell Ramon about keeping the baby. Not if she didn't want to.

Lexy stood and went to the kitchen. She unloaded the dishwasher and then sat at the kitchen table. It was eleven o'clock, almost lunchtime. Mary Catherine and Sami had gone to Marcus's house to help get ready for their big dinner. Again they had invited her.

But she needed this time.

She'd been reading some of the Bible verses Sami had

given her the first week she was here. Verses about strength and courage and hope because of Jesus. She needed to remember all of that because she'd made a decision. One that would affect her life and the life of her baby.

Last night she'd asked Mary Catherine if she and Marcus would come early to pick her up. She needed to talk to them. The time was right. Mary Catherine was doing so much better. She looked really good. The doctor said she could live with the mechanical heart for lots of years.

Sure, she had to take care of herself and plug her battery pack into the wall each night and she couldn't swim. But other than that Mary Catherine seemed as healthy as anyone else. Lately she and Marcus had started taking walks to the beach again. Mary Catherine said she felt like she could walk all the way to San Diego. So that had to be good.

There was just one thing she couldn't do with a mechanical heart.

Mary Catherine couldn't have a baby.

Lexy put her hand over her stomach. It was still flat, but she could feel something growing there. The doctor said her baby would be strong and healthy. Already they could tell that. It was too soon to know if the baby was a boy or girl, but Lexy didn't mind. She wasn't going to find out. Why make things hard on herself?

The baby wasn't hers. It never would be.

Tears came from nowhere and made her eyes hurt. She breathed deep and tried to imagine life after the baby. Would she stay with Sami or Mary Catherine? The Wayne family?

Or maybe . . . if Ramon was nice to her . . . she would move back with her grandma and her mama. The three of them would be different now. Her mom 'was clean and her grandma was happy and Lexy . . . well, she could take online classes. The three of them could go to church together. And if Ramon was okay with her having a baby, maybe they'd get married. Do things right. It could work.

They were happy thoughts, but for some reason she was crying. *God, why am I so sad?*

Lexy heard the sound of people talking outside the door and then the key in the lock. Marcus and Mary Catherine walked in and saw Lexy sitting at the table. They could probably tell she'd been crying.

"Hey." Mary Catherine set her keys down on the table and took the seat beside Lexy. "What's wrong?"

Tears blurred Lexy's eyes. She shook her head. "I'm fine."

Marcus sat down on the other side of Mary Catherine. The two of them looked worried.

Lexy shook her head. "I'm sorry." She sniffed and wiped the tears from her eyelashes. "I'm fine. I'm happy, really."

"Okay." Mary Catherine put her hand on Lexy's shoulder. "You still wanna go to your grandma's house for Thanksgiving?"

"Yes." Lexy sniffed again and looked from Mary Catherine to Marcus. She was making the right decision. This was the best thing for her and the baby. She had no doubts. "I'm ready."

Marcus put his arm around Mary Catherine's shoulders. He looked at Lexy. "You feeling okay?"

Lexy shook her head. She needed to just say it. But after this she couldn't change her mind. She took a deep breath. "I've made a decision about the baby." *Not my baby,* she reminded herself. *The* baby. She had to think about it the right way. Otherwise she wouldn't make the best choice. It didn't matter what Ramon thought, or whether he had changed for the better. Having a child inside her made her wish—in some ways—she could keep it.

But she couldn't do that. Her baby deserved the best life.

She rushed ahead. "I've been thinking about how I didn't have an abortion and how I want to give my baby up for adoption." Lexy looked at Mary Catherine and then Marcus.

They were both quiet, waiting.

"Anyway." Lexy felt the tears again. "I've decided." She paused. "I'd like to give my baby to you both."

Mary Catherine leaned into Marcus, like she might fall off the chair if he wasn't there. "Lexy . . . what do you mean?"

"I'm placing this child up for adoption." She felt stronger just saying the words. At the depths of her heart she believed this was best. "I'm not ready to be a mama. Maybe in another five years or ten. After I go to college and stuff. But not now."

"So." Marcus's eyes were wide. "You want us to take care of your baby until someone adopts him or her? Is that what you're saying?"

Lexy shook her head. "I'm saying . . . I'd like you and Mary Catherine to adopt my baby." She hesitated. "If you want a baby this soon. I'm due in mid-April."

Mary Catherine turned to face Marcus and at the same time he wrapped his arms around her. At first it looked like they were only hugging, but then Lexy could see Mary Catherine's shoulders shaking. After a minute, Mary Catherine turned back to Lexy and brought her close.

Finally she pulled back and stared at Lexy, right through to her heart. "You really mean it? You want us to adopt your baby?"

"I do." Lexy was crying now, too. "I have this crazy love for this child already. And since I can't be a mama, I prayed about who the very best mama would be. And I thought about you."

Lexy stood and got a box of tissues from the kitchen counter. She brought them back to the table and handed one to Mary Catherine, who was still crying. She looked really long at Lexy's face. "Are you sure? You want to do this?"

"I'm sure." Lexy felt much better now that her decision was out in the open. "My baby will have dark skin." She smiled at Marcus. "Like you." She wiped her eyes with the tissue. "People will think you're his real parents. I like that."

Again Mary Catherine hugged her. "We never imagined this."

"Not at all." Marcus still had his arm around Mary Catherine's shoulders. They both looked shocked. "Can you give us a day to talk about it? So we're on the same page."

"Of course." Peace—warm and calm—spread through Lexy's body. "I prayed. It seemed like God really wanted me to ask you. But if it's too soon or if you don't want to adopt, that's fine." She smiled. "Sami told me that somewhere out there, God had the perfect parents for this baby. She was sure."

"I'm sure, too." Mary Catherine dried her eyes again.

Lexy hoped she was right, and that God had handpicked Mary Catherine and Marcus for her baby. But if not, she believed that there was a husband and wife somewhere praying for a baby.

For now, it was time for her to go to her grandma's house. And if things went like she hoped they would, sometime later today she would see Ramon for the first time in months.

Lexy had a feeling it would be the best Thanksgiving ever.

SINCE HEARING THE NEWS from Lexy, Mary Catherine hadn't been able to stop her tears. She wasn't sobbing or breaking down with emotion. The tears just kept coming. One or two at a time, with every thought about Lexy's unborn baby.

They dropped Lexy off at her grandma's house and then headed straight to the stadium. The place where Marcus said he could think more clearly. Marcus called Tyler and told him they'd be a little later than expected.

Something had come up.

MARCUS USED HIS KEY to let them in and they found a place on the bleachers near the top of the stadium. Where the sky felt close and God felt closer. They didn't talk about the baby until then.

"I'm in shock." Mary Catherine leaned her head on Marcus's shoulder. After a few moments, she looked up at him. "Did you see this coming?"

"Never." Marcus shook his head. "I had no idea why she wanted us to come over early."

A warm Santa Ana wind whispered through the stadium. Mary Catherine narrowed her eyes. "When I was in Africa—a

few months before I came home—something happened."
Mary Catherine turned so she could see him better. "A local
mother had died, and someone brought her newborn baby to
our orphanage."

Mary Catherine remembered how the baby felt in her
arms. The warmth of his little body against hers. "I held that
child for the longest time." She pictured the moment. "One of
the volunteers made a bottle and I fed him." Mary Catherine
lifted her face to the sky, to God. "Marcus, all I could think
was how that would never be me. I'd never hold my own baby
and feed him and know what it was like to be a mommy."

They were quiet, letting the dramatic, unthinkable possibility dangle in the air between them. Marcus put his arm
around her. "So what do you think?"

"Adopting a child . . ." She sniffed and shook her head.
"It's not something you can make a quick decision about."

"Exactly." Marcus took her hand and eased his fingers between hers. "That's why I brought you here."

She angled herself a bit more and put her free hand on his
shoulder. "But you already know how I feel, right?"

"You'd adopt that baby in a minute." Marcus had tears in
his eyes now. "You would've signed the papers right there at
your breakfast table."

"Yes." Mary Catherine nodded. "It's sooner than I
thought."

"A lot sooner." Marcus ran his finger and thumb along his
brow. He laughed. "But so what. Who says there's a right time
to have kids?"

Mary Catherine faced the ball field again. A slight bit of
laughter came from her. "You were the one who said you'd

have kids now or ten years from now." She grinned at him. "Remember?"

His look was deeper than before. "I meant every word."

"So we get married in a week and bring home our first baby in April?" Mary Catherine still couldn't grasp the possibility. "What about my heart? We both know—"

"Shhh." Marcus held his finger to her lips. "Don't." He shook his head. "God saved your life. He gave you a device that will pump blood through your body for a decade. And sometime along the way you'll get a heart transplant."

"I know." Mary Catherine didn't want to think about this, but what choice did she have? "But a baby deserves a mom who can be at his graduation . . . wait with her in the bride room at her wedding." She blinked and two more tears slid down her cheeks. "You know?"

"Mary Catherine." Marcus looked at her, his kindness and compassion so strong it took her breath. "Who of us by worrying can add a single day to our lives?" He kissed her lips and searched her eyes again. "None of us is guaranteed tomorrow."

She thought about the Scripture he was quoting. He was right. If God wanted her to live another twenty years or forty, then He would make that happen. Whether she needed five more surgeries or whether God gave her the miracle some other way.

Mary Catherine refused to voice more fears or concerns. "You think . . . this is God's plan? This baby?" She studied Marcus's reaction. But the only thing she saw was the beginning of a smile. One that eventually filled his entire face.

"Yes!" He helped her to her feet and faced her, his hands on her shoulders. "Yes, I do."

"So we'll have a baby in less than five months?"

"We will." Marcus's smile faded. "Then we bring that baby home and we raise it as our own." Each word was like a declaration. "We teach him or her about Jesus and we believe that God will use that child to change the world."

Mary Catherine nodded. She was too overcome to speak.

"We do that . . ." Marcus took gentle hold of her face, his words more of a proclamation. "And we remind ourselves every day along the way that the Lord chose us to be that baby's parents."

There was no need to ask him if he was serious. Other than the day in the hospital when he had asked her to be his wife, Marcus had never been more serious. Mary Catherine was certain.

She threw her arms around his neck and hugged him. Both of them had tears on their cheeks when they pulled back. She wondered whether she'd ever been this happy. "We're going to have a baby!" She tipped her head back and said it louder. "We're going to have a baby! I can't believe it!"

Marcus pumped his fist in the air and shouted across the stadium. His words were something Mary Catherine wasn't sure she'd ever hear him say. "I'm going to be a father!"

They called Lexy on the way home and told her the news. Yes, they wanted to adopt the baby. They couldn't be more excited. They asked if they could tell everyone at Thanksgiving dinner that night.

Lexy sounded a little subdued, but still happy. "Tell everyone." Her smile filled the phone line. "I'll see you all later."

When they reached Marcus's house, they sat in his car and tried to grasp all God had done. Then Marcus took her hands and they prayed, thanking God for saving Mary Catherine's life and letting her live. They thanked Him for giving them another chance at love and for their wedding coming up in just a handful of days. And finally they thanked God for the tiny baby He had chosen for them.

All things Mary Catherine never dreamed she'd have.

The prayer brought new meaning to the holiday and Mary Catherine was convinced that whatever Thanksgiving Days the future held, none of them would ever be as rich and meaningful as this one. The day the Lord revealed his very great plans not only for them.

But for their child.

25

THE MURDER WAS SET to go down at eight o'clock that night.

Beck had been stalking Ramon since that morning, when he first got word from Orlon. He knew the full story now. Until today, the leader of the West Knights had no idea what happened to Lexy. He'd been by her grandmother's house and even thought about shooting the older woman. Just to make Lexy think about what she'd done. In the end he spared the grandmother's life for one reason.

She wasn't worth serving time for.

Lexy, on the other hand . . . she was a different story.

Beck knew all of this, because he'd been watching Ramon for seven hours, ever since the texting that started between him and Lexy. Beck had been listening to him, waiting on him. Aspyn and Ember were nearby. They'd called on a team of angels to stand guard at Lexy's grandma's house.

But even then Beck knew it would take all they had to

stop Ramon from killing Lexy tonight. Lexy and her unborn baby. From the place where Beck and Jag waited, invisible, Ramon stood and paced the alleyway. "No girl dumps me, the leader of West Knights, and gets away with it."

Beck watched three other West Knights sitting on trash-cans, smoking pot. "Take her out, Ramon." One of the guys raised his joint in the air. "That'll teach her."

"What about her grandma?" Another one took a long drag from his joint. "You gonna shoot her, too?"

Beck saw Ramon glare at the guy. "I'll kill anyone who gets in the way." He rattled off a string of cuss words. "That whore is finished."

Jag was suddenly at Beck's side. "I'll call the police."

"Yes. You and Aspyn." Beck kept an eye on Ramon. "She's a volunteer for the Youth Center. The police will believe her."

"You'll stay here? With Ramon?"

"Yes." Beck clenched his jaw. "I won't leave his side." Beck was already moving closer to Ramon.

"Good." Jag looked relieved. "People like Ramon . . . they don't bring out the best in me."

The two angels committed to pray about the night ahead. Whatever happened, the outcome was highly critical to the mission. Every one of them knew that much. Beck watched Jag leave. Then he anchored himself a few feet from Ramon. In the near distance the air filled with silent screeches, the hissing of an army of demons.

An hour and a six-pack of beer later, Ramon coughed. "I'm ready." He pointed to the youngest gang members. "Load my gun. You're going with me." He looked at another. "You, too."

The two guys—both sixteen years old—immediately responded. One loaded Ramon's revolver. The other took up his place at Ramon's side. "Let's do this."

Ramon smiled as he took his gun. "She won't know what hit her."

Beck trailed them as they walked three blocks past the Youth Center, turned left, and headed straight for the house where Lexy and her grandmother and her mother were finishing Thanksgiving dinner. A cloud of darkness gathered around the place, held off only by a hedge of angels—all called in especially for this stage of the mission.

The enemy's forces hissed and bellowed in anticipation of what was coming.

In a rush, Aspyn was at Beck's side, the two of them moving just above Ramon and his boys. "She's expecting him." Aspyn had never looked more concerned. "They've been texting all day. She thinks it's a reunion."

Beck felt sick. "You think she'll come out to meet him?"

"I do." Aspyn pointed at three unmarked police cars parked in an empty lot across the street from Lexy's house. The officers were armed and hiding behind their cars. Ready. "The police have been notified. They know something's going down."

Beck had never been more concerned. "But Lexy . . . if she runs out now . . ."

"Exactly." Aspyn breathed deep. "She'll get caught in the crossfire."

If Ramon weren't so drunk and drugged, he would've noticed the police cars. They weren't that well hidden. Instead he reached Lexy's house, pulled out his phone, and sent a text.

Beck could see every word.

Baby, I'm here . . . come on out.

"Father, delay her! In Jesus' name!" Beck shouted the prayer. All around him he could hear other angels doing the same thing. Aspyn and Jag and Ember. But also a host of angels. The battle had never been so intense. Beck raised his voice again. "Keep her inside. Please, God."

Jag appeared then, towering in his police uniform. He stepped out of the bushes between Lexy's house and the waiting police officers and shouted at Ramon. "Hey! What are you doing?"

In an instant, Ramon drew his gun and aimed in Jag's direction. But Jag disappeared before the kid could fire. At the same time the waiting police officers used a bullhorn. "Drop the weapon and put your hands up."

Instead, Ramon fired three rounds at the officers. The policemen ducked behind their cars, and chaos followed. Ramon's fellow gang members opened fire, too. But one of them was too close to Ramon.

Beck held his breath, praying Lexy would stay inside until the danger passed.

On the fourth shot, Ramon took a bullet in the upper back. He dropped to the ground, motionless.

"No! What'd you do?" The other gang member screamed at the one who had made the mistake. "You shot Ramon! Are you serious?"

"Get your hands up!" It was one of the police officers, still behind the line of squad cars. "Now!"

Both gang members threw their hands in the air. One of them yelled. "Someone call 9-1-1. Ramon's been shot!"

Thank You, Father . . . thank You." Beck rose to his full height and looked the darkness straight on. "Be gone. In the name of Jesus!"

The cloud of evil withdrew, but not completely. Never completely.

Lexy ran out the door then and immediately she saw Ramon bleeding on the ground, his friends with their hands up. "No! Ramon . . . no!"

She ran toward him, but at the same time Ramon reached for his gun. He cussed because he couldn't grab it. His injuries were too grave. Instead he glared at Lexy. "No one walks out . . . on the leader of . . . the West Knights!"

"Ramon, what are you doing?" Lexy shrieked. "What happened?"

Again he tried to grab his gun, but before he could find the strength, he passed out.

Police rushed the scene and handcuffed the younger gang guys. A paramedic was called for Ramon. Beck was suddenly surrounded by Jag and Aspyn and Ember. The four of them hugged for a long time. Then they formed a circle and prayed. They thanked God that on this Thanksgiving Day, Lexy Jones had been allowed to live.

Light had overcome the darkness—at least for Lexy and her baby.

And then the angels prayed for a single mom seven blocks away who—later tonight—would get word that her son wasn't only in trouble again.

He was dead.

26

Even the weathermen said it was the most beautiful December third that Southern California had ever seen. Sami wasn't surprised. God had done the miraculous time and again to bring this day together.

Of course He would give them beautiful weather, too.

Before the guests arrived, Sami and Mary Catherine walked out to where a hundred and fifty chairs were set up. The management of the Ritz-Carlton had given them the prettiest grassy knoll on the property. Each of the chairs was covered in white satin with white bows tied in the back. The only thing that would separate their guests from the stunning view of the ocean were two lattice archways.

The spot where later today Sami would stand with Tyler, and Mary Catherine with Marcus.

"It feels like a dream." Mary Catherine stood beside her best friend.

"Especially with that view." Sami stared out at the ocean.

The temperature was sixty-eight and climbing. By the time the wedding started at four o'clock it was supposed to be in the low seventies. "It couldn't be more perfect."

They had three hours before the ceremony, thirty minutes before they'd do hair and makeup in the bridal room. They would be each other's maids of honor. Sami had three of her UCLA friends as bridesmaids. Mary Catherine's bridesmaids were three of her friends from Nashville, girls she'd grown up with.

They had each written their own vows and picked their own cakes. Most of the Dodgers organization had been in-vited—guests Mary Catherine would've invited, too. The idea of a double wedding not only worked—but it was giving them the chance to share their special day in a way they would re-member forever.

"Lexy will be here soon." Mary Catherine checked the time on her phone. One of the bridesmaids was bringing her earlier than the other guests. She wanted to be in the bridal room—just to have a reason to be happy. "Poor girl."

"I told her not to respond to Ramon's texts or calls." Sami sighed. Her heart broke for Lexy. "Now she thinks it's her fault. That if she hadn't been texting Ramon, he wouldn't have come to her grandmother's house to kill her." She paused. "No logic at all."

"I'm glad she's seeing a Christian counselor." Mary Cath-erine looked out at the ocean. "She can't go back to the old neighborhood again. Lexy knows that now."

"Yes." Sami stared at the expanse of blue. "She needs full-time help. Just to believe God really has a plan for her. Even now."

They were quiet for a moment. The tragedy of that night was something Lexy would live with forever.

After a while, Sami turned to Mary Catherine. "We need to remember this moment. Just before getting married." She smiled.

"Definitely." Mary Catherine used her phone, and the two of them grinned for the picture.

Sami looked at the photo for a long time. "I wouldn't be here if it weren't for you." She gave Mary Catherine a side hug, holding her phone up so they could both see the picture.

"I remember when you were dating Arnie. You were actually going to marry him." Mary Catherine sat on the nearest wedding chair and patted the seat beside her. "Sit for a minute."

"Dear old Arnie." Sami sat next to Mary Catherine. The bluff was quiet, serene. Just the two of them and the gentle breeze off the Pacific. "So very safe."

"I kept telling you to break up." A soft laugh slipped from Mary Catherine. "Your heart was never into Arnie. Not once."

"And what if you hadn't pushed me to see Tyler, during that business trip to Pensacola?" Sami smiled at her friend. "I'll be forever grateful for that."

"It was your way of skydiving. Taking a risk." Mary Catherine tilted her face to the early-afternoon sky. "You had to see him."

Sami could hardly get her mind around all the changes that had happened since then. Tyler had gone from injured and homeless to one of the top pitching coaches for the Dodgers. Just last week he'd gotten word that his position was permanent. "I would've loved him anyway . . . till the day I died."

Sami leaned back in the chair. "I just didn't know it. Not until you pointed it out."

A peaceful feeling settled around them. Mary Catherine grinned. "That's what friends are for."

"And what about you? Going off to Africa and nearly dying." Sami still couldn't believe the miracle of Mary Catherine's healing. The fact that she was alive at all. "You should've told me."

"I should have." Mary Catherine nodded. "I knew you'd tell Marcus."

"Good thing I did." Sami felt the depth in her smile. "You wouldn't be here."

Mary Catherine stood and drew a deep breath. "I guess we're both here because of each other."

"And the grace of God." Sami rose to her feet and for a moment the two of them stayed there, side by side, facing the ocean and looking at the place where they would say their vows later that day. "It's going to be a perfect day."

"Yes." Mary Catherine linked arms with Sami and they headed back into the resort toward the bridal room. Mary Catherine looked back just once. "The most perfect day of all."

SAMI DIDN'T OFTEN THINK about her parents. She was so little when they were killed. But today in the bridal suite, she couldn't stop wondering how it would feel to have her mother here, beside her. Helping her into her dress.

The way Mary Catherine's mother was helping her a few feet away.

At first Sami had thought about asking her grandmother to take her mother's place. But that didn't feel right. Her grandmother was a special person, a kind woman who had given up much of her life to raise Sami. Still, they weren't particularly close. And so Sami had simply asked her bridesmaids to join her a little earlier.

Their hair and makeup was already done. Now all that was left was the dress.

"It's time!" One of Sami's friends nodded to the pretty white dress hanging elegantly from a hanger on a hook nearby. "Let's make you into a bride."

Across the room, Mary Catherine's mother was fastening a row of thirty small buttons down the back of her gown. As she finished, Mary Catherine turned and held out her hands. "Well? How do I look?"

Sami felt her heart melt. There would never be another friend as dear to her as Mary Catherine. "You're the most beautiful bride ever."

"The two most beautiful brides." Mary Catherine's mother smiled at Sami. "Your dress is stunning, dear."

"Thank you." Sami held her hands up while her friends lifted her dress and let it fall into place. The room had mirrors everywhere, and already Sami felt like a princess. "I wish we could wear these dresses again."

"Like once a month for a special date night." Mary Catherine twirled around, swishing her long skirt back and forth.

Sami laughed. "Exactly."

"Every girl should feel like this at least once in her life." Mary Catherine smoothed her lacy dress and the layers of taffeta beneath it. "I've never felt so alive."

That was saying something for Mary Catherine. Sami held her arms up while one of her friends eased her zipper up. "Better than skydiving?"

A smile lifted the corners of Mary Catherine's mouth. "So much better."

Her friends finished with her zipper, and after fluffing out her train, Sami turned and faced Mary Catherine. "Here I am!"

Mary Catherine had been fixing her hair. Now she turned to Sami and gasped. "You look absolutely stunning." She walked closer. "Tyler won't be able to take his eyes off you."

The bridesmaids were all ready and they'd taken dozens of photos. Now there were just ten minutes before the wedding was set to start. Sami took hold of Mary Catherine's hands and smiled at the group. "Let's pray before heading out." She felt a surreal sort of peace surround her and the others.

"God is with us, His presence is here." Mary Catherine smiled at the faces around her. "This wedding . . . marrying Marcus . . . I've never felt so sure about anything in all my life."

They all held hands and Mary Catherine's mother began the prayer, asking for God's blessing over the two weddings and the marriages that would begin today. Several of the girls prayed, too. Some of them thanking God for bringing them all together, and for the gift of marriage, others asking for His continued presence in the lives of Sami and Mary Catherine and the men they were marrying.

Sami closed her eyes and suddenly she was there again. Sitting on her grandparents' roof, looking at stars next to the cutest boy she'd ever seen, and he was looking into her eyes and asking her to be his girlfriend. And they were sharing a million happy high school moments and then she was watching his bus drive off as he left to play for the minor leagues.

And she was walking through the doors of Merrill Place Retirement Center, seeing Tyler for the first time in years and wondering whether that would be their final goodbye, and she was opening her laptop one night and seeing a letter from him and knowing she would never love any man the way she loved Tyler Ames.

And she was standing on the beach meeting him again for the first time since his return to Los Angeles. And he was taking her hand and telling her he couldn't live without her and she was learning that because of a sweet old woman named Virginia, Tyler had changed. He was real in his faith and his character, and he forever would be. And like that the year flew by and Sami was once more on the rooftop of her grandparents' house and Tyler was asking her the only question that remained between them.

And she was saying yes. Yes, a million times yes.

In a single moment she could see it all.

As the prayers ended, Sami whispered to her friend, "Thanks for helping me find my way back to Tyler." She hugged her. "I love you, Mary Catherine."

"You, too." Mary Catherine grinned at Sami. "You taught me how to love. Otherwise I would've run from Marcus forever."

The photographer stood on a nearby chair and captured their hug. Sami was grateful. She could picture herself some far-off day, ninety years old, sitting in a rocking chair and having the photo from this moment somewhere nearby.

A reminder of the forever friend who had taught her how to live.

How to really live.

TYLER HAD HEARD from a few of his married friends that a man's wedding day was the most profound page in the story of his life. Now that he and Marcus were standing inside the back foyer of the Ritz-Carlton, dressed in their tuxes, ready to walk out and meet their brides, Tyler could only say he agreed.

All day God had brought to mind images of His faithfulness. The way He'd loved Tyler through his minor league days and His grace in healing his arm and restoring his career. And even the way God had connected him with Virginia Hutcheson.

Tyler had thought about her today, too.

Virginia had taught him about love and grace and second chances. Despite the dementia she faced in her final days, the two of them had shared many beautiful, profound conversations. And in those conversations dear Virginia had thought she was talking with her son. All of which made Tyler miss his own parents. Virginia believed in family. And how a family was forever, no matter what.

Joy filled Tyler's heart. His parents were here this evening because of Virginia Hutcheson. More than that, *he* was here today because of her. Even when Sami walked back into his life, he would've been too embarrassed to ever talk to her again if it weren't for Virginia. And something else the woman did for him.

She helped him find his way back to God.

Waiting for the cue to walk out to the ocean bluff, Tyler lifted his eyes to the blue sky beyond. *Maybe you can give her a window tonight, God. So she can know how much her words mattered to me.* Tyler smiled. *Every one of them.*

Marcus took a quick breath. "Any minute now."

"Feels like forever." Tyler peered out the window. The wedding coordinator was within sight. She would signal to them when it was time. After the guests were seated and the violinists were in position. "I've waited for this day since I was a junior in high school."

"You're lucky." Marcus patted Tyler on the shoulder. "I only wish I'd known Mary Catherine that long."

"True." He nodded, his soul full. "I hadn't thought of it that way." He slipped his hands in his pants pockets. The wedding today would be followed by dinner, and then both couples would take off for Shutters, a beachside hotel in Santa Monica.

Tomorrow morning Marcus and Mary Catherine would leave for the Bahamas. Tyler was taking Sami to Maui. Their bags were loaded in the vintage car Marcus had rented for the occasion. Everything was set.

Tyler couldn't wait. He steadied himself. "Earlier . . . I was thinking about Virginia."

Marcus's smile softened. "Sweet Virginia. Such a wonderful person."

"She was just what I needed." Tyler nodded. "I don't know where I'd be today without her."

"Mmmm. God definitely lined up all the right people."

"At just the right time." Tyler thought about the pastor

who gave him a bag lunch and then sent him looking for a job at Merrill Place. "In some ways it feels like God has been working behind the scenes this whole time. Otherwise this day would've been impossible."

Marcus nodded. "What if that volunteer hadn't pushed me out of the way of that bullet? That night at the Youth Center?" He shrugged, as if he had no words. "The odds of Mary Catherine and I being here today? Beyond impossible."

"You rescuing her from Africa?" Tyler chuckled. "They make movies about stuff like that."

"I had help." He hesitated. "Did I ever tell you about the Jeep?"

"In Africa?" Tyler shook his head. "Tell me."

"I needed a Jeep to get her out of the orphanage. At first the guy behind the counter said there wouldn't be one for a day or so." Marcus leaned against the nearest wall, the story clearly still very real to him. "But you know how sick she was. I didn't have that kind of time. I needed a Jeep immediately."

Tyler had heard much about Marcus's time in Uganda. But he hadn't heard this. "So what happened?"

"All of a sudden this mechanic comes in and says he's got a Jeep. He'd fixed one that was broken." Marcus's laugh showed that he still couldn't believe what had happened that day. "Things like that. Over and over again."

"A series of miracles."

"And that Ember girl," Marcus added. "The one who helped Mary Catherine at the orphanage."

"The one who convinced her to fight for her life."

"Yes." Marcus's eyes grew distant. "Mary Catherine called her . . . to let her know about the surgery and to invite her to the wedding. Just in case she could make it." He looked at Tyler. "The woman who answered the phone said she'd never heard of an Ember. No one by that description had ever worked there."

"Which is obviously a mistake." Tyler felt confused. "Clearly the woman worked there. You met her, right?"

"Of course." Marcus shrugged. "Mary Catherine never did find her. Maybe she's moved on." He paused. "I don't get it. I just know God worked a miracle. It's like we could see His fingerprints with every passing hour right up until this."

"So true." The moment lightened and Tyler caught the signal from the wedding coordinator outside. He nodded to Marcus. "Hey, best man. It's time."

Tyler led the way with Marcus a few feet behind him. They had decided that after the pastor gave the message, Tyler and Sami would say their vows first, then Marcus and Mary Catherine. So they would each have their own special moment.

Unlike the girls with their bridesmaids, Tyler and Marcus had decided to pass on the idea of groomsmen. They were close to the entire Dodgers team, so choosing a handful of special friends would've been difficult. Just as Sami and Mary Catherine were each other's maids of honor, the guys were each other's best men.

In life and here, at their weddings.

Tyler felt their friends and family turn and watch as the guys made their way to a place at the front of the wedding setup. Already Coach Wayne was there. He stood to one side, grinning as Tyler and Marcus walked up. Tyler took the left side and Marcus the right. They stood side by side and stared down the aisle, ready for their brides.

Tyler felt the sting of tears. *Lord, I don't deserve Sami. Only You could've brought us here . . .* Tyler watched the bridesmaids leave the building and head to the back of the chair setup. The violinists played Bach while one at a time Sami's friends walked down the aisle and took their places on the far side of the left archway. They each smiled at Tyler as they walked by. A few of them had tears in their eyes.

Next came Mary Catherine's bridesmaids, each of them taking a spot on the far right side. The music changed, and the guests stood, all eyes on the back of what felt like an outdoor church.

And suddenly there she was, his Sami. His forever bride. Her eyes shone with the light of the setting sun, and everything about her looked stunning. The vision of her took his breath, and in a single heartbeat he could see the two of them through the years, celebrating life in their twenties and thirties, with babies and a busy, happy family. He could see them as empty-nesters and even into their eighties and nineties, holding hands and rocking on the front porch together.

But however long they lived and whatever the years ahead held for them, Tyler knew one thing for sure as Sami walked toward him.

He would never forget how she looked in this single moment.

27

IN THE MINUTES BEFORE Mary Catherine would walk down the aisle and become his wife, a flashback hit Marcus. The hot afternoon when he learned about his teammate Baldy Williams dying from a drug overdose.

Marcus hadn't known where to turn.

So he'd gone to the stadium and started running. Just running the stairs until he thought he might pass out. And the whole time all he could think about was Baldy's success, Marcus's own success, and how none of it mattered. How there had to be more to life than baseball and money and the fame that came with it.

The violins played as Sami walked down the aisle, her eyes locked on Tyler's.

Even still Marcus was back in that moment, there in the empty stadium crying out to God, *Okay, if You're there . . . show me! Give me a reason to believe. If You're real . . . give me meaning.*

Marcus blinked back tears at the memory.

God had been answering him ever since.

The music changed, and in a blur of white, Mary Catherine was there, walking beside her father. Her dress was simple and elegant, satin and lace that made her the most beautiful bride Marcus had ever seen. She wore a white lace bag that carried her battery pack, a reminder that there was nothing ordinary about Mary Catherine Clark.

There never had been.

He couldn't stop the tears if he wanted to. *You've done what I asked, Lord.* His bride was walking closer, joining him for now and as long as they lived. Marcus couldn't take his eyes off her. *Father, You proved You were real. You've given me meaning beyond anything I could have asked for.*

That day at Dodger Stadium, a swirling of dust had risen from the baseball diamond. As if the finger of God were moving the dirt, speaking to Marcus, assuring him that he was not alone and that life did hold meaning. Today the sign from God was different.

It was Mary Catherine, his bride, walking toward him.

All the proof Marcus could ever need—now and forever.

HALFWAY DOWN THE AISLE, Mary Catherine looked at her dad through teary eyes. "I feel perfect."

Her father wiped a finger along his own damp cheek and smiled at her. "Thank you."

"You don't have to worry about me." She glanced at Marcus and then at her father again. "I'll be fine, Daddy. Marcus has me. God figured it all out."

"I know, honey." Her dad nodded, even as a few tears ran down his face. His smile never wavered. "I believe that."

Mary Catherine turned her attention to Marcus again. Him and only him. Their eyes locked and held. Through all her high school and college years, in the long seasons in Los Angeles when her health took a turn for the worse, Mary Catherine never believed she'd have a moment like this. Sure, she could skydive and swim with the dolphins.

But love? Finding a man whose heart belonged to God first? Allowing him to love her when she didn't know if she had a year to live? Everything about it had seemed impossible.

She felt the tears on her cheeks, but she didn't care. Marcus was crying, too. In all the world there was no other man who would've raced to Africa and rescued her from certain death—all so he could prove how much he loved her. God had known the condition of her heart—both physically and emotionally. And he had brought her the only man who could help heal her in both ways.

When she reached the end of the aisle, Coach Wayne stepped forward. His eyes were kind and familiar, filled with his obvious deep joy for the weddings at hand. After all, he and his wife had been there from the beginning. For both couples.

Ollie Wayne lifted his Bible. "Who gives this woman to be married?"

Mary Catherine's father nodded. "Her mother and I do."

Her dad kissed her cheek. "Love you, baby."

"Love you, Daddy." They had practiced this, but even still Mary Catherine wasn't prepared for the emotion she felt as her dad turned and took a seat next to her mother. The action was as profound as it was symbolic.

After today, forevermore she would belong to Marcus Dillinger.

She stepped up and took her place next to her handsome groom. "You're so beautiful." He leaned close and whispered the words. "I'm in love with you."

"Happiest day of my life." She breathed the near-silent words in response, as one of her bridesmaids helped straighten her train.

On the other side of Coach Wayne, Sami had done the same thing. They shared a quick smile as they each handed their flower bouquets to another of their bridesmaids. Then, at the same time, they turned and linked hands with their grooms.

Mary Catherine could feel their guests reacting, touched by the double wedding. But she and Marcus might as well have been the only people there. The ocean spread out like a scene from heaven over her left shoulder. Marcus's eyes held more love than Mary Catherine thought possible.

He's Your gift to me, God . . . no man could ever love me more.

Marcus seemed to read her thoughts, because he lifted his eyes toward the deep blue sky and then he grinned at her. The slight shake of his head told Mary Catherine he was thinking the same thing. God had given them this day and each other. They would spend their lives thanking Him.

Coach gave a talk about marriage, how God designed it from the beginning. He read from Genesis chapter 2, where God made woman specifically for a man, and then He directed them with words that held deep meaning today.

"And so the Bible has the answer for marriage." Coach

Wayne's voice was kind, compassionate. "Scripture tells us in verse twenty-four, 'That is why a man leaves his father and mother and is united to his wife, and they become one flesh.'"

He talked about marriage being a mystery because literally the two would no longer be separate, but one. The way Christ was one with His church. Marcus looked deep beyond her eyes to her soul. He ran his thumbs lightly over hers, adoring her, loving her.

"I can only tell you, Sami and Tyler, Mary Catherine and Marcus, marriage—God's form of marriage—is the most beautiful gift He has given us outside salvation." The coach's words rang with compassion and conviction. "You have the privilege from this day forward of guarding this gift, protecting it. Fighting for it. When you look at your spouse in the days and years to come, you must see that perfect gift, designed by God for you alone. The way you see each other here, now."

Marcus grinned. "Every day," he mouthed. "Every hour."

Her heart certainly didn't feel mechanical. She had so much love bursting from her she wanted to rush to his arms right now, before the vows. Instead she waited, lost in his love.

When Coach Wayne was finished, he moved to the spot between Sami and Tyler. Like they had rehearsed, Marcus turned and put his arm around Mary Catherine, so the two of them could watch their friends say their vows. Both couples had written their own, and Mary Catherine had already heard them yesterday at the rehearsal.

Good thing.

Because here, with the ocean so close, and their families and friends nearby and her head resting on Marcus's shoulder,

Mary Catherine couldn't quite concentrate on the words Tyler was saying. Something about having loved Sami forever, and how always when he looked at her he would see the grace of God. Because only God's grace would've given them a second chance at love.

It was Sami's turn. She promised to always see Tyler through the eyes of her heart, the place where she had always known he loved her. She talked about how God had created her to love him, and how she wanted nothing more than to spend the rest of her life living out that purpose.

Something like that.

Their friends exchanged rings then, and the pastor smiled. "Tyler, you may kiss your bride."

Tyler lifted the veil out of the way, dipped Sami low, and kissed her in a way that brought applause from their guests. Mary Catherine felt fresh tears in her eyes. She had never seen Sami so happy. To think she'd had the privilege of insisting Sami take that meeting with Tyler more than a year ago.

She couldn't imagine Sami with anyone but Tyler Ames. And now the two of them would have forever together.

"All right." Coach chuckled. "Time for act two."

The guests laughed, same with Mary Catherine and Marcus.

Then—as they had planned—Marcus returned to his spot facing her. He whispered to her, "Finally!"

"I can't wait."

Coach Wayne looked up at the guests. "You get the feeling these two are in their own world?"

Again light laughter from their guests. Marcus chuckled and hung his head for a few seconds, guilty. Mary Catherine stifled another laugh and then, like that, it was time for their vows.

Not only had they written them, they had memorized them. Same as Sami and Tyler. Marcus went first. He held Mary Catherine's hands gently in his. "There was a time when I struggled to find meaning in life. Wins . . . losses. Failure . . . success . . . it meant nothing. So I asked God to give me a sign that He was real, to give my life meaning." Marcus's eyes grew watery, and his smile faded a little. "And God gave me you."

Mary Catherine blinked so she could see him clearly through her tears.

"Now, Mary Catherine, I promise to give you myself. I will love you as long as you live. And along the way I will be strong when you are weak, I will carry you when you fall. I will pray alongside you . . ." He paused, his eyes marked by the deepest intensity. "And I will believe every day that God will give us a lifetime together. I am here for you now and always, Mary Catherine. I would go to the ends of the Earth to find you again and again and again."

She couldn't stop her tears, but they didn't matter. Every word he spoke was etched in her soul, where they would stay forever.

"I promise to hold your hand . . . and your heart . . . forever in mine. Till death do us part."

How could she possibly speak after that? Mary Catherine leaned her forehead against Marcus's, and then, because weddings didn't have to all be the same, she put her arms around his neck and leaned into him. The hug lasted a few seconds before she felt composed enough to step back.

One of the bridesmaids passed a tissue to Mary Catherine. "Thanks." She sniffed and laughed at the same time. She dabbed at her eyes and cheeks and handed the tissue back to her bridesmaid. Then she turned to Marcus. "Sorry."

Once more the guests laughed. But Mary Catherine could see that most of them were crying, too. They all knew her story. How only by the miraculous healing power of God she was here at all. Let alone marrying the man who had rescued her. The one God had created to love her.

It was her turn.

And with Marcus's beautiful vows still ringing through her heart and soul, Mary Catherine steadied herself and began. "Marcus, I take you this day as my forever husband, my other half. My hero and rescuer sent by God." She smiled. There could be no truer words. "You pursued me even when I told you no, and you saw past my shallow words to the deepest part of me. Past my fears to the dreams I didn't dare voice. You are not afraid of tomorrow. You are brave, and so you have made me brave, too."

Marcus's eyes welled up again. He didn't blink, didn't look anywhere but straight into her soul.

"And so I promise to give you myself. My honesty and my concerns, my health and my sickness. My whole life long." She hesitated, finding control again. "I cannot promise you decades. But you have taught me that no one can promise that. All we have is today."

He nodded, his head angled slightly. She knew he was feeling for her. Believing in her.

"So here, in the power of Jesus, and with our friends and families as witnesses, I give you today . . . and tomorrow. And every day God gives us after that." This time she ignored the tears on her cheeks. "I promise to believe in our future and the child that will join us in April."

Mary Catherine thought about Lexy, watching from one of the front rows.

She pressed on. "I want to live a long life with you, Marcus. And so I promise to do everything in my power to guard my heart—physically and emotionally. Because my heart belongs to you."

Joy shone brighter than his tears. He nodded, encouraging her even here.

She felt her entire face light up. "Till death do us part."

Coach Wayne wiped at a tear on his cheek, the same way many of their guests did. Then Coach walked them through the exchanging of rings, and again they'd written their own words.

Mary Catherine's left hand didn't waver as Marcus slipped the ring on her finger. The feeling was something she had longed for since the day she said yes. She was Marcus's wife now. She always would be.

It was her turn. She took his hand and slid the wedding band into place.

Coach Wayne raised his voice. "With the power vested in me by the State of California, I now pronounce you husband and wife." He smiled at the two of them. "Marcus, you may kiss your bride."

He framed her face with his hands. "I love you, Mary Catherine Dillinger."

"I love you." Her eyes were dry now. The joy of the moment left no room for anything but happiness.

Marcus kissed her and in all the world there was only him and her.

Yes, the baby would come in April, and along the way there would be doctors and hospitals and maybe even a heart transplant. Marcus would travel with the Dodgers and ride the ups and downs of being a professional ballplayer. But all of that seemed a world away as Marcus held her right here, right now. And in those seconds, Mary Catherine knew that together she and Marcus would pray for God's strength and courage and help. They would be brave and intentional. And they would truly live in the moment.

Moments like this.

Because in the end that was all anyone ever really had.

28

LEXY CRADLED THE BABY close to her chest. The memory of the pain and pushing and agony of delivery all faded the minute they placed him in her arms. The baby was a boy. Her son. Whether he ever knew her or not.

He was beautiful. His light brown skin and wide, beautiful eyes. Like hers. The nurse had taught her how to wrap him in a blanket so he felt safe and secure. Swaddling, she called it. Lexy pulled her knees up in the hospital bed and held the baby out in front of her. "Hello, beautiful boy. Your mommy loves you." Tears made her voice shaky. "Always know how much your mommy loves you."

This day would be too difficult, too painful if it weren't for one thing: Mary Catherine and Marcus. They would be the perfect parents for her perfect little boy. Lexy had no doubt. Besides, God had worked out the details.

Every one of them.

A month ago her mother had gotten a call from her brother. The one in Texas. He told her he should've called sooner, but he'd been busy. Busy with things that in the scope of life didn't really matter. At least that's what he told Lexy's mother.

Her mom gave the man Lexy's cell number, and the next day her phone rang. She had relived the phone call every day since. The man, her uncle, was on the other end.

"Lexy, my family and I have discussed this. We'd like you to come live with us." He sounded confident and kind. "You'll get your high school diploma and then we'll help you get accepted to Texas Christian University—which is very close to our house." He paused. "If you're interested, that is."

If she was interested? Even now Lexy smiled at the possibility that she might be anything but interested. Mary Catherine and Sami had moved out of the apartment after their weddings, and Lexy had lived with the Waynes ever since. But that wasn't a long-term solution. Especially now that the baby had been born.

She brought him to her face and kissed his cheek. If she lived with him even one more day, she couldn't give him up. She could barely imagine letting him go now. *You'll help me, won't You, God? You'll get me through this?* Her baby's cheek was soft against hers. *You'll give me another little boy one day, right? Please?*

The thought of God brought more tears to her eyes. She'd been talking to God a lot, getting closer to Him. Rhonda and Ollie Wayne had been reading the Bible with her. Picking up where Sami and Mary Catherine had left off—in the book of

Acts. God had become like the daddy she didn't have, and she'd learned how to talk to Him about even the tough things. Like memories of her time in the gang.

For a minute she thought about Ramon, her baby's father. His dead body lying in a pool of blood outside her grandmother's house. How could she have thought for a minute that he maybe cared about her?

When the whole time he'd been trying to kill her?

Lexy ran her hand over her baby's soft head. They both would've died. That's the crazy thing. Somehow God had protected them both.

Her baby closed his eyes and fell asleep. He would never know what it was to be in a gang, never get caught up in drugs and stealing and killing. From the moment his parents came to pick him up in an hour, he would be loved.

And he would be good.

Lexy had already asked God about that. That He would use her son to help people. That He would be an example to others. She smiled at the infant, even as her eyes welled up again. He was so perfect. She had no idea how she would let him go, only that she would. It was her decision.

Mary Catherine had been really nice about the whole thing.

Last week she and Marcus had sat down with Lexy and talked to her. "We want you to know something." Mary Catherine took her hand. Her voice was kind and understanding. "You can change your mind about this. Giving up your baby has to be your decision, Lexy. Yours and God's alone."

Lexy thought for half a minute, trying to imagine raising the baby and finishing school. She didn't have a job or a driver's license or any money. Still . . . the idea was tempting. For those few seconds she wondered what it would be like to keep him, to watch him learn to sit and stand and walk. To hear his laugh and his first words.

Then she thought of something else. "Are you not sure about the adoption?" Lexy had to ask. Just in case.

Marcus put his arm around Mary Catherine. "We already love your baby like our own." His voice was gentle. Marcus was nothing like the guys Lexy had known. "We want this adoption to work. But we want you to know it's your choice."

Reality had settled over her then, the way it always did whenever she even thought about keeping her baby. She wasn't ready. Her baby deserved a good life with good people. So he could be everything God wanted him to be.

Lexy had smiled at Mary Catherine and Marcus then. "I'm not going to change my mind. He's your baby." She had put her hand on her baby bump. "God wants you to have him."

The memory of that time would always stay with Lexy. Whenever she thought about the warm feel of her sweet-smelling baby boy in her arms, if she ever wondered whether she'd done the right thing, Lexy would remember that it had been her decision. And that this was what God wanted her to do.

Her uncle's phone call had been the proof.

That day he had explained to her that they would take her in as their own and help her finish college. "This is something only God could've set up," her uncle told her.

Then he shared the most amazing story with her. How her mother had written him a letter when she was still in prison, asking him to take Lexy in and help her find a future. "But I put the letter in a drawer somewhere and forgot about it." Her uncle had sounded upset with himself. "It was nothing personal, Lexy. Please know that. I was just so busy I couldn't even imagine the idea."

But something had happened, something her uncle still couldn't explain. "Every week or so the letter would turn up. All of a sudden it would be sitting next to my computer, or lying on the kitchen counter. Next to my bathroom sink." The man had sounded surprised by this. "I'd put it away and it would turn up again."

Finally her uncle had read the letter once more. Then he sat down—just him and God. "I asked the Lord what He wanted me to do about the situation." A smile had filled her uncle's voice. "And God told me to talk to my family and take you in. To love you like one of my own."

Lexy had talked to both her aunt and uncle a number of times since. They'd Skyped with the whole family and gone over some of the house rules. Already she felt close to them. Once this day was over, and her baby was home with Marcus and Mary Catherine, Lexy would live with the Waynes for a few more days and then get on a plane and head for Texas.

Her uncle had arranged more counseling for her there. To help her heal and process everything that had happened. Everything she'd lost.

She pressed her cheek lightly against her little boy's face again. "Including you, little guy."

The baby opened his eyes and for a long while he looked at Lexy. Like somehow he knew what was happening. As if he wanted Lexy to know it was okay, that he would be happy with his new parents. But he would never forget her, like he knew she loved him enough to let him go. He might only be a few hours old, but Lexy could read all of it.

Right here in her little boy's eyes.

"We're each going to find a new life, little man," she whispered to him, and he blinked a few times. "God has a plan. That's what Mary Catherine always says."

Lexy had just one request for Mary Catherine and Marcus. A special name that she hoped they might give her baby boy. A way for him to know the story of his birth. How God had somehow made a letter to her uncle appear over and over again. All so Lexy would know for sure she was doing the right thing in giving him up.

Lexy studied her tiny son. She would remember the look on his face for the rest of her life. The gentle curves of his cheeks and forehead, his beautiful eyes. And maybe . . . maybe one day they would meet again. Mary Catherine and Marcus were open to the idea. But Lexy had asked that the paperwork be closed. She trusted God and her friends with this baby. Better not to have visits and a string of goodbyes to mess up his childhood.

At least that's the way she saw it.

Maybe one day she would change her mind. By then her boy would be older. He would know how God had given Lexy a family and a future in Texas. And that Lexy had done the same for her little boy. The child would know that Lexy had absolutely made the right choice.

All because of his name.

Now all she had to do was convince Mary Catherine and Marcus.

MARCUS WAS A FATHER.

He could hardly contain his joy, hardly wait to hold his son. But here, halfway to the hospital, that wasn't all Marcus was thinking about. He and Mary Catherine were both quiet, aware of the weight of the next few hours.

And the gravity of Lexy's decision.

"I'll remember this day forever." Marcus took Mary Catherine's hand.

"Yes." On and off all morning she'd been wiping tears. "Every minute of it."

Marcus tried to picture how after tonight there would be three of them. Their son's crib was waiting for him, along with blankets and teddy bears and a nursery filled with things their friends and family had bought for them.

Back in January they'd contacted an adoption agency and a home study had been done. Marcus understood the only problem, of course. Mary Catherine's heart. But that wasn't a deal-breaker. As long as Marcus and Mary Catherine were both willing to raise the child if one of them died, then there wasn't an issue.

Especially because Lexy had chosen them, despite Mary Catherine's heart issues.

A representative from the adoption agency was meeting them at the hospital—assuming Lexy still wanted to go ahead with the plan. Mary Catherine leaned her head on Marcus's shoulder. The two of them were quiet for a few minutes.

Mary Catherine was the first to speak. "I wonder how Lexy's doing."

"I've been thinking about her. It has to be hard." Marcus thought for a moment. "She's felt the baby growing under her heart all these months. Then holding him for the last hour." He raised his brow. "Only God could give her the strength to let go."

Marcus replayed the past twenty-four hours. He and Mary Catherine had been at the hospital last night and earlier today for the delivery. Several times they came in to pray with Lexy and comfort her. Those times with the three of them had been very sweet.

They were even in the room for the birth, there to celebrate his arrival and to make sure Lexy and the child were healthy. But neither Marcus nor Mary Catherine held the baby. Instead, the two of them went home—just like they had all agreed before the birth. Lexy had requested an hour alone with the infant, before Marcus and Mary Catherine officially met him.

Her last hour with her baby.

Marcus and Mary Catherine had used the time to drive home, change clothes, grab the diaper bag, and fasten the car seat into their SUV. They had prayed before they climbed into Marcus's truck. Neither of them had felt very chatty.

"I'm glad we haven't named him yet." Mary Catherine shifted, facing him. "You know . . . just in case."

Marcus nodded. He didn't say anything, didn't want to put words to the idea that even now Lexy could change her mind. But the truth was, she could. Marcus and Mary Catherine had given her that option. Legally she had time to change her mind. Lexy had assured them that wouldn't happen. The plan was for the three of them to sign adoption papers when they were all together.

They would name their son in the next few days.

Lexy had told them many times that she wasn't going to change her mind. She was certain about her decision. But what if she was supposed to keep the child? It was a thought Marcus couldn't voice.

After Lexy asked them to adopt her baby, Marcus and Mary Catherine had talked often about the chance of the plan falling through. Recently, though, they rarely brought up the topic. The heartbreak if Lexy decided to keep the baby now would be more than Marcus could imagine. But even still he and Mary Catherine wanted God's will.

Whatever that was.

And so Marcus spent the remainder of the drive to the hospital praying. Asking God to guide them and to speak to them in the next hour or so. *We need Your will, God. Please help Lexy make the right decision, the one that lines up with Your plans.* Not just for each of them.

But for the tiny baby whose future would depend on it.

29

A PART OF MARY CATHERINE refused to fully accept the possibility that she was going home today with a son. She didn't dare let herself believe it. Not when there was still a chance Lexy could keep the child. As she and Marcus walked through Cedars-Sinai Hospital and rode the elevator up to the maternity wing, Mary Catherine could barely breathe.

"I only want what's best for him," she whispered as they stepped off on the seventh floor.

"Me, too." Marcus put his arm around her as they headed to the nurse's station. "Pray for that."

"I am." They were directed to Lexy's room, and along the way Mary Catherine could hardly focus. Was it really just six months ago that she'd nearly died in this very hospital? Back then she couldn't imagine having another week of life, let alone a husband and a child. Already her life was a miracle. That would be true whether she left here today with a baby or not.

Lexy's door was partially closed. Marcus was about to knock when they both heard something from inside the room. The soft sound of Lexy crying. Mary Catherine looked at Marcus and then hung her head. What was happening? Was Lexy having doubts? Should they have someone check on her? In case she wasn't ready for them?

But before she could say anything, Marcus leaned toward the opening. "Lexy?"

"Come in!" The girl was definitely crying. But she sounded almost relieved. "Please."

They stepped inside and the scene took Mary Catherine's breath. Lexy looked so small, so young. But she also looked very much like a mother. She held the bundled baby in her arms, cradled close to her. The swelling around her red eyes told how difficult the past hour had been.

Lexy spoke first. "He's your baby." She looked down at the infant. "This has been one of the best hours of my life." She lifted her eyes to Marcus and then to Mary Catherine. "But I'm not ready to be a mother. I'm just not. I want what's best for him."

"You're sure." Mary Catherine held her breath.

"Yes." Lexy wiped her eyes with her free hand. "God's opening up one plan for me. And a different one for my little boy." She smiled at Mary Catherine. "Jeremiah 29:11. Just like you always said."

For the first time since they left the hospital more than an hour ago, Mary Catherine felt herself draw a complete breath. Lexy had been working with a counselor from the adoption agency, keeping her options open and making sure of her decision.

Lexy ran her hand over the baby's head. "My counselor said it's not like I'm giving my baby away." She gave Mary Catherine a sad smile. "I'm placing him in a better life. Giving him a better future. Which is the best way I can love him."

Just then the woman from the adoption agency knocked on the door. "Lexy." She peered into the room. "Is this a good time?"

"It is." Lexy introduced the woman to Mary Catherine and Marcus. "I'm ready to sign the papers."

The woman nodded. "Very well. They're right here." She moved slowly, respectfully. It took her a minute to pull a folder and a pen from her bag. "Would you like to hold the baby while you sign?"

"Yes, please." Lexy's tears returned. Quiet tears, as if they came from a place deep in her soul.

Mary Catherine felt strangely awkward and peaceful all at the same time. She and Marcus stayed toward the back of the room, waiting, watching. She didn't dare look at the baby. Not yet.

The woman handed Lexy the papers positioned on the folder. "We've gone over this . . . where you need to sign."

For a brief moment Lexy closed her eyes and pinched the bridge of her nose. The woman handed her a tissue. "Would you like more time, Lexy?"

The idea of taking more time seemed to snap Lexy out of her obvious grief. She dabbed at her eyes and blew her nose. "No, thanks. I don't need more time." She took the pen and paperwork from the woman and with the baby cradled in her left arm, she began to sign the documents.

Mary Catherine's tears came like a flood. The picture of Lexy holding her baby with one hand and using the other to sign away the rights to her child was something she would hold on to always. The cost of this gift was more than Mary Catherine could comprehend.

After she was finished, Lexy asked the woman from the adoption agency to give them some time. Mary Catherine and Marcus would sign papers later. The next few minutes were not part of the legal transfer of rights for the baby.

They were more personal than that.

When they were alone, Mary Catherine and Marcus came up alongside Lexy's bed. Mary Catherine spoke first. "How do you feel?"

"Sore." Lexy winced. "But I've asked God to let me do this again. When I'm married. When I can be the mom I want to be."

Mary Catherine nodded. Marcus put his hand on Lexy's shoulder. "We would always welcome you to visit him, Lexy. You know that."

"I do." Lexy looked at her baby again. "But I don't think that would be good for me or for him." She turned her attention back to Marcus. "You understand, right?"

Marcus nodded. "I do."

Lexy brought the baby close to her face. She kissed his cheek and then, fresh tears streaming down her face, she held him out to Mary Catherine. "Here." She released a few quiet sobs. "He's yours."

With all the love she could have possibly felt, Mary Catherine took the child into her arms and held him close to her heart. For the first time, she looked into his face and as she did he opened his eyes. "Hi, baby boy." Mary Catherine held him closer to Marcus. "He's perfect."

Marcus leaned in and kissed his cheek. He looked at Lexy. "He's beautiful."

"I know." She smiled, clearly proud. "He looks like me when I was born."

Lexy had already been discharged from the hospital. She had made it clear she didn't want to stay any longer than she had to. Rhonda and Ollie Wayne would pick her up and take her back to their house.

Then in a matter of days Lexy would move to Texas.

Mary Catherine wasn't sure what to say or do next. She wanted to give all her attention to Marcus and the baby. But that didn't seem sensitive to Lexy. Most birth moms would allow a social worker or adoption agency representative to take their baby from their arms. In this case, Lexy wanted to hand him directly to Mary Catherine and Marcus.

But this moment could only last so long.

"You're ready for Texas?" Marcus must've sensed that it was about time to leave.

Lexy nodded. "I've been talking to my aunt and uncle every day. My mom and grandma are so happy for me." Her eyes lit up. "I didn't tell you! I think my mom and grandma might move to Texas, too. We all need a new start." She hesitated, her voice softer. "My mom's learning to read. She wants to finish high school. My uncle said he'd help her, too."

Mary Catherine reached for Lexy's hand. "You said they have a strong church?"

"They do." Lexy smiled at Mary Catherine through watery

eyes. "You saved my life. I mean it." She looked to the baby. "And Sami saved his."

"The Lord saved us all." Marcus's eyes were damp, too. He looked from Mary Catherine to the baby, and back to Lexy. "None of us would be here otherwise."

Lexy took a fresh tissue from the box near her bed. "I do have one thing I wanted to ask you." She sat up a little straighter, wincing at the pain. "I thought of a name for him. I can't get it out of my head." She looked nervous, like she wasn't sure if she should say this next part. "You can name him what you want, of course. I just thought . . . maybe . . . This would mean a lot to me."

The idea of Lexy naming the baby wasn't something they had talked about. But Mary Catherine was completely open to the idea. After all, she and Marcus hadn't allowed themselves to think about names yet. Mary Catherine still had hold of Lexy's hand. She nodded. "Tell us."

"Okay . . . so God is giving me a second chance in Texas. It was my uncle Garner's idea. He felt like God was telling him and his wife and kids to take me in. So I could be part of their family. And they live in Dallas." Lexy paused. She looked from Marcus back to Mary Catherine. "So the name Dallas Garner keeps coming to mind." Lexy let her eyes fall to the baby once more. "Dallas Garner Dillinger." She smiled through new tears. "Sounds like a president or something, right?"

"Dallas Garner Dillinger." Marcus said the name first. He looked at Mary Catherine. "I like it. I really do."

The name was beautiful. Mary Catherine looked into the face of her son and suddenly she was absolutely certain. "It's the perfect name for him."

"That way . . . you can tell him about me. About how God rescued me out of LA to Dallas, Texas. And how He used my uncle Garner to change my life."

All three of them were in tears as the name settled into their hearts. "All right . . ." Lexy held up her arms. "Let's say goodbye."

Still cradling baby Dallas in her arms, Mary Catherine leaned in and hugged Lexy. "We'll always be here for you. If you ever need anything." She pulled back enough to look into Lexy's eyes. "Stay close to Jesus."

"I will." Lexy's voice was a choked whisper. But in her eyes Mary Catherine saw something she desperately needed to see.

Certainty.

Marcus prayed for them then, for Lexy and the future God had for her, and that one day she would have more children of her own. He prayed for himself and Mary Catherine, for their health and for a lifetime of raising Dallas Garner. And he prayed for God's protection over all of them. Then Marcus hugged Lexy. "Thank you. For trusting us with him."

Lexy smiled through her tears. "He's yours." She took one final look at the baby. "Tell him how much I love him." She could barely speak the words. "Will you do that?"

"Of course." Mary Catherine tried to see clearly through her tears. "We'll tell him that and we'll tell him about his name."

"Thanks." Lexy nodded. She pressed the tissue to her face again. "Okay . . . you can go now. Please."

They said a final goodbye, and Mary Catherine, Marcus, and Dallas left the hospital room. They signed the paperwork in the hallway and on the elevator down they didn't speak.

Marcus kept his arm around her shoulders, the two of them staring in awe at the beautiful baby in their arms. "I love the name Dallas." Mary Catherine looked into her husband's eyes.

"Me, too." He kissed her lips just before the elevator door opened. "But I love you more."

"We're a family." Mary Catherine had no words to describe how she felt. The love exploding through her was something she couldn't have understood until now. With their first baby cradled between them.

In the lobby, they immediately found Sami and Tyler. The two of them stood as Mary Catherine and Marcus walked up with the baby. "Here he is." Mary Catherine turned so her friends could see the child.

Sami gasped. "He's absolutely perfect." She touched the baby's cheek. "Look at his eyes. So handsome."

Tyler said something similar. Mary Catherine wasn't sure exactly what. All she wanted was to be home with Marcus and Dallas, so she could try to believe what had just happened. The fact that she was a mother.

They talked for a few minutes and then the Waynes joined them. The six of them talked for a few minutes, everyone marveling at baby Dallas Garner. Then the Waynes headed up to get Lexy. Tomorrow they would all get together and celebrate the arrival of the baby. Marcus's parents would stop by also, and over the weekend Mary Catherine's parents would arrive for a week.

Mary Catherine was grateful for the support. She felt like she was floating on clouds as she waited in the lobby for Marcus to pull up his truck. He brought the car seat inside and they buckled the baby in. Then—like something from a dream—Mary Catherine and Marcus climbed into the front seats and they drove off.

A few miles from the hospital, Mary Catherine reached for Marcus's hand. "Know what I'm thinking?"

"That it feels like a dream?" Marcus grinned at her.

"Yes." Though Mary Catherine had been wiping away tears all morning, now her eyes were clear. "He's our little boy. It's more than I can take in. God is so great."

They talked about the name Lexy had chosen. Dallas Garner. A name they already loved. Mary Catherine looked over her shoulder at the top of her son's small head. "You know what *I* think?"

"What?" Marcus hadn't stopped smiling.

"I think God's going to use our little boy for something very special."

"Mmmm." Marcus chuckled. "I agree, of course. But we sound like all new parents."

"I know, but I really mean it." Mary Catherine couldn't shake the feeling. "Like God has destined this child for great things." She hesitated, looking back at her son again. "Maybe he's going to change the world for God. You know?"

"If the miracle of how we all got here is any indication, then I'm sure you're right." Marcus's eyes were full of depth and emotion. He gave Mary Catherine a quick smile. "I'm sure God has very special plans for him."

"Exactly." She looked straight ahead, still pondering everything that had happened today.

They were a mile away from home when the song came on the radio.

Francesca Battistelli's song—"Hundred More Years."

Last time Mary Catherine had thought about this song she could only think of everything she would never have, the husband and children she would miss out on, the years she wouldn't live. But this time . . .

The words played out like an anthem.

All those dreams and now they're finally here . . .

Every line spoke straight to Mary Catherine's soul. She could've written the song herself. *All this life still left to live and they can hardly wait . . .*

Marcus exchanged a look with her. Neither of them needed any words. The song said it all. The lyrics rang with hope about a bright and beautiful future and God smiling down on them.

Again tears filled Mary Catherine's eyes. But this time because the song was her life. She really did have everything she'd ever dreamed about. Everything she never dared ask for. The song told about the future looking beautiful and bright . . . and God smiling down on them.

Mary Catherine sang the last lines quietly, like a prayer to God. "'And they want to stay right here . . . make it last for a hundred more years.'"

Yes, God had answered every one of her prayers. She was alive and her body felt whole and healthy and strong. Marcus wasn't some far-off memory she needed to forget. He was her husband, her best friend. Her lover.

And Mary Catherine really did have a feeling that amazing things lay ahead for all of them. There was no way to tell whether she'd get her heart transplant or if she and Marcus would ever have more children. It didn't matter. Because they

were a family. They had God and each other, and the greatest
gift God could've given them.

A baby boy named Dallas Garner.

THE CELEBRATION COULDN'T BEGIN until Jag and the
others arrived at the meeting. Jag was convinced it would be
a time of rejoicing they would always remember. Orlon and
the others were already inside. But first he and Aspyn, Beck
and Ember gathered together outside the door of the meeting
place.

On what felt like holy ground.

All of heaven knew about the victory that had taken place.
Jag looked at his peers. "It's a miracle. Really, it is."

Beck nodded. "How many times did we all feel like we
were being led by the Holy Spirit?"

"Constantly." Ember looked at peace. "Failure was around
every corner. And yet . . ."

Aspyn smiled. "God prevailed."

"Yes." Jag took a deep breath and looked at the other
three. First Ember, then Aspyn. And finally Beck. "We were
the exact angels for the job. Orlon had it right." He hesitated.
"But it was by prayer that we succeeded. The prayers of
heaven and Earth."

The baby would be tended by guardian angels from this
day on. That was the job of others. For now, the four of them
could simply join the rest of the team and rejoice. They would
spend the day thanking God for the victory. Their work had

been nearly impossible at every turn. And there would be other jobs ahead, other Angels Walking adventures they would embark on. But for now they would enter the room together.

The four of them.

And they would hear the words they all longed to hear. Words they had longed to hear from the beginning.

Well done, good and faithful servants.

Mission accomplished.

Dear Reader Friend,

It's never easy to wrap up a series. Angels Walking was no exception. As I finished the scenes with Marcus and Mary Catherine, Tyler and Sami, I kept writing slower and slower—not wanting to say goodbye.

People ask me why I wrote the Angels Walking series, and the answer has stayed the same. These books allowed me to peel back the layers of a very real spiritual dimension and give us all a fictional glimpse at what's going on behind the scenes—not just in the lives of my characters.

But in your life and in mine.

Hebrews 13:2 says, "Do not forget to entertain strangers, for in doing so some of you have entertained angels without knowing it." That tells me that on occasion someone has given me a word of encouragement or helped with a rescue or prayed with our family when my father was suffering his heart attack in 2007—and just possibly that person was actually an angel.

Your letters throughout this series have encouraged me. While you've enjoyed the story line, most of you have taken away more than an entertaining diversion. Rather, you have closed the cover of the book and realized just how much God loves you. How He would send angels on your behalf for any number of reasons. But mostly because He loves you.

Of course the angels in this series are fictional.

But angels are very real. Have you interacted with an angel? None of us will ever know for sure, but maybe reading the Angels Walking series has helped you take a closer look at your own life. Sometimes when we look for the fingerprints of God at work in our stories, we're more likely to see Him.

More likely to experience a deeper faith.

I'd love to hear your thoughts on this series, and how you've seen God at work in your life. Stop by my Facebook, Twitter, or Instagram! I'm there all the time! Also, visit my website—KarenKingsbury.com—for announcements about upcoming books and movies. And sign up for my newsletter and weekly blog. One more way I can encourage you to stay the course!

God is on your side.

Love you all!
Karen Kingsbury

Reading Group Guide
Brush of Wings

Questions for you and your group to help you take a deeper look at *Brush of Wings*.

1. Mary Catherine was afraid of hurting Marcus. What impact did that have on her life?

2. Have you ever adjusted your life because of fear? Explain the situation.

3. Tyler took Sami back to her grandparents' house to propose to her. Why was that such a special idea for the two of them? Talk about a sentimental marriage proposal—either yours or someone you know.

4. Why was Africa so important to Mary Catherine, especially in relation to her fading health?

5. When has something been as important to you as Africa was to Mary Catherine? Explain.

6. Ember was a significant help to Mary Catherine, and yet she was an angel. Talk about a time you or someone you know may have interacted with an angel.

7. Which angel was your favorite—Jag, Beck, Aspyn, or Ember? Why?

8. What did you like most about Mary Catherine in *Brush of Wings*? Give some examples.

9. Why did Mary Catherine change her mind about falling in love with Marcus? What was the tipping point?

10. Mary Catherine was on the verge of death when she had her heart surgery, but she was given another chance to live. Talk about a situation like that in your life or in the life of someone you know.

11. Do you believe in miracles? If so, tell about one you or someone you know witnessed.

12. What was your favorite part of the double wedding of Marcus and Mary Catherine, and Tyler and Sami?

13. Why were Tyler, Sami, Mary Catherine, and Marcus, along with Lexy, all so important to seeing the successful completion of the Angels Walking mission?

14. Were you surprised by the fact that Lexy's baby was Dallas Garner? Why or why not?

15. What is God doing in your life right now? How has the Angels Walking series helped you to see beyond the black-and-white details of life to the spiritual?

One Chance Foundation

THE KINGSBURY FAMILY IS passionate about see-ing orphans all over the world brought home to their forever families. As a result, Karen created a charitable group called the One Chance Foundation.

This foundation was inspired by the memory of her fa-ther, Ted C. Kingsbury. Ted always said, "Life is not a dress re-hearsal. We have one chance to love, one chance to truly live!"

Karen often tells her reader friends that they have "one chance to write the story of their lives!"™ Now, with Karen's One Chance Foundation, readers can join her in the belief that all of us have one chance to make a difference in the lives of orphans.

In the Bible, James 1:27 says that people with pure and genuine religion care for orphans. The One Chance Founda-tion was created with that truth in mind.

If you are interested in giving to Karen's One Chance Foun-dation and having your dedication printed in one of Karen's upcoming novels, visit www.KarenKingsbury.com. Below are dedications from some of Karen's reader friends who have contributed to the One Chance Foundation:

- **Jill Reilly:** Happy 50th Pat & Jack Socola! I love you, Jill

- **Daniel and Tanya Brand:** Brenda Hagler-Mom, you're beautiful inside & out, cherished by many. Love, Your Kids

- **Cindy Tschann:** Chris Tschann, you're forever in our hearts.

- **Kelly Haye:** Happy Birthday Cathy Eldredge—love you!

- **Judy Resley:** Violet Studer, Best Mom Ever, Love Judy

- **Bethany Danner:** All I am I owe to my mother. Love, B

- **Cheryl Sales:** Patty Nagasawa BF 4ever! Love you. Cheryl

- **Lee-Anne Diggs:** Noelene Diggs, the best Mum ever!

- **Martha Oskvig:** Creative Friend: Martha Mensink Oskvig

- **Becky Gardner:** In memory of Jared Gardner, We Miss You!

- **Richard and Mary Howrigon:** Elias & Titus Howrigon Welcome Home

- **Patti Bunje:** To Honor Bruce Bunje, Jerri & Roy Nygren

- **Karen C. Allen:** In loving memory of Mama, Daddy, and Karee

- **Stacia Haney:** Myrna Carter, great mom and friend—BGLU!

- **Lisa Turner:** Happy 21st birthday, Emma Turner. 10/11

- **Pamela C. Alden:** In memory of John & Helen who adopted me

- **Pamela C. Alden:** In memory of Cara! We love & miss you! XO

- **Pamela C. Alden:** In honor of my angels Joshua & Hannah

- **Roxann Pishnick:** Michael Carl, LOVE—Always and Forever.

- **Diane K. Weimer:** For my son Theron Edward Weimer, Jr.

- **Herbert L. Lacassagne:** To my wife Puppsy, What A Wonderful World

- **Mona Milbrandt:** To Thelma Bradley—My Loving Mom!

- **Patti Mullin:** Katelyn, I love you more! Aunt Patti XOX

- **Kimberly O'Connell:** Many thanks to our parents—Kim & Kevin

- **Susan L. League:** For Stephanie Brown—Love, Susan & Ray

- **Sharon K. Evers:** God bless our precious PIE, Grandma E.

- **Brian Connolly:** I luv u more than rocks Kaitlyn Connolly

- **Mr. & Mrs. Joseph J. Malloy, Jr.:** Sara Blair Brakebill—Ever in our Hearts

- **Joan Smith:** In memory of David Geoffrey Smith by his loving wife, Joan

- **Linda Simpson:** Celebrating Forever Families! Linda, Danny & Chris Simpson

- **Anne Kingsbury:** Karen! Your dad, Ted Kingsbury, would be so proud of you!—Love Mom

- **Karen Dobson:** Heather Barrett-Forever in our hearts. Forever in His arms.

- **Phyllis Mifflin:** My beautiful Granddaughters Jenna and Kylee ~ Love Nana

- **Ann Holden:** To my children: Be kind and merciful. Love, Mom Ann G.

- **Jennifer Cochrane:** Lori, grateful to God and KK for our friendship! Jennifer C.

- **Teresa Pisani:** My dear friend Dawn, enjoy this book as all the others! Teresa

- **Joan Hawbaker:** Jolene and Chad Haffner, adoptive and foster parents, THANKS!

- **Jennifer Hansen:** Cyndi Enea-Trust in GOD-HE has your back! Love you! BFF's Jennifer

- **Camille Pinkerton:** Lovingly dedicated to Cathi Carpenter, the best mom ever!

- **Cyndi Wydner:** Roxie Maudean Cagle 9/7/39-9/19/10 Forever in my heart!—Cyndi

- **Lori Kennedy-Stewart:** Love of my life-Bobby/Our unborn child/TeamKK-Jenn C/Lori KS

- **Rebecca Waszak:** With love, Gregory and Rebecca Waszak

- **Patricia Patterson:** With love, Wiley L. Patterson and Patricia B. Patterson

- **Michelle Ferris:** May God bless those who benefit from this donation!—Michelle

- **Grace McCain:** For Garry and Marsha with much love—Grace McCain

- **Janet Bowles:** In loving memory of our Mamaw, Hazel Etter, love—Stella

- **Helene Selvik:** With love, Helene Selvik

- **Robyn Stiles:** With love, Robyn Stiles

- **Carol Foose:** To my six blessings, Isaiah 49:15

- **Maybelle Reichenbach:** In memory of my grandma—Love, Carrie

Life-Changing Fiction™

by #1 *New York Times* bestselling author

KAREN KINGSBURY

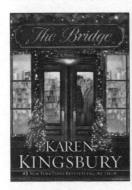
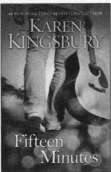

Available wherever books are sold
or at **SimonandSchuster.com**

HOWARD BOOKS
A Division of Simon & Schuster
A CBS COMPANY

Look for the ongoing stories in the
LIFE-CHANGING
BIBLE STUDY
series!

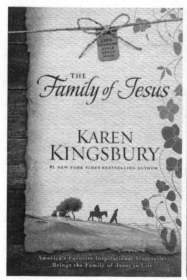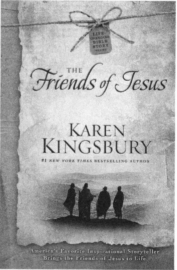

AVAILABLE WHEREVER BOOKS ARE SOLD OR AT SIMONANDSCHUSTER.COM

HOWARD BOOKS
AN IMPRINT OF SIMON & SCHUSTER, INC.
A CBS COMPANY

49875

Look for the first two books in the

ANGELS WALKING SERIES

and experience the unseen miracles
happening all around!

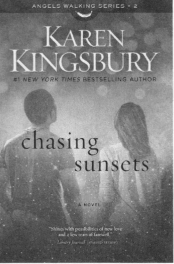

Available wherever books are sold or at SimonandSchuster.com

HOWARD BOOKS®
An Imprint of Simon & Schuster, Inc.
A CBS COMPANY

49876

Karen's Newsletter, Blog, & FREE Chapters!

Sign up to receive upcoming news, inspirational blogs, and life-changing moments from Karen. It's easy. And once a month receive a new, FREE Chapter on the Baxter Family!

Sign up at
KarenKingsbury.com